Critical Acclaim for Robin Lee Hatcher's Historical Romances

Catching Katie, named a "Best Book of 2004" in Christian fiction by Library Journal

"[In *Catching Katie*,] Robin Lee Hatcher delivers a delightful, thought-provoking romp with characters readers are sure to adore."

Romantic Times Book Review Magazine

"Robin Lee Hatcher is not afraid to challenge us with thought-provoking issues and valid spiritual insights. A truly enjoyable read!"

Cindy Swanson, host of the Weekend Rockford radio show

Patterns of Love, winner of the RITA Award for Best Inspirational

"This heart-warming prairie romance [*Patterns of Love*] promises to establish Hatcher as a noteworthy Christian romance author."

CBA Marketplace

The Victory Club, winner of the 2006 Award of Excellence

"[In *The Victory Club*,] veteran Christian fiction author Hatcher weaves epistolary elements with third-person omniscient narration in this moving novel about a year in the life of four Idaho women working at a Boise airfield during WWII ... Three of them are Christians, and rather than making them cardboard saints, Hatcher depicts each one struggling with and giving in to sin ... Hatcher includes V-mail and news clippings to good effect, making this novel's wartime setting believable without resorting to cliché ... This novel embraces complexity rather than eschewing it. A well-paced and genuinely suspenseful plot plus Hatcher's pleasingly smooth prose make this novel a delight."

Publishers Weekly

The Shepherd's Voice, winner of the RITA Award for Best Inspirational

"Capturing the essence of the early 1930s, author Robin Lee Hatcher crafts an endearing story about a young shepherdess who rescues a wayward soul in her latest work, *The Shepherd's Voice* ... Hatcher has a real warmth in her writing style and the relationship between the characters comes across as natural and honest, rather than contrived and superficial. There is an authentic luster to the story, which gives the reader a genuine feeling, together with a plot that is suspenseful enough to keep the pages turning until the very end."

Christian Retailing

Wagered Heart

OTHER BOOKS BY ROBIN LEE HATCHER

The Perfect Life

Return to Me

A Carol for Christmas

Loving Libby

The Victory Club

Beyond the Shadows

Catching Katie

Speak to Me of Love

Firstborn

Ribbon of Years

Promised to Me

In His Arms

Patterns of Love

Dear Lady

The Shepherd's Voice

Robin Lee
HATCHER

Wagered Heart

A NOVEL

ZONDERVAN.com/
AUTHORTRACKER
follow your favorite authors

Wagered Heart

Requests for information should be addressed to:

Zondervan, *Grand Rapids, Michigan 49530*

Library of Congress Cataloging-in-Publication Data

Hatcher, Robin Lee.
Wagered heart / Robin Lee Hatcher.
p. cm.
ISBN 978-0-310-25926-8
1. Young women—Fiction 2. ?????—Fiction. 3. Montana—Fiction. I. Title.
BV2082.A9 M485—2001
266'.0092—dc21

2001017679

All Scripture quotations, unless otherwise indicated, are taken from the King James Version of the Bible.

Interior design by Michelle Espinoza

Printed in the United States of America

08 09 10 11 12 13 14 • 20 19 18 17 16 15 14 13 12 11 10 9 8 7 6 5 4 3 2 1

In God have I put my trust:
I will not be afraid what man can do unto me.

Psalm 56:11

Wagered Heart

ONE

Bethany Silverton swept her lime green and white striped gown out of the way and closed the picket gate of her family's new home. Then with gloved fingers, she opened a matching striped silk parasol and rested it against her shoulder. From down the street, the sounds of laughter mixed with the brassy tinkle of piano keys spilled from the nearest saloon and into the main street of Sweetwater, Montana.

Bethany's friend, Ingrid Johnson, shook her head. "It is shameful that those men drink so early in the day." The words rolled off her tongue in a soft Swedish accent. "I do not know why the good reverend wanted to build his church here. He could have settled in a more civilized place long before this."

Bethany hid her amusement behind her parasol. She couldn't admit to Ingrid how much she liked this raw frontier town. After all, she had complained without ceasing when her father announced they were leaving Philadelphia to go west. She had declared to both of her parents she would never forgive her father for withdrawing her from Miss Henderson's School for Young Ladies, for making her leave all of her friends behind, for removing her from the glittering society of which her wealthy grandmother—and by extension, Bethany herself—was a part. She had pouted when they traveled, and she'd pouted whenever they stopped along the way, waiting for her father to hear from the Lord if they had reached the place God meant for them to call home.

Now, two years after bidding Philadelphia farewell, she could admit to herself how much she loved the rolling plains and majestic mountains that surrounded her, how much she admired the men, women, and children who had left everything in hopes of making a better life for themselves in the West.

Even more, she loved her newfound freedoms. Her grandmother—the venerable Eustace Vanderhoff Silverton—would be horrified to know Bethany sometimes went riding without a chaperone or spoke to complete strangers without a proper introduction. Such things were not done by young ladies in her grandmother's world.

Bethany shifted the parasol to her other shoulder and looked at Ingrid. "There were saloons in every town we passed through. You simply must ignore them." She turned and began walking, Ingrid hurrying to keep up.

Sweetwater, Montana, was in its youth, a town flowering to life in service of the ranchers who laid claim to the vast grasslands. Its main street was lined with false-fronted buildings, including a mercantile store, two saloons, a small restaurant, a bakery, a livery, an apothecary and doctor's office, and the sheriff's office and jail. When the Silverton family arrived less than a week ago, the reverend had purchased a two-story home on the edge of town from a widow who was returning to Missouri.

This, he'd said, was where the good Lord would have them stay.

The first business the two young women reached was the apothecary. A small bell jingled overhead as Bethany opened the door and she and Ingrid entered.

A green-visored man looked up from his paper-strewn desk. His weathered face cracked into a grin. "How do, ladies. Can I help you?"

She stepped forward. "I'm Miss Silverton. My father is Reverend Silverton." She motioned toward Ingrid. "This is my friend, Miss Johnson."

"I heard we'd got us a preacher. Glad to meet you, Miss Silverton. You too, Miss Johnson. My name's Wilton. John Wilton. My brother's the doc here in Sweetwater."

"It's a pleasure to meet you, sir. Miss Johnson and I don't want to take up your time, but we wanted you to know that my father will be holding a church service this Sunday morning in a field tent behind our home. The service will start at ten."

"Me and the missus will be there. My Sarah's been praying for a pastor to come through these parts ever since we settled here. She'd want me to tell you she's been eager to come calling on you and your mother, but she's been feeling a might poorly. We've got us a new baby coming real soon now."

"How wonderful, Mr. Wilton. Children are a gift from God. Please tell your wife I look forward to meeting her too."

"That I'll do. And good day to you, miss."

The next business was the livery stable, where Bethany tacked up a notice of the church service near the main doors. Then they crossed the street to Mrs. Jenkins's Restaurant. Once inside, Bethany introduced herself to the proprietress while Ingrid—ever shy around strangers—waited in the background. Again they received a warm welcome. The same was true in the mercantile and the bakery.

But as they left the sheriff's office almost an hour later, their way was blocked by a man with a week's worth of whiskers on his chin and a dusty, battered hat on his head.

"Well, would you look at what we got here. Ain't you a couple of pretty little fillies."

Bethany lifted her chin and leveled a cool stare at the grizzled cowpoke. "A gentleman, sir, would step aside and allow us to pass."

She spoke with an air of authority, one she'd learned from observing her grandmother. With her eyes, she dared the man to block their path.

In an instant, his face reddened. " 'Scuse me, miss." He stepped down into the street.

She resisted a triumphant grin. "Come along, Ingrid."

Her friend's eyes were wide with awe. "Are you never afraid of anything?"

Bethany laughed. "You are altogether too meek, Ingrid. You must overcome it if you're to be happy here. We must be as bold and fearless as the land itself."

She stopped walking at the far corner of the Plains Saloon and tacked another notice to the clapboard siding. The noise coming from inside was louder than ever. Twice she glanced toward the door, battling an almost irresistible temptation to peek inside and learn the cause of so much merriment. But, of course, she couldn't do anything so unbecoming. She might relish her many new freedoms, but as a preacher's daughter she had to be mindful of her position. Besides, Ingrid would go straight to the reverend if Bethany did anything so brash as look inside a saloon.

She turned from her task, ready to head for home, then stopped when she felt the hem of her dress catch, cringing as she heard the tearing of fabric. This was one of her favorite dresses, a gift from her Philadelphia cousin, Beatrice Worthington. She'd taken great care of it, and if it was ruined, she would be heartsick. There would be no replacing it in Sweetwater.

"Allow me," a deep voice said.

She glanced over her shoulder in time to see a stranger bend down to free her skirt from the troublesome nail. When he straightened, she found her head tilting backward, ever backward in order to look him in the face.

He was over six feet tall with broad shoulders, lean but exuding an aura of power. She had never felt so slight as she did now. His features were boldly spaced, his skin dark, his jaw smooth and square. Blue-black hair brushed the collar of his shirt. She could read nothing in his expression, but his midnight blue eyes seemed to look right inside her head, reading her mind, judging her thoughts.

She gasped and stepped backward.

One corner of his mouth lifted, suggesting a smile. He turned away without a word.

"Bethany?" Ingrid's hand clasped her arm.

She took another step back, her gaze still on the man.

"Look at this, Hawk." A second cowboy, one Bethany hadn't noticed before, pointed at the notice she had tacked on the wall. "They're startin' a church here in Sweetwater. We're gonna get civilized. You gonna come to the service on Sunday?"

The man named Hawk looked behind him, his enigmatic gaze meeting Bethany's once again. She held her breath, awaiting his reply.

"No," he said and walked away.

"Come on, Bethany." Ingrid tugged at her arm.

"Did you see him?"

"Of course I saw him."

"I wonder who he is. Have you ever seen anyone so … so …" She didn't know what she wanted to say about him. So handsome … so mysterious … so dangerous.

"He looked like every other cowboy we have seen in Montana. And certainly not the kind of man you would find in church."

Bethany turned. "Why do you think that?"

"He said so himself. Weren't you listening? He would not come even if you invited him."

"But it's our Christian duty to encourage everyone to come to church. How else are we to reach them with the good news?"

Ingrid shook her head. "Many are called, but few are chosen."

His eyes were as wild and raw as this land. As if he's a part of it. Surely that is why God called Papa to this place, to reach men like him.

A delayed shiver of reaction ran through her.

"I can see what you are thinking, Bethany, and I tell you, it will not happen."

"Who says?" She tossed her head. "I'll wager I could get him to services if I tried hard enough."

Ingrid shot her a frown. "Gambling is a sin."

"Oh, pishposh. This isn't gambling. It's a little game between friends."

"Bethany— "

"I'll wager you five dollars I can get him to come to church within thirty days."

"I do not have five dollars."

"Well, we'll pretend you do. See. Then it isn't gambling."

"The reverend would not approve."

"Then we simply won't tell him."

TWO

Hawk Chandler glanced at the clear sky. Judging by the sun, they ought to reach the Circle Blue Ranch before nightfall. He swung into the saddle of his copper-colored gelding. His friend, Rand Howard, mounted his own horse, and they rode west down Main Street. Once outside of Sweetwater, they settled into a smooth canter, riding in companionable silence.

Hawk scanned the grasslands. The terrain undulated with benchlands and cutbacks, draws and coulees. The eastern plains were rich in native buffalo grass, a grass that withstood the heat and drought of Montana summers, that survived the frigid, snow-covered Montana winters, that was unharmed by the trampling of hooves. It grew and flourished and filled the bellies of Circle Blue cattle.

From the moment he laid eyes on this range back in '78, he'd known it was where he would stay. Plenty of grazing. Natural brush shelter in the form of plum thickets and chokecherry trees. And most important of all, water.

The boundaries of the Circle Blue began at the foot of the mountain range. That's where Hawk and Rand had built the ranch house. Nothing fancy. Just a solid place to keep them from freezing in the winter. They'd brought up the Circle Blue starter herd from Texas in the spring of 1879, and after three years, Hawk had introduced shorthorns from Oregon to the range. He wasn't rich, but he was doing okay. Plenty of others had come and gone. He was here to stay.

He was a lucky man. There wasn't much more he could want than hard work to keep him busy in the daytime, good food to fill his belly at night, and a friend he could trust through thick and thin.

Then he remembered a pair of green eyes, wide with surprise, and heard again the soft gasp that had slipped from a shapely mouth.

Maybe there was something more he wanted.

He clenched his jaw and forced the delicate image from his memory. He'd learned his lesson when it came to young ladies like her. They weren't for him, and he'd do well to remember it.

"We thank you, Lord, for bringing us safely to our new home. We ask that you bless our work in Sweetwater. Amen."

Nathaniel Silverton lifted his head even as three soft "amens" echoed his from around the supper table. His gaze settled first upon his bride of twenty-seven years. To him, the former Virginia Braddock was as lovely as the day he'd married her, even though her sable hair was now highlighted with strands of silver. Throughout their marriage, she had served beside him. When he'd told her God was calling him to leave Philadelphia—a life made comfortable by the wealth of his family—she hadn't questioned him or uttered a word of complaint.

God bless her.

The same had not been true of their only child.

At this moment, Bethany looked as submissive and gentle in spirit as her mother. Ah, but looks could be deceiving. His daughter was filled with a fire for life. If he could, he would protect her, shelter her from the trials he knew would come to her — many, he feared, of her own making. Some of her willfulness was his fault; he had spoiled her as a child. Truth be known, he spoiled her still. He couldn't resist her impish grins and sweet pleadings. She had charm and knew how to use it to her advantage.

Oh, Father. Protect this child of mine. Teach her to be humble and kind.

As if knowing he prayed for her, she looked up, unmistakable mischief in her eyes. What bit of tomfoolery was she up to now? Then she smiled, and he forgot to worry, his heart melting in response.

Nathaniel knew she'd forgiven him for taking her away from Philadelphia, though she was too willful to admit it yet. Not after all the fuss she'd made during their slow journey west. He would have to pray harder about her stubborn streak. Pray and hope it wouldn't bring her too much heartache before she surrendered it to God.

His gaze moved on, arriving at last to Ingrid. What a contrast she was to his daughter. Where Bethany's coloring was bright and vibrant — auburn hair, green eyes — Ingrid was pale. Her blond hair was more silver than gold, her blue eyes so light as to be almost gray. While Bethany's curvaceous body highlighted her young womanhood, Ingrid was tall and almost as straight as a boy. Likewise, their personalities were as night to day. Bethany looked for adventure at every turn; Ingrid sought peace.

The Silvertons had befriended Ingrid and her father, Sven Johnson, on their journey from Minnesota to Colorado. It was in

Denver that Sven crossed over to eternity, leaving his daughter with little money and no family. The Silvertons had taken her as one of their own, and so she remained.

"Papa?"

Drawn from his memories, Nathaniel looked at Bethany. "Yes?"

"Ingrid and I met as many of the townspeople as we could today, and we posted notices about church services in several places. But I was thinking. What about the ranchers and homesteaders who only come into town on occasion? How will they know we're here? Shouldn't we seek them out and let them know Sweetwater now has a church?"

"Well, I—"

"I'd like to go with you. Some of the ranchers must have wives and children. They should know you have a family too."

"Your mother—"

"Oh, of course Mother should come. And Ingrid too. We could pack a picnic lunch and make a day of it. Wouldn't it be fun?"

It pleased him that Bethany was interested in helping him in his work, that she wanted to become a part of this community. While it was true she could be stubborn and willful, it was also true she had a good heart.

"You're right, daughter. We should pay our respects to those who live outside of Sweetwater. If the weather's good tomorrow, we'll take the buggy and go calling." He turned toward his wife. "Virginia, when should we leave?"

"If it's all the same to you, dear, I'll decline. There's much to do here before I'll feel settled. The house is at sixes and sevens. You and the girls go and have a good day together."

"As you wish." He turned toward Ingrid. "We should get an early start."

Ingrid glanced toward Bethany, a peculiar look in her eyes. Then she shook her head. "Thank you, Reverend Silverton, but I will stay and help Mrs. Silverton if that is all right."

"Well"—he turned to his daughter—"I guess it's just you and me. We'll leave right after breakfast."

THREE

It was hot for May. Too hot for Hawk's liking. It shouldn't be like this until July.

He yanked the pump handle up and down until cool water gushed from the faucet, filling the tin cup in his hand. It took several cupfuls to quench his thirst. Afterward, he leaned down and stuck his head beneath the flow of water. Air whooshed from his lungs at the cold, both startling and welcome. As he straightened, he shook droplets of water from his hair, like a dog just out of the river.

He returned the cup to its nail before starting across the dusty yard, long strides eating up the distance between pump and barn. But he stopped when he saw a horse and buggy approaching at a smart clip, the identity of the vehicle's inhabitants hidden in the shadow cast by the fringed top. He heard the driver's "Whoa!" seconds before the horse slowed to a walk. It stopped not far from where he stood.

"Good afternoon." The man—a stranger to Hawk—stepped from the buggy. He wore a fine black suit. Attire not often seen in these parts. "I'm Reverend Nathaniel Silverton of Sweetwater."

"Afternoon."

The reverend held out a hand toward the buggy. "This is my daughter, Bethany."

He watched her alight, a petite foot and ankle peeking from beneath her flounced and ruffled gown of sunshine yellow. The preacher's daughter. Pretty as a picture—and the very lady he wanted to avoid.

"I see we are interrupting your work, Mr.— " The reverend's voice rose in question as he extended his hand.

Hawk wiped his palm on his trousers and shook the proffered hand. "Chandler. Hawk Chandler. The Circle Blue is my ranch." He pushed his damp hair back from his face. "I've been shoeing horses most of the morning." It irritated him that he felt the need to explain his appearance.

"And we are sorry to have intruded. We won't keep you, Mr. Chandler. We only wanted to extend an invitation to you and your family to attend services in Sweetwater this Sunday."

Hawk's gaze moved once more to the young woman at her father's side. Bethany. The name fit her. Ladylike. Elegant. Lovely. Her rosy lips parted slightly as she returned his gaze, and he felt his gut tighten.

"Thanks for the invitation, Reverend. I'm not much on church-going, but it was good of you to stop by." He stepped back one length and nodded. "Good day to you." Then, without waiting for them to leave, he strode toward the barn.

Bethany had never seen anyone like him. The muscles of his upper arms bulged beneath his rolled up shirtsleeves. His wet hair glistened in the sunlight, droplets of water shining like diamonds against the black. And his eyes, the way he'd looked at her. It had left her breathless.

"Come along, Bethany," her father said, his hand on her elbow. "I believe we've overstayed our welcome."

"But Papa, shouldn't we try to change his mind? We've come all this way." A new thought sprang into her head, one that made her stomach sink. "We don't know if he's married. Perhaps we should talk to his wife. She might want to come to church, even if he doesn't."

Her father shook his head. "We aren't giving up, my girl. There will be other occasions to see Mr. Chandler. If he has a family, we will learn that too."

Reluctantly, she allowed herself to be moved toward the buggy, taking her place once again on her father's right side. He clucked at the horse and turned the vehicle around.

Hawk Chandler. She recalled the sculpted angles of his face, the heavy brows, the deep-set, brooding eyes. Blue eyes, yet so dark they were nearly black.

"Hawk," she said softly. "An unusual Christian name, isn't it?"

"My guess is he's part Indian."

"Do you think so?" She twisted to look behind her at the retreating ranch. "But I thought Indians were ..." *Savages. Heathens.* The words caught in her throat. While Hawk Chandler seemed many things to her, those words didn't fit.

Her father understood what had gone unsaid. "My child, never judge a man because of his race. Never. God looks at the heart. So should we. We are all made in God's image. Whatever the reason Mr. Chandler doesn't go to church, we'll pray we can overcome it so that he will join us soon."

"I'll do everything I can to make that happen, Papa."

Vince Richards leaned against the high-backed leather chair, nodding every so often as the reverend spoke, but he wasn't listening. His thoughts were locked on the auburn-haired beauty seated beside her father.

From the moment she entered his home, she'd held him captivated. She was perfection—her laugh, her sweet smile, the lyrical sound of her voice. Even the way she drank the tea that Hutchens, Vince's manservant, had delivered to the drawing room a short while before. Lovely. Absolutely lovely. It wasn't often one found a truly genteel young woman in Montana.

"We've taken up enough of your time, Mr. Richards." The reverend stood. "It was a pleasure meeting you. I hope we'll see you in church on Sunday."

"I'll be there, Reverend Silverton." He rose and stepped forward to shake the man's hand. Then he turned toward Bethany and bowed. "It was a distinct honor to meet you, Miss Silverton. I look forward to the pleasure of your company again soon."

Nathaniel took Bethany's arm. "Until Sunday then. Good day, Mr. Richards."

Vince saw his guests to their buggy, then watched as they drove away. Now there was a young woman who would make a proper wife for the future governor of Montana. And that's who he meant to be. Not just governor of the territory. He would see that Montana became a state, and, when it did, he would be its governor. Bethany Silverton would make a perfect first lady. Beautiful, cultured, refined. Everything a governor could want in a wife.

He turned toward his house, pride welling at the sight. It had taken a long time to have the materials brought here, a long time for the large brick structure to be built and furnished. But now it was the finest home in all of Montana Territory.

He stepped onto the veranda and took a cigar from his shirt pocket. As he smoked, his gaze scanned the rolling countryside that made up the Bar V Ranch. Five thousand head of cattle roamed the range. Soon there would be ten thousand, then twenty thousand. Perhaps even more. All he needed was time and more grazing land—and more water.

Water.

He bit down on the cigar, eyes narrowing as they slid toward the mountain range to the west. Chandler's ranch was at the foot of those mountains—the ranch and a spring that never ceased to flow, providing life-giving water for livestock for miles around. If Vince was to own the largest cattle operation in Montana, he needed ownership of the Circle Blue. Once it was his, control of the water rights from the mountains all the way to the Musselshell would be his too.

And there was no mistaking that the Circle Blue would be his. He wouldn't allow anything or anyone to stand in his way.

He tossed his cigar into the dust of the yard and went inside.

Rand set his bowl of stew on the table opposite Hawk. "Did you get the last of those horses shod? If not, I can do it in the mornin'."

"I finished. Except for the roan. He's gone lame again. I figured to put him out to pasture for a while, see if he doesn't heal up." Hawk took a couple bites of his supper. "We had visitors today."

"Who? Richards? When's he gonna believe you're not sellin'?"

Hawk shook his head. "It wasn't Richards. It was the new reverend and his daughter. Came to invite us to church."

"They did, huh?" Rand chuckled. "Guess if they're gonna go to all that trouble to bring a personal invitation, we oughta go."

Hawk resumed eating without comment.

"I don't suppose the reverend's daughter was that blonde we saw outside the saloon."

"No."

Rand swallowed his disappointment. "Well, I reckon I'll go anyway. You gonna change your mind and come with me?"

Hawk shook his head.

Rand understood his friend's reluctance to mingle with the town's growing population. He'd come to know Hawk pretty well in the five years they'd been together, well enough to know that he'd suffered his share of scorn from folks when they learned he was a quarter Sioux. Didn't matter that Hawk had spent his whole life living with white folks, that he was as upright and honest as any man Rand ever knew.

Never ceased to amaze him how otherwise kind and caring folks—even some who called themselves Christian—could act like that. Made him ashamed, it did. Downright ashamed.

FOUR

Bethany stared at the ceiling, watching as the encroaching dawn lightened her bedroom, all the while twirling a strand of hair around her index finger and worrying her lower lip.

Now that she'd found Mr. Chandler, how was she to get him to church? She couldn't wait for her father to go visiting again. Papa would take his own sweet time. How could she win her bet with Ingrid that way?

I wonder if he's married.

Oh, how very much she hoped not. She could still win the wager if he was, but it wouldn't be as rewarding if he had a wife.

She pushed away the blankets and swung her feet over the side of the bed. A ride would help clear her thoughts. And if that ride happened to take her near the Circle Blue, perhaps she would learn if there was a Mrs. Chandler. Her father wouldn't approve of her riding out so far from town, of course. Well, she needn't tell him. Besides, as long as Ingrid was with her, what harm could there be?

She poured water from the pitcher into a bowl and quickly performed her morning ablutions. Then she ran a hasty brush through her unruly curls before capturing her hair into a bun at the nape. As she slipped into her riding habit, she heard a door open and close, then the creaking of the stairs. Her father was up for his morning prayer time. She and Ingrid would have to wait until he emerged from his study before they could leave.

She checked the mirror one more time, approving her appearance and dark umber riding habit. Then she hurried down the hall to Ingrid's bedroom. "Get up, sleepyhead."

Sprawled on her stomach, Ingrid opened one eye. "What time is it?"

"Time to get up if we want to go for a ride."

"What ride?"

"Our ride. Don't you remember?" Bethany pulled back the coverlets on the bed. "We wanted to go for a ride today."

Suspicion clouded her friend's face as she sat up. "I do not recall anything about a ride."

"Oh, you're so forgetful." Bethany swept over to the chair near the window and perched herself on it. "Look outside. It's going to be a beautiful warm day, and I'm not leaving this room until you're up and ready to go riding with me. I had such a lovely time with Papa yesterday. The countryside is beautiful. Especially over by the—" She caught herself. "Over by the mountains. I want you to see it. Maybe we'll see some buffalo. Wouldn't that be exciting?"

While Bethany chattered, Ingrid got out of bed, washed, and went to her wardrobe. Not until she was dressed did she speak again. "You do not fool me, Bethany. It is not buffalo you wish to see."

Bethany feigned hurt feelings. "Must you be so suspicious of me?" Then she laughed, her excitement bubbling to the surface despite her best effort.

The stallion quivered, his eyes wild with fright, his legs braced. Rand gripped the rope, holding the horse steady while Hawk stepped into the saddle.

"Okay. Let him go."

For one moment after Rand stepped backward, the rangy black didn't move. Hawk wasn't fooled. He tightened his hold. A second later, the horse erupted into the air with fury, his body twisting in a vicious attempt to unseat its rider. All four hooves struck the hard earth with teeth-jarring impact. Horse and human grunted in unison.

Hawk heard Rand's yell of encouragement as the wild horse took flight again. The stallion echoed the sound with a shrill neigh as he dropped his head between his legs, back arched. Hawk's body flowed with the animal's movements rather than against them, his free arm acting as a balance as the stallion bucked and twisted and spun around the corral. Dust filled Hawk's nostrils and stung his eyes. Sweat poured from beneath his hatband and down his back.

Fight all you want. I'll win in the end.

As if he'd heard, the horse stopped bucking and stood dead still in the middle of the corral. Surprised—he'd expected this to take more time—Hawk looked at Rand, who shrugged in response. In that same instant, the animal threw his back legs toward the sky, his nose almost touching the ground.

Hawk parted company with the saddle and somersaulted toward the corral fence before hitting the dirt. The force of connecting with the ground knocked the air from him as he tumbled onto his back. He lay still, eyes closed, trying to drag a full breath into his lungs.

Rand laughed. "You took wing on that one. A flyin' hawk if ever I seen one."

Ignoring his friend, Hawk painstakingly sat up, his gaze turning toward the quivering horse.

One of us is the boss here, and it isn't you.

With a grimace, he pushed himself up from the dirt and brushed off his trousers as he strode across the corral. The stallion's breathing was labored; white rings circled his eyes as he watched Hawk's approach. Tension passed between them.

"Easy," Hawk crooned, picking up the rope and reaching for the saddle horn. "Easy, boy."

As soon as his leg swung over the animal's back, the twosome went airborne again.

As Bethany and Ingrid rode around the side of the barn, a wild scene met their eyes. The man they'd seen with Hawk Chandler outside the Plains Saloon sat on the corral fence, shouting encouragement and waving his hat. In the corral, Hawk rode a horse that looked as if it meant to kill both the rider and itself.

Bethany nudged her mare forward, drawn by the drama of man against beast. Reaching the corral, she dismounted, then stepped onto the bottom rail of the fence. Her gaze never wavered from Hawk. She forgot Ingrid and the man on the fence, too captured by the battle of wills taking place inside the corral to notice anything else.

The struggle between horse and rider continued for a long time before the exhausted animal accepted defeat. The fight gone out of him, the stallion stood in the center of the corral, dragging in noisy gasps of air. Hawk Chandler waited a few moments before he nudged the horse with the heels of his boots, moving him forward at a walk, then a trot. He didn't look at her as he rode by, yet she sensed his awareness of her presence. A tiny thrill raced along her spine.

"He's good, ain't he?"

She looked at the man on the fence. "I've never seen a wild horse ridden before."

He hopped to the ground and stepped toward her, putting his hat back on his head as he did so. "I'm Rand Howard." His brow lifted in question.

"Bethany Silverton. And this is my friend, Ingrid Johnson."

"The new preacher's daughter. Pleased to meet you, Miss Silverton. Miss Johnson."

Bethany returned her attention to the corral.

Hawk Chandler had drawn the lathered stallion to a halt. Without haste, he stepped down from the saddle, all the while speaking softly to the horse, his voice but not his words carrying to the observers. His hand stroked the sweaty black neck. Then he placed his foot in the stirrup once again and remounted. The stallion's ears twitched forward, then back, listening to the soothing murmur. Several more times, Hawk guided the horse in a wide circle around the corral. When he dismounted again, he gave the stallion another pat on the neck before loosening the cinch and removing the saddle and pad.

It was a pleasant thing, watching him work. Bethany could have stood there all day.

Hawk turned from the horse, and his gaze, hard and unflinching, met hers. Heat rose in her cheeks, but she couldn't look away. He walked toward her, his gait easy, his stride long. The closer he got, the more intimidating he seemed.

She forced herself to smile. "Good day, Mr. Chandler." She tilted her head to one side. "My friend and I were out for a ride and heard a commotion. This was exciting to see."

"You're a long way from Sweetwater." There was nothing welcoming in his tone.

"I know, but the day was warm, and it's such lovely country."

"It's not safe for you to ride out this far from town on your own."

"But I was here with Father just yesterday. We saw nothing to be afraid of."

"You don't always see danger coming in this country, Miss Silverton."

She didn't care for his advice, but perhaps she could take advantage of it. "I … I didn't think of that, sir. Perhaps … would you mind escorting us back to town?"

Not for all the world would she admit, even to herself, how much she hoped he would agree. She wanted to talk to him, to get to know what went on behind those dark eyes. And if he had a wife? Well then, she would want to know her too.

Wouldn't she?

Unsure of herself—an uncharacteristic feeling—Bethany lowered her gaze.

Rand broke the silence. "How about if we offer these nice ladies something to eat and then I'll see them back to town."

An escort home by Mr. Howard wouldn't serve her cause. It wasn't him she desired to know. It wasn't him she wanted to come to church. "We wouldn't want to put you or your wife out, Mr. Chandler." She looked at Hawk, anxious for his answer.

"There's no Mrs. Chandler. And we'll go into town together. I mean to have a word with the reverend and tell him to keep you at home before you wind up in trouble."

At that, a flash of anger replaced all other emotions. "My father has no need of your advice, sir. I may be a woman, but I assure you I'm not helpless."

For the first time, she saw him grin, and it had a startling effect on her equilibrium. She forgot everything in that moment.

He climbed over the fence and dropped to the ground near her. "That's debatable, miss." The humor vanished as quickly as it had come. "And I still mean to talk to your father. Next time you might not find the men you meet as friendly as we are."

Her irritation returned, even stronger than before. "Less friendly than you, Mr. Chandler?" She tossed her head as she turned toward her mare. "I shouldn't think that possible." After she was mounted, she looked at Rand. "Ingrid and I thank you for your kind invitation to dine, Mr. Howard, but we must decline. Good day."

She hoped Ingrid followed as she rode away. She didn't dare look back. Not until she'd put more distance between her and Hawk Chandler.

Hawk and Rand rode behind the two women. By now, Bethany had to know they were there, that she hadn't cowed him with her superior air or swayed him with her coy glances. But she never looked back. Not even once. She rode that mare with her head high and her shoulders straight as an arrow.

Maybe she had a point. Maybe he shouldn't take it upon himself to tell her father how to manage her. But once he'd suggested it, he had to carry through. Besides, he was right. A woman alone without even a gun or a rifle could get into all sorts of trouble, if not from disreputable men, then from snakes or wolves or other wild animals.

Up ahead, Bethany stopped her horse. "Ingrid, look. What on earth is that?" She pointed toward a mound of sun-baked bones.

Hawk rode up beside her. "The remains of a buffalo herd."

She looked at him, obviously considering whether or not she should deign to acknowledge him. Curiosity apparently won. "What killed them?"

"Greed."

Her brows rose as her eyes widened in question.

It was Rand who elaborated. "Hides pay about three fifty each in Miles City. Maybe more by now. The buffalo herds of the southern plains were wiped out in the seventies. Now this territory's about the last place for the buffalo, and I reckon we won't find any here in another year or two."

Hawk touched his heels to his horse's sides. "Most cattlemen think they can't raise their herds where there's buffalo."

"You don't agree?" Bethany asked, catching up with him.

He shrugged.

Once again, his friend filled the silence. "Buffalo come through; they sweep away horses and cows right along with them. Chances are you'll never see your stock again. Besides, they eat the grass the cattle need. Now that the railroad's reached Montana, there's going to be more and more men coming to build their ranches, men with big plans for the grasslands here. Those plans don't include buffalo herds. Anyways, long as there's people willing to buy their hides, there'll be hunters willing to kill 'em."

"We saw some buffalo on our way to Sweetwater," Bethany said softly, sadness touching her face. "I thought they were magnificent. They were frightening and yet so noble."

She confused him, this girl. One moment, the flirt. And the next—

"Have you ever killed a buffalo, Mr. Chandler?"

"No, Miss Silverton, I haven't."

She smiled, and it was as if the sun had come from behind a cloud. "I'm glad."

In that moment, completely against his will, so was he.

FIVE

"I wish I'd never made that miserable wager." Bethany passed a dripping dish to Ingrid. "Then I wouldn't have to see Hawk Chandler ever again." She groaned. "The way Papa carried on. All I did was go for a horseback ride like I've done countless times before."

"We can forget the wager if you would like."

"We will not!" Bethany dropped a dirty skillet into the wash water, splashing soapy suds onto her apron. Her eyes narrowed as she began to scrub, imagining it was Mr. Chandler beneath the wire brush. "I'll win that wager, and I'll make him pay for the trouble he's caused me."

Even now, five days later, her father's angry scolding echoed in her mind. "I'll not have a daughter of mine behaving like some wild street urchin. Riding out alone so far from town without protection. Calling on unmarried men without a chaperone. I won't have it, Bethany Rachel. I will not have it."

"But Papa—"

"You'll not sweet-talk me out of this. I forbid you to ride that horse of yours for two weeks. You'll have so much to do around the house you won't have time for more shenanigans."

"But Papa—"

Her protests had been to no avail.

So here she stood, up to her elbows in dishwater on a sunny morning, her mare locked up in the stable. This was Hawk

Chandler's fault. If he hadn't insisted on coming back to town with her ... If he hadn't told her father how dangerous it was for her to be out riding on the prairie ... If he hadn't told the reverend about their visit to his ranch ...

It was his fault, and by hook or by crook, she meant to get even.

Ingrid touched her shoulder. "You should not be thinking such things."

"What things?" She scrubbed the skillet even harder.

"You know what things. You should forgive Mr. Chandler. He was only trying to protect us."

"Don't you stand up for him. Don't you *dare* stand up for him. I'm almost as mad at you as I am at him."

Her friend's hand fell away and her gaze dropped to the dish she was drying.

Bethany knew she should apologize. Ingrid's feelings were easily hurt. But right now she didn't care. It stung her pride that Rand Howard had been the first person to arrive at church on Sunday. Even a blind fool could tell he was there because of Ingrid. Worse still, he'd come alone. After all the trouble Hawk had caused Bethany, he hadn't had the decency to come to church and apologize.

She stepped back from the counter and tore off her apron. "I'm going for a walk. I can't stand it in here one more moment."

She hurried out the back door without even a bonnet. What did she care if the sun darkened her complexion? Who would notice as long as she was a prisoner in her own home?

Holding her skirts out of the way, she walked across the open field behind the house, making for the cottonwoods and willows. On the bank of Spring River, she sat in the shade of the leafy trees. But even here she felt confined. As if it would help, she plucked the pins from her hair, setting it free to fall down her back.

It wasn't fair. It truly wasn't fair.

She was fond of Ingrid. She loved her like a sister and was happy Rand Howard was interested in her. He seemed a nice sort.

But, oh, it stuck in her craw that Rand had asked permission to call on Ingrid when all Hawk had done was scold her, treating her like a child and getting her in trouble with her parents.

The nerve of that infuriating man.

Wretched, uncouth cowpoke. You're a beast, that's what you are.

As she acknowledged the hurtful words spewing from her heart, her anger turned to shame.

"I'm sorry, God."

This morning her father had called her petulant. Perhaps it was true. Maybe she had behaved like a spoiled child.

"I don't mean to be this way, Lord."

She closed her eyes, meaning to pray and to seek God's guidance, but instead, her thoughts returned to Hawk. They'd returned to him all too often since the day she met him outside the saloon. Even her dreams betrayed her.

There is no earthly reason why I should think of him. He's nothing to me.

Many a young man had called upon her since her coming out, but there'd never been anyone who caught her fancy, no one who made her heart race. And now, to have this taciturn cowboy infiltrate her thoughts … Oh, it wasn't to be borne! He wasn't even a believer.

God, help me stop thinking of him. I don't care about my silly wager. She sighed. *Well, maybe I do just a little.*

Rand whistled as he and Hawk rode toward Sweetwater. He couldn't wait to see Ingrid again.

In all his twenty-five years, he hadn't felt this way before. It seemed as if he'd been looking for her all along. He wasn't about to let her get away now that he'd found her. He meant to sweet-talk that gal into marrying him. It didn't matter that he owned little more than his clothes, tack, a couple of horses, and a piece of land. It was enough to make a start. He would build a house, warm and tight against the cold Montana winters. They would be happy there.

He grinned. If he and Ingrid were happy as man and wife, could be he'd build a bigger place than originally planned, just in case they were blessed with a baby before the first year was out.

"What's got into you?" Hawk asked.

"Nothin' in particular. Just glad I'm havin' supper at the Silvertons. You oughta join us. The reverend invited you too."

"I don't think Miss Silverton feels the same."

"So what are you going to do? Head on back to the ranch after you check on those supplies you ordered?"

"I haven't decided."

"Miss Silverton's mighty pretty to look at across a supper table."

This time Hawk replied with a grunt.

Rand chuckled. "Suit yourself."

Hawk dismounted in front of the mercantile and watched his friend continue down Main Street toward the reverend's house. No way would he admit that he'd like to see Bethany again. Ever since he'd left the Silverton home last week, he'd been haunted by the memory of her angry gaze following him out the door.

He turned away from the store and cut between two buildings, headed for Spring River, hoping a walk would clear his head. The trees were in glorious spring foliage, a stark contrast to the brownish-green grasslands. A welcome breeze rustled the leaves overhead as he followed the river's edge.

He stopped when he saw Bethany, seated in the shade near the riverbank, knees pulled close to her chest. A vision to behold. Her hair fell in a mass of curls, touching the ground behind her. Her eyes were closed, but her lips were moving. Talking to herself or to God?

He stepped closer to a tree, melting into the shadows.

Bethany opened her eyes and released her legs, then stretched her arms high over her head. A smile played across her mouth. She pulled up the hem of her skirt and, with nimble fingers, untied her shoes and removed them. Then she rose and stepped to the river's edge, testing the water with the toes of her right foot, drawing back with a gasp at the cold water. But she didn't give up. She pressed her lips together in determination, lifted her skirt almost to her knees, and stepped into the river.

In the years since Hawk had left Chicago, he'd avoided women for the most part, except for the ones who worked in saloons from here to Texas. A man couldn't compare those painted, hardened faces with Bethany's fresh-faced beauty. Rand was right. It would be a pleasure to look at her across the supper table.

It would be better, of course, if he didn't allow himself said enjoyment. There was no room in his life for a woman. Any woman. This one in particular. She was the daughter of a preacher. He didn't have much use for church. She was a lady. He was no gentleman. She was used to the finer things that came with money and a place in society. That same society had no use for someone like him.

If he was smart, he would turn around and walk away, straight back to the mercantile. Better yet, he ought to mount up and ride his gelding back to the Circle Blue as fast as the horse could carry him. Instead, he stepped from the shadows and moved toward the river.

"Afternoon, Miss Silverton."

She jerked as she looked up. Her foot must have slipped on the slick rocks that lined the riverbed. Eyes wide and arms flailing, she fell backward into the swift-flowing water.

SIX

Bethany felt Hawk Chandler's hands grab her as the current drew her under. He pulled her to her feet, then scooped her into his arms, sodden gown and all. Coughing and sputtering, she wrapped her arms around his neck, holding tight as he carried her out of the river.

She looked into his eyes, his face close to her own. His gaze was disconcerting to say the least, and in response her heart fluttered like a hummingbird's wings.

"I'm getting your shirt wet," she said softly.

"It will dry."

"Hadn't you best put me down?"

He complied.

"Thank you for rescuing me."

The corners of his mouth lifted. "You made quite a splash for such a small thing."

His words begged a sharp retort, yet she felt no irritation with him, made helpless by the magnetic pull of his grin. She couldn't resist smiling in return. "Yes, I suppose I did."

"I'd better see you home. You should get out of those wet things."

"You'll want a change of clothes as well, Mr. Chandler. You're nearly as wet as I am."

"I'll dry off on the ride back to the ranch."

"Nonsense. You must stay for supper. Mr. Howard will be there." Her heart was racing again. "Won't you please stay?"

Hadn't she been furious with him only a short while ago? She'd even sworn to get even. But those thoughts were forgotten now.

Please stay. Please don't disapprove of what I do or say. Let me see your smile again. Please.

"Please," she repeated aloud.

Something in his expression said he regretted his teasing comment, that he would much prefer his own company to hers. But he surprised her. "I guess I can't refuse after causing you a dunking in the river." There was no denying he acquiesced with great reluctance. It was clear in the less-than-pleased set of his mouth and the grudging tone of his voice.

"No, Mr. Chandler, you most certainly cannot. Having supper with us will be the only way to make up for giving me such a fright." She didn't care that his acceptance lacked enthusiasm. Given a little time, she could change his mind. She was sure of it.

"Then I guess I'll stay, Miss Silverton."

They walked side by side in silence back to the house. Once there—after a quick explanation for her wet appearance and disheveled hair—she excused herself and left Hawk in the parlor with the others while she flew up the stairs to her bedroom. The water-soaked skirt fell in a puddle of fabric on the floor, followed by her blouse. She was pulling on clean drawers when a soft tap sounded on her door.

"May I come in?" Ingrid asked.

"Yes."

Bethany quickly donned a fresh chemise and ruffled muslin petticoat. "What dress should I wear, Ingrid? Help me decide."

Her friend joined her at the wardrobe.

"Do you think he would like the rose sateen? Mother says it brings out the red in my hair. Or maybe I should wear the dark blue." *It's almost the same color as his eyes.*

"You look lovely in anything."

Her hand stilled. "I'm acting like a fool, aren't I?"

"Are you?" Her friend shook her head. "I think he is very handsome. I would want to look my prettiest too."

"You are pretty," Bethany insisted, grabbing Ingrid by the shoulders and turning her toward the mirror. "Mr. Howard can't take his eyes off you. I saw that the moment I entered the parlor, even as wet as I was."

This was a lie. She hadn't been aware of anything or anyone except Hawk Chandler. But Ingrid needn't know that, and it was only a small lie meant to give her friend some confidence. Surely that was forgivable.

Ingrid's voice was whispery soft, breathless with hope. "Do you really think so?"

She nodded.

"Bethany?"

"Yes?"

"I am not sorry we came to Sweetwater any longer. Even if the saloons are noisy."

Bethany smiled as she squeezed her friend's arms. Then she turned away and withdrew the rose-colored gown from the wardrobe. Ingrid helped slip it over her head, fussing with the skirt while Bethany buttoned the bodice down to its pointed waist. Then Ingrid brought a towel and dried Bethany's hair as best she could before coiling it into a chignon at the nape and capturing it in a rose-colored net to match the gown.

As Bethany cast a critical eye at her reflection, Ingrid said, "You do like him, don't you?"

"I ... I don't know." She worried her lower lip. "He's so ... so different from any man I've known before. He either makes me feel unsure of myself or angry when I'm with him. Usually both."

"You did not bring him here today in order to win your wager?"

Bethany laughed as she rose from her dressing table, her uncertainty vanishing. "Oh, I intend to win the wager. *You* are going to owe me that five dollars yet."

Hawk turned when he heard the muffled whispers of the two young women. They entered the room arm in arm, but it was only Bethany he noticed. A sharp longing shot through him. Had he ever seen a more delightful and beguiling—

The cold splash of reality hit him. A young lady of position and wealth was not for Hawk Chandler. Wasn't even what he wanted. He liked things the way they were now. Women—especially of Bethany's ilk—would bring nothing but misery into his life. He could count on it.

A gray-haired woman in a black dress and crisp white apron appeared in the parlor doorway. "Mrs. Silverton, ma'am. Everything is ready."

"Thank you, Griselda." Bethany's mother turned toward her guests. "Gentlemen, shall we go in to supper?"

The reverend stepped forward to take his wife's arm, and the older couple led the way to the dining room. Rand and Ingrid followed next, leaving Hawk and Bethany alone in the parlor. Left with no choice, he held out his arm to her. When she slipped her fingers into the crook of his elbow, he felt her quivering.

He looked at her. Petite, delicate, and fragile. Too fragile for the hard land outside of a home like this one. He caught a whiff of her toilet water, something like wildflowers on a spring morning, and was tempted to lean down, press his face to her hair, and breathe in. She tipped her head to look at him, and their gazes met. Her eyes widened, as if she'd guessed his thoughts and was alarmed by them. Good. She ought to be afraid of him. It would be better for them both.

They sat down at the dining room table, Mr. and Mrs. Silverton at either end, Bethany and Ingrid on one side, Hawk and Rand opposite them. The reverend spoke a blessing over the meal, and then Griselda brought the food from the kitchen.

"I understand you raise cattle, Mr. Chandler." Virginia Silverton passed him the platter of meat as she spoke.

"Yes, ma'am."

"Is it a family ranch?"

"No, ma'am. My parents were never ranchers."

"Do they live nearby?"

"My parents are both dead."

Compassion filled her eyes. "Oh, I'm sorry. I didn't know."

"No reason you should have." Hawk looked down at his plate. "They passed away quite a few years ago now. Back in Chicago where I grew up. They died in the great fire."

The woman murmured her sympathies.

"You grew up in Chicago?" Bethany said, surprise in her voice. "I thought you had always lived in Montana."

He shook his head. "Not always."

"Hawk and I met on a cattle drive from Texas," Rand said. "He was fresh from the city and didn't know a steer from a mule. Me, I've been on my own since I was thirteen. So I figured I'd try and make a cowboy out of the greenhorn. Didn't do too bad of a job, if I say so myself. Been together ever since. Truth is, he couldn't've done it without me."

Nathaniel chuckled. "Why do I have the feeling, Mr. Howard, that your story is somewhat exaggerated?"

"Guess I should know better than to try to pull the wool over a minister's eyes." Rand winked at Hawk.

But the reverend was wrong. Rand hadn't exaggerated much. As Hawk acknowledged his friend's words with a nod, he felt Bethany watching him, wondering about him and his past. Might as well tell it all. Get it over with.

He turned a purposeful gaze on her. "My father was a newspaperman. Traveled all over the West when he was young. He met my mother in the Dakotas. My grandmother was a full-blooded Sioux, and my grandfather was a French fur trapper. Crying Wind, my mother, was their only child." He waited for some reaction. No one said anything. "When my father took a job with the newspaper in Chicago, they went there to live. That's where I was born. My mother was never happy in the city. She felt closed in and longed for the plains. And people weren't kind to her." *Or to me.* "But she loved my father. Her home was with him to the end."

"Have you met any of your mother's family since you left Chicago?" Bethany asked, her voice soft.

The question brought back a long-ago memory. He was seven years old and had been in a fight with some of the boys at school—the ones who called him names and said even worse things about his mother. He'd come home with a black eye and bloody nose. Crying Wind had cleaned his wounds and put him to bed.

As she tucked the blankets around him, she leaned close and said, "Never be ashamed that you are of the Sioux, my son. Our people are a proud race. But you are also a white man. Be proud of that as well. There are cruel people like those boys in both worlds. It is up to you to be different. Do not learn to hate. Rise above it."

Her smile had been tender, her eyes misty. "If you grow up to be like your father, you will be the best kind of man."

Hawk shook his head, both in answer to Bethany's question and to shake away the memory that brought tightness to his chest. "I didn't belong in the Sioux world." He looked at each person around the table, ending with Bethany. "But I make no apologies for my heritage."

She didn't bat an eye. "Why should you, Mr. Chandler?"

It was not the response he expected, and he felt something soften in his heart. Something hard and unyielding that had been there since he was a boy of seven, fighting for his mother's honor.

SEVEN

Bethany tossed another gown across the bed and eyed it with disgust. "It's not right. Not a one of them is right." Clad in chemise and drawers, she turned toward the wardrobe.

"But you have many pretty gowns." Ingrid picked up the blue gingham from the floor where Bethany had dropped it earlier. "What is wrong with this one?"

"Half the women in town will be wearing one just like it." *Hawk will never notice me if I look like every other female.*

"I think you want to please Mr. Chandler."

"Certainly not!" It was a lie, and they both knew it.

Ingrid turned toward the bedroom door. "He may not even come to the dance," she said as she left.

Bethany flounced down on the bed, pushing the pile of clothes onto the floor. "He'll come. He's got to come."

When she'd first heard there was to be a barn dance, she had written to Mr. Chandler and Mr. Howard that she had enjoyed their company at supper and she hoped they would be at the dance. Her father would be appalled if he learned of her bold behavior. But how else would she win her wager with Ingrid if she didn't have the opportunity to see Hawk Chandler?

Cupping her chin in her palms, elbows resting on her legs, she recalled once more the way she'd felt when he pulled her from the river. She wanted to feel that way again. She would if he were to dance with her. She knew she would.

A glance toward the window told her the hour was growing late. She had to decide on something to wear. She slid off the bed and returned to the wardrobe. There must be something that would catch his eye.

Phil Potter's new barn smelled of fresh-cut lumber. The hard-packed dirt floor had been swept free of straw, and a long table, covered with a white tablecloth, had been set near the far wall. It was laden with cakes, cookies, and pies, as well as a large crystal bowl. Laura Potter, Phil's wife, stood behind the table, filling cups with punch.

As soon as the Silvertons were inside the barn, Virginia said, "I'm going to give Mrs. Potter a hand."

Bethany glanced around the large, airy structure, looking for Hawk, her eyes roaming from one person to the next. When someone smiled at her, she smiled in return, but didn't allow her gaze to linger. The search proved futile. He wasn't there. He hadn't come. She'd been certain her personal invitation would bring him here tonight.

"Good evening, Miss Silverton."

She turned, swallowing her disappointment and forcing her face to a pleasant expression. "Good evening, Mr. Richards."

"I'm flattered you remember me." He bowed, then turned toward her father. "Good evening, Reverend. I wanted to tell you how much I enjoyed your service on Sunday. Truly inspiring."

"I'm glad you thought so."

As the two men fell into conversation, Bethany's attention wandered once again, this time to see who else she knew.

There was John Wilton, the pharmacist. No sign of his wife, Sarah, who was close to the end of her confinement. Next to John was Sweetwater's doctor. Doc Wilton was taller than his brother and had a full head of brown hair, graying now at the temples. Like John, Doc wore spectacles, and it amused her to see them push their glasses up their noses in unison.

A fiddle began to play. Soon other instruments — more fiddles, a flute, a mouth organ — joined in. A young man in a too-large suit set aside his cup of punch and walked across the barn to speak to Martha Eberlie. The girl blushed lobster red. The color didn't suit her.

An unkind thought, to be sure.

The music drew more people inside the barn, and soon it echoed with happy voices and shared laughter.

Ingrid tugged at Bethany's elbow and whispered, "They are here."

Bethany looked toward the entrance, her pulse quickening. There were five men — Hawk, Rand, and three others. But Bethany had eyes only for Hawk. How handsome he looked in his white shirt and dark trousers.

Rand said something to him, and he nodded as his gaze traveled the room, stopping upon Bethany. Her heart skipped a beat, then raced again as he turned away.

Rand walked toward Bethany and Ingrid, whisking his hat from his head as he drew near. He came to a halt in front of Ingrid. "Evenin', Miss Johnson."

"Good evening, Mr. Howard."

"Evenin', Miss Silverton."

"Good evening."

He repeated the greeting to her father, but when he looked at Vince, his good humor disappeared. "Richards."

"Howard."

It was obvious the two men felt a mutual dislike.

Rand looked at Ingrid again, and his smile returned. "Care to join me for a glass of punch, Miss Johnson?"

"Thank you. I would like that very much."

He offered his arm and escorted her away.

Bethany looked toward the entrance, hoping Hawk might follow the example of his friend. Instead, she saw that he and the other cowboys had moved away from the door and now leaned against the wall of the barn, visiting among themselves. He didn't even glance her way.

The musicians struck up a lively tune, and soon the center of the barn was filled with dancing couples, Ingrid and Rand among them.

Vince turned from her father and held a hand toward Bethany. "May I have the pleasure of this dance, Miss Silverton?"

She didn't want to dance with him, but neither did she want to remain standing with her parents. Perhaps it would be good for Hawk to know others desired her company, even if he didn't.

"Thank you, Mr. Richards. I'd be delighted."

Hawk watched Bethany. He hadn't stopped watching her since he arrived. There was no lovelier woman in the room, no one else to command his attention. Not that he was glad of it.

When Vince Richards walked her to the dance floor, he felt his jaw clench. He didn't like seeing that man put his hand on the small of her back. He was a snake. A wealthy one in fine clothes, but a snake all the same.

It wasn't his concern, of course. She could dance with anyone she chose. Still—

"Evening, Hawk." Fred Eberlie, owner of Sweetwater's mercantile, stepped up beside him. "I got in those supplies you were waiting on."

He pulled his gaze away from the couple on the dance floor. "That's good. I'll bring the wagon for them tomorrow."

"We don't often see you at these shindigs."

"Not often." From the corner of his eye, he saw Bethany whirl past him, her skirt flaring out almost far enough for him to touch it. Against his will, his gaze followed her.

"Have you met the reverend and his family?" Fred asked. "I'd be glad to introduce you."

"I've met them."

"They're nice folks. Guess you heard we'll be building us a church now. Can't keep meeting in a tent come winter."

"Guess not."

"Can we count on you and your men to give us a hand when it's time?"

Hawk nodded as he watched Vince escort Bethany back to her father. "Sure, Fred. We'll all help."

Bethany danced twice with Vince Richards, three times with her father, and one dance each with four young men whose names she forgot as soon as they walked away. And still Hawk stood in that dim corner of the barn. What on earth was wrong with him? Was he afraid? Didn't he know how to dance?

Squaring her shoulders, she slipped away from several women who were visiting near the refreshment table. She didn't allow herself to consider what her parents would think of her actions. As she approached Hawk, he turned his head and their gazes met.

In a fluid motion, he pushed off the wall, straightening to his full height. She couldn't tell if he was pleased or annoyed to see her. Blood pounded in her temples and her mouth went dry.

"Hello, Mr. Chandler."

"Miss Silverton."

"I'm glad you came tonight. Are you having a pleasant time?"

He gave her one of his looks.

"Don't you like to dance?" She glanced toward the couples on the dance floor, then back at Hawk, hoping her expression wasn't too eager.

"I like it well enough."

Oh, he was an infuriating man. But at least she'd learned he could dance.

The strains of a waltz came from the loft.

One of the men who stood nearby said, "Go on, Hawk. Don't disappoint the lady. Ask her to dance."

Heat rushed into her cheeks. What if he refused? She would die of mortification.

His dark eyes seemed to bore into hers, warning her of something she didn't understand. Then he took her by the hand and led her onto the floor.

Bethany had been introduced to society two seasons before her family left Philadelphia. She had danced beneath glittering crystal chandeliers to the music of full-piece orchestras. She had glided in the arms of handsome young men from the finest families in the East. Clad in yards and yards of satin and lace, she had whirled past walls lined with gilded mirrors. But never could she remember an evening so brilliant, a moment so wonderful, as the one she knew now, dancing in the arms of Hawk Chandler.

She wished the music would go on forever.

Hawk sensed people watching them, could feel the disapproval. There were those who thought him not good enough for a young lady like Bethany Silverton. Maybe they were right. Maybe he wasn't good enough. But he didn't want to stop dancing with her. Not yet.

It was the cessation of music that made the decision for him. He stepped back and reluctantly released her. "Thank you for the dance, Miss Silverton."

Her cheeks were flushed, her eyes bright. "It was my pleasure."

For a moment, his gaze lingered on the fullness of her bottom lip. A mouth made for kissing.

But not by me.

He placed a hand beneath her elbow and steered her across the barn toward her parents. After a slight nod to her father, he turned to leave.

"Wait!"

Warily, he turned.

"I . . . I hope we'll see you on Sunday." The color in her cheeks deepened. "In church, I mean."

With a noncommittal nod, he turned and left the barn.

EIGHT

Bethany awoke long before the sun was up on Sunday morning. The moment her eyes opened, she thought of Hawk.

Would he come to church as she'd asked?

She slipped from her bed and padded on bare feet to the window. Sweeping aside the lace curtains that her mother had brought with them from the East, she looked outside. Her father's white tent reflected the last traces of moonlight. A gentle early-morning breeze ruffled the canvas flaps and stirred the buffalo grass. Overhead, a canopy of fading stars filled the lead-gray sky.

She leaned her elbows on the windowsill and cupped her chin in her palms as her gaze moved past the tent toward Spring River. Her thoughts returned to the moment when Hawk had pulled her from the water. No man had made her feel this way before. It was a terrible and wonderful ache that wound around her heart and tumbled her stomach. In Philadelphia, boys and young men had surrounded her even before she was of age. She'd loved to flirt and laugh with them. It was great fun to be the center of so much male attention. But no one in her past had come close to making her feel the way Hawk Chandler did with nothing more than a glance or a touch.

Certainly not Martin Phillips, who had kissed her when she was thirteen. She hadn't given him an opportunity to do that again.

Certainly not Stephen Patrick. She was sixteen when he asked her father for permission to come calling. Their families, the Patricks and the Silvertons, were longtime friends, and everyone thought Stephen and Bethany would make a good match. But as nice as Stephen was, Bethany was always glad when his visits ended. No, Stephen never made her feel the way Hawk did.

Nor Harold Masters, her constant suitor while the Silvertons resided in Denver. Harold's family had made their fortune in the gold and silver mines of Colorado, and he was building a fine mansion at the time they met. His proposal came as no surprise to anyone, but her refusal astonished them all. No, Harold never made her feel the way she felt now.

Only Hawk did that. Just his name made her skin prickle with gooseflesh. She scarcely knew him, and yet she could think of little else.

Am I falling in love?

She turned from the window and sat on the floor, back against the wall, tucking her feet beneath her nightgown as she hugged herself, hoping to calm the wild sensations inside her.

She couldn't be in love. Mother said love needed time to grow. Her parents had known each other a number of years before her father approached her mother as a suitor. Surely that was the way one fell in love. It couldn't happen so quickly. Not with a stranger. And a non-Christian at that— at least as far as she could tell.

She closed her eyes and pictured him once more, standing beside the corral at the Circle Blue. His face was dusty, his shirt sweaty, his hair tousled. His expression was stony, eyes unreadable. And then she imagined his rare smile, and she went weak inside.

Could this be love?

"I'm going to church," Rand said. "You comin'?"

Hawk peeled another strip from the wood he whittled. "No. You know how I feel about church."

"Yeah, I know. Just thought you might change your mind."

"I can worship God easier on horseback."

"Miss Silverton will be disappointed."

Hawk grunted without looking up and was relieved when he heard Rand leave.

He wished his friend hadn't mentioned Bethany. He'd managed to put thoughts of her out of his head for a short while. Now they returned in a rush.

"I make no apologies for my heritage," he'd said to her.

"Why should you, Mr. Chandler?"

He couldn't describe how those words made him feel, both the night she'd said them and now as he remembered them.

She'd invited him to church more than once. Would it be so onerous to oblige her?

His parents had been faithful members of a Chicago congregation when he was a boy. He'd spent most Sunday mornings of his youth sitting in a pew between them. He'd heard the preacher talk about the love of God—and then he'd seen church members turn their backs on his mother.

If that was God's people in action, he could do without them.

"Why should you, Mr. Chandler?"

He remembered Bethany's expression when she'd asked that question. Guileless. Earnest.

He gave his head a shake. It didn't matter if she was different and without prejudice. There were a hundred other reasons why he needed to keep his distance.

Her father was not some itinerant preacher. He was a man of means and culture. Their home, though modest, was beautifully furnished. They had a housekeeper, brought with them from Philadelphia. The women in the family wore tailored gowns, not the sort one could buy ready-made from the mercantile.

And who was Hawk? Nobody special. He owned his land, and he had a good herd of cattle. But it was only a beginning. His cabin would never do for a girl like Bethany, a young lady of quality used to the finer things. She wouldn't last one winter on a place like his. And while most folks in these parts accepted him and gave no thought to who his mother or father were, there were some who would disapprove if he had anything to do with Bethany Silverton.

He threw his pearl-handled knife at the cabin. Its sharp point slid with ease into the wooden door, the handle vibrating from the impact.

Women.

He got to his feet, a scowl furrowing his brow as he jerked the knife from the door and slipped it into the sheath on his belt.

The last thing I need is to get mixed up with her or her kind.

❧

Taking her eyes from the hymnal, Ingrid cast a furtive glance toward the man at her side and found Rand watching her. He stopped singing and grinned. She dropped her gaze as the heat of embarrassment rose from the neckline of her gown all the way to the cowlick in the middle of her bangs.

She'd never before had a suitor, and it was beyond belief that any man would single her out when he could have chosen Bethany instead. Ingrid wasn't pretty, and she was too tall and too thin. She had no family, no money of her own. Yet there he was, standing beside her, for all the world to see.

The hymn ended, and the congregation sat on the wooden benches. Reverend Silverton took his place at the makeshift pulpit. Ingrid tried to concentrate on his words, but she couldn't keep her thoughts from straying to the man seated on her right. Something told her the day would come when he would ask her to marry him, and she knew with equal certainty she would accept.

For the first time since her father died, Ingrid wasn't afraid of the future.

Bethany was miserable. Not only hadn't Hawk come to church, but for the second week in a row she was forced to sit beside Ingrid and Rand. Not that she begrudged Ingrid her happiness. Truly she didn't. Still, if Rand was here, why wasn't Hawk?

He must have understood how much she wanted him to come. She'd made it clear—and in front of half the town too! He could have done it to be polite, if for no other reason.

Oh, for pity's sake. It didn't matter to her if he came or not. She couldn't care less. She wasn't falling in love with him. She wasn't interested in him. Not one little bit. Her competitive nature had gotten the better of her. That was all. So what if she lost that stupid wager? It was only a game, and Ingrid didn't have five dollars anyway.

And yet . . .

Her father spoke the last amen, and Bethany rose from the bench, hoping to get away by herself so she could sort through the confusion roiling inside her.

"Good morning, Miss Silverton." Vince Richards tipped his hat as he addressed her. "Wonderful sermon today."

"Yes, it was. My father's a fine preacher."

"Miss Silverton, would you do me the honor of dining with me? I had my cook prepare a basket lunch, in case you were agreeable."

"Well, I ..." She glanced behind her, looking for an excuse to refuse. She didn't feel like being with anyone. But when she saw Ingrid and Rand speaking to each other, smiling all the while, suddenly it seemed worse to be alone. "I will have to ask my father."

"Allow me. We'll picnic within view of the house, and if you or he would prefer, we can bring Miss Johnson along."

She swallowed a sigh. "I believe Miss Johnson has other plans."

A short while later, with her father's blessing, Bethany walked beside Vince toward the river. She steered him away from the place where Hawk had pulled her from the water. She didn't want any reminders.

Vince carried the blanket and picnic basket to a place with a clear view of the house and church tent. She watched as he spread the blanket over the level ground, wishing all the while she hadn't accepted his invitation.

"Here." He held a hand toward her. "Let me help you."

Sometimes, Bethany thought as she settled herself on the spread, her impetuous nature got her into terrible pickles. This was one of those times. She had no desire to encourage this man's interest. He might be handsome and wealthy, and it might not be unusual for girls of eighteen or twenty to marry men in their late thirties—which he most certainly was—but she didn't want him for a suitor. She wasn't interested.

Because he isn't Hawk.

Everything about Vince paled in comparison.

Dark, irritating, wonderful, enigmatic Hawk.

She sighed.

"Is something wrong, Miss Silverton?"

"What?" She looked at Vince, half surprised to find him still there. "Oh, no. I . . . I was daydreaming. I'm sorry."

"No need to apologize." He reached for the basket. "Let's see what my cook has prepared for us."

Hawk spotted Rusty Andrews's sorrel in the distance, grazing at the edge of a draw, reins dragging the ground. But the Circle Blue cowpoke was nowhere in sight. Ever vigilant, Hawk drew his rifle from its scabbard and nudged his gelding into a canter, eyes scanning the countryside, looking for signs of trouble.

The riderless horse shied backward as Hawk drew his own mount to a halt. "Rusty?"

"Down here."

He followed the sound of the cowboy's voice and found him crouched over a dead cow in the dry creek bed.

"What happened?" He dismounted.

The cowboy looked up, his weathered face crinkling as he squinted into the sun. "Neck's broke. Happened early this morning, I reckon."

Digging his heels into the loose soil, Hawk descended into the draw. His eyes studied the area around the brindled cow. It hurt to lose cattle, especially after they'd made it through a rough winter.

"There's tracks up there you oughta look at." Rusty straightened, pushing his hat back on his forehead. "I think someone was driving her down into the draw."

"Rustlers?"

"Probably."

Hawk removed his hat and drew his shirtsleeve across his forehead, wiping away the beads of sweat.

"I tried to follow 'em, but the tracks disappear down the creek bed a ways."

"How many riders?"

"Couple of them, it looks like."

"Horses shod?" No shoes meant Indians. Shod meant white men—and maybe a bigger problem than just a few missing cows.

"Shod."

Hawk looked again at the brindle. If the rustlers could have been followed, Rusty would have done it already. "Tell the boys to keep a sharp eye out for any signs of more unwelcome visitors."

"I'll tell 'em."

The chances were slim they would find anything. Besides himself and Rand, the Circle Blue employed Rusty and two other cowboys. They were kept busy enough without looking for a trail left by rustlers.

But neither could Hawk let himself be robbed.

Rusty seemed to read his mind. "With that new herd of shorthorns you got comin' in from Oregon next month, you're gonna be needin' more men on this place."

Hawk nodded.

"Matt says there was some boys in the Plains last night on their way to Miles City, lookin' to hook up with an outfit on the Big Dry. Might see if you can still catch 'em."

Hawk glanced at the midday sun. "Think I'll do that. If I run into Rand, I'll tell him to come give you a hand." He climbed out of the draw, mounted his horse, and set off for Sweetwater.

Nine

Bethany smoothed her skirt over her knees and folded her hands in her lap, hoping her impatience didn't show. Would her father never stop asking Vince Richards questions about Montana Territory? She longed to excuse herself from their company, but her parents would consider that rude.

Her hour by the river with Vince had been the most intolerable of her life. If only he would leave.

What she wouldn't give for a solitary ride on Buttercup. To feel the sunshine on her face and the wind in her hair. To canter her buckskin mare across the rolling plains or walk her along the river's edge. To be anywhere but here.

Finally Vince made a motion to leave. "Well, Reverend, it's been a pleasant afternoon, but I must return to the Bar V." He looked at Bethany. "I hope we can do this again, Miss Silverton."

Smiling—not in response to his suggestion, although he probably thought so—she rose and wasted no time in leading the way to the front door.

As he stopped before her, he took one of her hands in his and lifted it to his lips. "You're a charming companion, Miss Silverton."

Uncomfortable, she withdrew her fingers from his grasp.

"The Bar V needs a young woman like you as its mistress."

What arrogance! As if she would ever marry him, after one hour in his company or after a thousand. She quelled the desire to shudder. "Then I hope that you will find her, Mr. Richards."

His voice dropped to a near whisper as he leaned closer. "*You* are that woman."

She took a step back. "I assure you, sir, I am not she. I am not interested in finding a husband. You will have to look elsewhere."

Vince straightened. "Don't be so quick to reject me." His smile contained no warmth. "I have a great future in this territory, and I want you to share it with me." With that, he placed his hat on his head and left the house without a backward glance.

Standing in the open doorway, Bethany felt utter revulsion. She scrubbed the back of her hand against her skirt, trying to remove any trace of the man's kiss. That would never happen again, she vowed. Never.

Piano music from the Plains Saloon drew her gaze down the street. Ingrid would be—

Her heart thudded when she saw the familiar saddle horse tethered outside the saloon. Hawk was in Sweetwater. He hadn't come to church this morning, but he was in town now. In town and in the saloon, no less. She moved onto the porch and leaned against the railing, her anger with him forgotten.

Walk through those doors, Hawk, and look this way. Please. Come out and see me on the porch.

But it didn't happen. The laughter and the music wafted through the swinging doors, but no one entered or departed.

If this was what falling in love was like, it wasn't the happy feeling she'd been told it was. She'd never been less happy in her life.

Hawk shook hands with the two cowpokes. "Matt here'll show you how to get to the ranch and where to bunk. Glad to have you with us, Caleb. You too, Westy."

Caleb Moore had worked a cattle drive with Hawk back in '76. He was a good hand and would fit in well at the Circle Blue. And while Hawk didn't know Westy, the man had a look about him that spoke of experience on the range.

"You comin', Hawk?" Matt pushed away from the bar.

"Not yet. Thought I'd wait and ride back with Rand if I can find him."

Matt flashed a crooked grin. "You'll probably find him at the parson's house. Been there all day, far as I know."

"You sure?"

"His horse is tied out back by the tent. He's sweet on that Miss Johnson in a bad way." Matt motioned for Caleb and Westy to follow him, and they left the saloon.

Hawk stood alone at the bar, undecided what to do next. When he'd ridden into Sweetwater about an hour ago, he'd recognized the carriage hitched outside the Silverton home. Was it still there? He doubted Vince Richards was there for spiritual guidance, which left only one other reason for the man to be there this long after the church service ended. Bethany. Richards' interest had been made clear at the barn dance. This just confirmed it. Hawk shouldn't care, but he did. He didn't like the idea of Vince Richards hanging around Bethany. She was too good for him.

Hawk had a lot of reasons to distrust the man. Vince had been after the Circle Blue ever since he came to this part of Montana and built the Bar V. Hawk wasn't fooled by his veneer of civility and manners. He was ambitious and ruthless—a dangerous combination.

He strode out of the saloon and looked east. The carriage was gone. Tension eased from his shoulders as he gathered his horse's reins in his hand and stepped into the stirrup.

"I've got to be gettin' back to the ranch soon." Rand cast a furtive glance at Ingrid, walking by his side.

"I thought you might."

"It's been nice spendin' the afternoon with you."

"It was nice for me too, Mr. Howard."

He stopped and reached out to lightly touch her elbow. "You think you could bring yourself to call me Rand?"

She blushed and dropped her gaze to the ground.

"I guess that's not proper."

"I would like to call you Rand."

He loved the soft rolling sound of her voice. He wished she would continue to speak. Words weren't easy for him to come by, especially sweet-talkin' words. At the dinner table after church, it had been the reverend and his wife who kept the conversation alive. And even after he asked Ingrid to take a walk with him, he'd spent most of the time thinking of what he wanted to say without ever saying it.

He motioned with his head toward a grassy spot on the riverbank. "Care to sit a spell 'fore I take you back to the house?"

She nodded, a hint of pink returning to her cheeks.

He waited until they were settled. Then he cleared his throat. "Ingrid, I been driftin' ever since I left Iowa back when I was a kid. I liked movin' around, seein' new things. Never thought of settlin' in one place 'til I met Hawk."

"You are a good friend to Mr. Chandler."

"He's about the best friend a man could ask for. I'd trust him with my life. I've had to a time or two." He glanced at her, then looked away again. "Anyways, I got me a piece of land near the mountains. Nothin' to ranch with. Just a spot to build me a house and barn of my own. Plenty of trees and a fine view of the range."

"It sounds pretty."

Not as pretty as you are.

A fleeting smile crossed her lips, as if she knew his thoughts.

"I haven't built nothin' there yet. Seemed just as easy to go on bunkin' with Hawk and the other boys at the Circle Blue." He cleared his throat again. "But, here lately, I been givin' it some thought. Seems like a good idea to get busy while the weather's good. Wouldn't be too fancy. Just a log cabin, but a place I could call home and ... and the sort of place a woman might not mind callin' home too." His last words came out in a rush.

A lengthy silence followed. He couldn't bring himself to look at Ingrid. He figured he'd made a mistake, that he'd spoken too soon. What would she want with some log cabin anyway? Look at the fine house where she lived. Why would she want to settle down with him?

It was as if she'd read his mind. "My papa and mama came to America from Sweden. We had a farm in Minnesota where I was born. When my mama died, my papa did not want to stay there. So he sold the farm. I have missed it. It was hard work, farming, but it was a good life." She drew a deep breath and sighed. "The Silvertons have made me a part of their family, and I love them. But sometimes I feel too idle. I wish I were building something for myself as you are going to do."

Their heads turned. Their gazes met. There was a glimmer of light in Ingrid's eyes, a gleam that told Rand she understood what he hadn't been able to say, that told him she wanted the same things too. It was all he could do to keep from letting out a whoop and grabbing her and kissing her smack on the mouth. But he couldn't do that. Not yet. He had to have something more to offer her before he proposed.

He got to his feet and held out his hand. "I better get you back before the reverend comes lookin' for us."

She placed her hand in his and allowed him to draw her up from the ground.

He would start work on the cabin this week.

Bethany opened the door. When she saw who stood there, her breath caught. She'd given up hope, but now he was here.

"Mr. Chandler."

"Miss Silverton. I'm looking for Rand. His horse is tied out back."

"He … he and Ingrid went for a walk. They should be back soon."

He glanced behind him. "Maybe I'd better go back without—"

"Don't go." She hated the pleading sound of her voice, but she didn't want him to leave. "I'm sure they'll return any minute. Won't you wait for him here? You could sit on the porch if you like." Before he could answer, she slipped by him, pulling the door closed behind her. "There's more shade on the side porch." She led the way. *Please make him follow me.*

He did.

She settled onto a cane-backed chair and took a moment to smooth the skirt of her floral-embroidered dress. Hawk chose to lean against the porch railing. Although he appeared relaxed, she sensed an undertow of tension, of power barely leashed.

"I looked for you in church this morning."

"I told your father I wasn't much on churchgoing."

Disappointment sluiced through her. "Yes, I remember. But I'd hoped ..." She let her words fade into silence.

He didn't seem to notice.

Any moment, Rand and Ingrid could return from their walk, and once they did, Hawk would ride away with his friend. What could she do to make him notice her, to make him want to stay?

How frustrating. She hadn't needed to do a thing to attract Mr. Richards, but she didn't want his attentions. She wanted Hawk's. There was something about him, something so different, so ... so unlike any other man she'd known.

She rose from the chair and stepped to the railing, an arm's length from where he stood. "Would you like something to drink? It's a long ride back to your ranch."

"No, thanks. I'm fine."

He was the most exasperating man. Did she have to throw herself at him?

She could hear her father's voice of warning in her head: "A woman's chaste and respectful behavior is her most appealing attribute, Bethany."

Somehow she doubted Hawk would notice any behavior, good or bad. He'd scarcely looked at her since he arrived. How could he tell what her behavior was like if he didn't look her way?

Tears sprang to her eyes. "Why don't I see if I can find Rand and Ingrid," she all but mumbled as she took a step away from the railing. But somehow her foot caught in the hem of her dress. She stumbled and tried to catch herself by grabbing the railing. Only it was out of reach.

Hawk caught her before she could hit the floor.

First the river, and now this. He must think her a terrible stumblebum.

He righted her, his hands holding her upper arms. He was so close she had to tip her head back in order to meet his gaze.

She didn't know how it happened. She didn't plan it. Never thought she would do anything so brash. But somehow she rose on tiptoes, pulled him toward her, and kissed him on the lips.

It lasted an instant.

It lasted an eternity.

Shocked by her own audacity, she drew back, covering her mouth with one hand. Her embarrassment worsened when she realized he looked more surprised than she felt.

He hadn't wanted her kiss.

Let me die. Let me die right now.

She whirled around and raced into the house.

TEN

On the following Saturday evening, Hawk sat in a washtub in the middle of the kitchen. He didn't dawdle. There was no room for a man to stretch out in the round tub. With a bar of soap, he scrubbed his hair and body, then stood and poured cold water from a bucket over his head to rinse himself clean. After he was dried off and dressed again, he checked his reflection in the small mirror that hung on the wall. He needed a haircut. He should have seen the barber the last time he was in town.

"Now I must say. You're lookin' right pretty, Mr. Chandler."

He turned to see Rand leaning against the doorjamb, a grin splitting his face. "If you plan to see Miss Johnson tomorrow, you'd better take a bath yourself. You smell like you've been tangling with a grizzly, and you don't look much better than you smell."

His friend laughed. "I reckon you got a point." He didn't move from the doorway. "You got plans in town tonight?"

"No." Hawk raked his fingers through his hair. "Not tonight."

"And tomorrow?"

"I thought I might ride in with you for church."

"Do tell." Rand came inside and sat at the table.

Hawk glowered at him.

Apparently his friend took note of the look for he changed the subject. "I was up on my land earlier this week. Laid out plans for the house I'm gonna build. Thought I'd get a start on it this summer. Have somethin' to live in before the first snow maybe."

Hawk took a seat at the table across from his friend, guessing what was coming next.

"I'm gonna ask Ingrid to marry me."

"I thought you might. Congratulations, Rand. I'm glad for you. She seems a nice girl." He glanced around the kitchen. "You know, I could move into the bunkhouse with the men and let you and Ingrid stay here if you wanted."

"Thanks, but I'd rather have our own place. I figure Ingrid deserves that."

"Sure. I understand."

Rand stood. "Reckon I'll go have that bath now. But I'll just use the creek. Easier than haulin' water, if you ask me."

Hawk stayed at the table for a long while after his friend left, thinking about this turn of events. Anybody with two eyes could see those two were crazy about each other. He'd figured it was only a matter of time before Rand would want to tie the knot.

What he hadn't figured on was feeling envious.

He rose, walked outside, turning when he was almost to the corral, and took a good long look at his house. It wasn't much. A log cabin with four small rooms. Plenty enough for two cowboys who did little more than eat and sleep there. But how would it look to a woman?

Like a shack. Not the sort of place a man would bring his bride.

Against his will, he thought of Bethany. Again. He thought of that unexpected kiss. Again. Whispery soft. Unbelievably sweet. Completely innocent.

More than once this past week, he'd wished he could turn back time, that he could undo the moment when he allowed her to step away from him. If he could do it over, he would pull her close and kiss her the way a man kisses a woman. He would hold her close and never let her go.

He'd long told himself he was better off alone. What if he'd been wrong about that? And what if a woman like Bethany... No, not a woman *like* her. What if Bethany could be happy with him? Shouldn't he give himself—and her—a chance to find out? Maybe the many things that should separate them weren't as insurmountable as he'd always thought.

Bethany stood on the porch, her cheek against the post, and watched the setting of the sun. The bright orange ball seemed to rest on the peaks of the mountains, turning the dark, pine-covered slopes a fiery red. Then the sun slipped behind them. The fire-hot colors of sunset faded to a deep purple, announcing the coming of night. As the sky darkened from blue to pewter to black, she saw the first twinkling star above the tallest peak.

Hawk's mountains. That's how she thought of them. Beneath their shadows, he was probably getting ready to turn in for the night.

She sighed.

"What's troubling you, dear?"

The question drew her from her thoughts. She'd forgotten she wasn't alone on the porch. "Nothing, Mother."

"You've been sighing and moping all week long. Is it because your father forbade you to go riding? That will end soon. It's been two weeks."

"That's not it." Again she sighed.

"Are you unhappy in Sweetwater? Perhaps you would like us to send you back to Philadelphia. I know your grandmother or Cousin Beatrice would—"

"I don't want to leave Montana. I love it here."

"Then what is it, dear? Please tell me."

How did a girl ask her mother about love and men and ... and kissing? She adored her mother, but somehow she couldn't talk to her about ... this. She couldn't tell her that she laid awake nights thinking about kissing Hawk Chandler. She searched for something—anything—to say, as long as it wasn't about him.

Looking at her mother, she said, "Ingrid's in love with Mr. Howard."

"Yes, she may be growing to love him." Her mother rose from her chair and came to stand before her, cupping Bethany's chin with one hand. "Is that what's troubling you?"

"No. Not really. It's just ... it's just that I was wondering. How does it feel to be in love?"

It was her mother's turn to sigh. "Quite wonderful, dear. And sometimes quite awful."

That was an apt description. Wonderful—and awful. "But ... how do you know when you're in love?"

"When it happens, you'll know. That's how it was with your father and me. He was always around because of his friendship with my brother, Frederick. I never gave him much thought. And then one day, after he came back from seminary, he was at our house for supper, and I looked at him across the table, and I knew I loved him. I'd grown to love him over time. That's the best kind of love."

"Ingrid hasn't known Rand very long. Don't you think their love will last?"

"Oh, my. That is how that sounded. I suppose love comes to a few rather quickly. Perhaps that is true of Ingrid and her young man. But remember, even if Mr. Howard asks Ingrid to marry him, they won't get married in haste. They'll have a period of engagement. That will give them time to be sure marriage is what they want. Ingrid is young, but she's a sensible girl."

She patted Bethany's cheek and stepped back from her. "Your turn for love will come. One day you'll meet the right man, someone who shares your faith and your dreams for the future. I pray that he will be as fine a man as your father." She paused, then added, "I think it's time we both said good night. It's growing late, and tomorrow is Sunday."

"Just a little longer, Mother."

"All right, dear. But not too long."

"I'll be in soon. Good night."

"Good night, dear."

When the door closed behind her mother, Bethany turned her gaze once again to the west. She could no longer see the outline of the mountains against the inky darkness of the sky, yet she stared hungrily in their direction.

Wonderful and awful.

She couldn't, she shouldn't be in love with him. He didn't match the description of the man her mother had prayed for her to find. He didn't share her faith. If he did, he would be in church on Sundays. And how could he share her dreams for the future if she didn't know what they were herself?

Oh, God. Do you have someone in mind for me? I fear if you don't that I'll make a terrible mess of things.

Her heart fluttered as she remembered the kiss she'd shared with Hawk on this same porch in this same spot almost a week ago.

But if it could be Hawk, Lord, I wouldn't mind. I wouldn't mind at all.

ELEVEN

On Sunday morning, Hawk rode into town with his ranch hands. The brim of his black Stetson shadowed his eyes, eyes that watched for one particular person in the flow of people walking toward the tent. As he drew his horse to a halt, he saw her with her mother and Ingrid.

Bethany saw him too.

He smiled.

She didn't.

He reined in, dismounted, and tied his horse to the hitching post. The other men followed suit.

When he turned, he found her still watching him. Her hair was mostly hidden beneath her bonnet, a satin ribbon tied in a bow near her right ear. A shawl, the same color as her eyes, was draped low across her back and through each arm. In her hands she held a Bible.

I shouldn't be here. He moved toward her even as that thought crossed his mind.

No, he shouldn't be here, but here he was. He didn't care if she was the daughter of a wealthy man and he was a working cowboy. He didn't care that some folks would censure them, that they would consider him unsuitable for her. He didn't care about any of the possible differences that might separate them.

"Mr. Chandler ... you're here." Her voice was soft and inviting.

"I decided I couldn't refuse your invitation again."

Color brightened her cheeks. "I'm glad." She lowered her eyes. "I hope you'll be blessed."

If he had her regard, then he was already as blessed as any man had a right to be. It surprised him, discovering he felt that way.

After church, Ingrid and Rand stood off to one side of the tent, watching the townsfolk and ranchers as they visited with one another. Silence stretched between them, and the silence made Ingrid anxious. Why couldn't she think of something to say?

Rand spoke at last. "I started clearing a spot on my land this week." He looked at her. "I know right where I'm going to build the house. Would you like to see it sometime?"

"I would like that very much."

"I want you to tell me if you like what I'm plannin' to do." He paused and that drew her gaze to him at last. "You see, I want it to be your house too."

She didn't know what to say. She'd hoped, even though she'd not dared to hope.

He cleared his throat. "I love you, Ingrid. I know most folks will think it's a mite fast, but it's how I feel. Will you be my wife? I haven't much to offer, but I sure will love you."

She opened her mouth but found her throat too tight to speak. Her eyes watered. Any moment her face would be tracked with tears.

"I'm sorry, Miss Johnson." The uncertain expression on his face turned to one of despair. "I knew I was bein' foolish, but—"

"Yes." She took his hand, whispering, "I want to be your wife. Yes, I will marry you."

It was as though the sun broke through his clouded face. He looked around, and then drew her through an opening in the tent. He didn't let go. "You've made me the happiest man in the territory." He kissed her cheek.

"I am happy too. But you must speak to Reverend Silverton. I cannot marry without his blessing."

"Of course. Of course." He grinned from ear to ear. "Wait until I tell Hawk."

"Not yet. Please say nothing until you speak to the reverend."

"Why don't I do that right now?"

Joy welled up inside her. She smiled even as she stopped him. "No, Rand. Do not speak to him today. I fear he will answer that it is too soon or that I am too young. I want to prepare him, as best I am able. Will you wait one more week? Just one."

He kissed her again, this time on the lips. "I'll do whatever you ask, long as it means you'll still want to marry me."

"I will. I promise."

They slipped back into the tent, and Ingrid searched for a glimpse of Reverend Silverton. She found him engaged in conversation with Hawk, Bethany, her mother, and a couple from town.

"Bethany said she would get him to come to church," Ingrid marveled to herself, "but I did not believe her."

"Who? You mean Hawk? Yeah, I was surprised. He hasn't darkened a church door since I've known him."

"Wherever will I get five dollars?"

"What'd you say?" Rand leaned closer.

Oh, gracious. She hadn't meant to say that out loud. "Nothing important. I should not have spoken of it."

"Of what?" He looked at her fondly. "We're gonna be married. You can tell me anything."

"I cannot tell you this."

"If it concerns you, it concerns me. Tell me, Ingrid, if for no other reason than you love me."

❧

Hawk had come to church because he wanted to see Bethany, but he had to admit, he'd enjoyed listening to her father's sermon. The message was one of hope for those who trusted in Christ, and the words the reverend read from Luke and Romans had tugged at his heart.

Memories of the nights when his mother sat beside his bed, reading aloud from her Bible, filled his head. "God will watch over you, my son. Trust him." Much had changed in his life since then, but he knew she would still say those words to him if she could. "God will watch over you, my son. Trust him."

Maybe the reasons he'd stayed away from church weren't valid ones.

"We hope we'll see you next week, Mr. Chandler."

He looked at Virginia Silverton, wondering what else she might have said while he was lost in thought. "I'll do my best." His gaze shifted to Bethany. "I'm glad you asked me."

Her smile was a wondrous thing to behold.

When would he have the chance to kiss her again?

❧

Hawk and Rand were halfway back to the ranch when Rand broke the silence with a chuckle.

"Something funny?"

"No. It's nothin'." Then he laughed again.

"Come on, Rand. Must be something."

"Nothing, really. Just something Ingrid told me."

"Well, tell me so I can laugh too."

"You cost her five dollars today."

He lifted an eyebrow in question.

"I swear it's the truth. Seems that first day we saw Ingrid and Bethany in town, Ingrid took one look at you and said they wouldn't ever see you in church."

He failed to see the humor in that.

"Maybe it's because we were outside the saloon. Anyway, Bethany made a wager that she could get you to come to church within a month."

"She what?"

Rand didn't seem to notice Hawk's darkening mood. "And she did it too. With a week or so to spare, I'm thinkin'. So now Ingrid owes her five dollars."

Hawk felt like he'd been hit dead-on by a buffalo. So it had all been a joke. Getting him to church had been a game to her. Her coy glances, her shy smiles, even her innocent kiss had been a sham. A lark. He should have known. He'd thought she was different, but she was just another hypocrite.

Something in his stomach tightened and twisted.

"You think that's amusing?" he said in a low voice. "How about a wager of our own?"

Rand's smile faded.

"Something a little more difficult." Something that would make Bethany regret playing games with the lives of others.

"Wait, Hawk. I don't think you want to—"

"Fifty dollars says I can get her to agree to marry me before the end of June." He turned a cold gaze on his friend. "And not a word to Ingrid, either. This is between you and me."

"But you don't want to marry Bethany. Do you? Why put her and you—"

"Marriage isn't part of the bet. I only have to get her to agree to it."

"Hawk, I—"

"Think I can't do it?"

Rand shook his head. "You're wrong about this. You're wrong."

"Is it a bet or not? Because I'm doing it anyway."

❧

The pale light of a first quarter moon fell through the hall window on the second floor of the Silverton home as Bethany tiptoed past her parents' bedroom. Reaching Ingrid's door, she tapped lightly, then slipped inside.

"Ingrid? Are you awake?"

"Yes," came a mumbled reply.

"I couldn't sleep. Can we talk?"

"Mmmm."

Bethany closed the door and hurried across the room. She sat on Ingrid's bed, tucking her feet beneath the quilt and drawing her knees up beneath her white nightgown to hug them against her chest.

All afternoon she'd wanted to talk with Ingrid about how Hawk made her feel, but there had been guests for Sunday dinner, and then Papa had wanted to discuss plans for the building of the new church, and then it was suppertime already.

Ingrid pushed herself up against the headboard. "What is it?"

"Are you ... are you in love with Mr. Howard?"

Silence.

"Are you?"

"Yes, I love him." Another pause. "I'm not supposed to say anything yet, but today he asked me to marry him."

"He did! Oh, Ingrid, what did you say?"

"Yes."

Bethany launched herself forward, giving her friend a hug. "Oh, I'm so happy for you." She settled against the headboard at Ingrid's side. "Tell me how it happened."

"We were talking and he told me he was starting to build his own house ... and then he said he wanted it to be my home too." Moonlight caressed her face. "He told me he loves me."

Gooseflesh rose along Bethany's arms. She envisioned the scene, but instead of Rand and Ingrid, she saw herself standing with Hawk. She imagined him bending low to whisper those three wonderful words in her ear. Her heartbeat quickened.

"I wasn't to tell you until Rand speaks to your father. You must swear you will not tell a soul. Not anyone. Promise me."

"I promise."

"And I will pay you the five dollars as soon as I am able."

"Five dollars?"

"The wager, Bethany. Mr. Chandler came to church. You won."

Bethany laughed softly. "I forgot all about it. I was just so glad to see him." She sobered. "Do you suppose I could be falling in love too?"

TWELVE

On Monday, Nathaniel Silverton received an invitation for the family to tour the Circle Blue. The note was delivered by one of Hawk's ranch hands, who said he would return for his reply before leaving town.

"Papa," Bethany said when she learned what the note said, "we must go. It would be rude not to accept."

"We can't, my dear. He's invited us for tomorrow, and your mother and I have another obligation."

"Then let Ingrid and me go. Mr. Chandler said he would escort us if needed."

Nathaniel scanned the invitation a second time, then lifted his gaze to his daughter. She stood beside his desk, her hands clasped at her waist. Her expression was eager, her eyes pleading.

Throughout his daughter's life, Nathaniel had given her more freedom than most girls enjoyed. He'd been told as much for years. But he wasn't so liberal that he would allow her to visit an unmarried man unaccompanied by a chaperone. After the trouble she'd gotten into because of her impetuous ride more than two weeks ago, how could she think he would change his mind now? He did not doubt that Hawk Chandler would treat his daughter with utmost respect, but she was high-spirited and impulsive. Who knew what mischief she might cause herself?

She cares too much for the man already.

Bethany reached to touch his cheek. "I'm not a little girl, Papa. Surely you can trust me to behave like a lady. It isn't like I would be alone. Ingrid would be with me."

He shook his head. "Ingrid is not a suitable chaperone. She is younger than you are. Not to mention that she's formed an attachment to Mr. Howard."

"Then Griselda can go with us."

"Griselda?"

"Why not? She's part of our family after all these years, and she is certainly old enough. A more proper chaperone couldn't be found."

"I don't know."

"She won't let us out of her sight for a moment. I promise."

"Well, I suppose—"

"Oh, thank you, Papa!" She threw her arms around his neck and hugged him tight. As she pulled away, she placed a kiss on his temple, then whirled away in a rustle of fabric and was gone from his study in a flash.

Nathaniel shook his head as he rose from his desk and walked to the window. How much simpler things had been when she was a little girl, her long hair in braids and ribbons. He'd been the only man in her life then. But she had blossomed from that pretty girl into a beguiling young lady, and now there were other men who vied for her attention. With a cock of her head or a bat of an eyelash, she could have almost anything she wanted.

He wondered if he'd been wise to take her away from Philadelphia. The men out West—men like Hawk Chandler—were different. They were toughened by a hard land. When the time came, would she be able to find happiness with one of them?

Lord, grant me wisdom. And protect Bethany from her own headstrong nature.

Hawk was no stranger to prejudice and duplicity. He'd seen enough of it as a boy, and as a young man he'd been spurned because of his mixed race by the girl he'd come to love. But his humiliation at Bethany's hands struck much deeper than anything in his past. She had played him for a fool. She'd made him believe she cared for him, but all she wanted was to win a bet. Nothing more.

As he jogged his horse down Main Street, he schooled his face to reveal nothing of his thoughts, nothing of the anger that throbbed inside him. He would woo her. He would win her heart. And then, after she agreed to marry him, he would tell her what he thought of her and her selfish tricks.

He stopped at the white picket fence and dismounted. A carriage and one saddle horse waited at the side of the house. It looked as if the women were ready to go.

As his gaze flicked toward the front door, it opened, and Bethany stepped outside. His chest tightened when she smiled and waved. She was clad in a tan riding habit. The bodice fit snugly; the skirt was short and simply draped, accentuating the narrowness of her waist. A yellow cravat was tied in a bow at her throat, and a matching yellow gauze veil was wound around the crown of her tan silk hat.

A ridiculous outfit for riding the range. She should be on some mincing mare parading through a park. She didn't belong in Montana.

Yet, even as he told himself those things, he couldn't deny how pretty she looked. It made him ache for what might have been.

"Good morning, Mr. Chandler." Her voice was melodic, like a mountain songbird.

Had he noticed that before?

Don't be fooled by her.

He wrapped the reins around a fence post and opened the gate. "Morning, Miss Silverton."

"Ingrid and Griselda will be ready soon. Won't you come in and say hello to my parents?"

He stepped onto the porch and removed his hat. "Be glad to."

"It was kind of you to invite us to see more of your ranch."

Hawk let his gaze slide to her mouth, full, pink, and inviting. He meant to kiss that mouth again before this month was out. Perhaps before this day was out. Winning his bet didn't have to be an unpleasant task, after all.

The day didn't turn out quite as Bethany expected.

Rand met them near the spring above the ranch house where they ate a picnic lunch in the shade of the willows. Afterward, they explored the area, Rand driving the carriage with Ingrid at his side and Griselda on the seat behind them, Hawk and Bethany riding their horses nearby.

Rand did most of the talking, sharing stories of past adventures on the trail, of the first summer he and Hawk were in Montana, of the birth of Sweetwater two years before.

Hawk said little, but it wasn't his silence that bothered her. It was the way he looked at her, the way he'd looked at her all day. His dark eyes seemed cool and emotionless, even when he smiled—which wasn't often. She didn't understand. She'd thought he cared for her. Why else invite her to see his ranch?

"What do you think, Miss Silverton?"

"What?" She looked at Rand. "I'm sorry. I let my thoughts wander. The countryside is so beautiful."

"Glad you think so, because right over there is where I'll be building my house." He glanced at Ingrid, who blushed as she stared toward the homesite.

Bethany wondered if Griselda noticed the look that passed between the couple in front of her.

Why doesn't Hawk look at me that way?

She swallowed a sigh. It would be awful to let his strange mood spoil her day. "Are we going back to the ranch house now?"

Hawk nodded.

"Then let's race. Buttercup needs a gallop." With that, she gave the mare her head.

The wind felt good on her face. She only wished she could lose the hat and let her hair fly free. And why not? Who was to stop her? She loosed the ribbon and sent her hat soaring. Laughter burbled in her throat. Oh, how she loved the freedom of this land.

The ranch house had come into view before Hawk caught up with her, the discarded hat in his hand.

She smiled as she called to him, "Isn't it wonderful?"

"Slow down."

She laughed again and leaned forward, urging more speed from Buttercup. But Hawk was too quick. His hand shot out and grabbed the mare's reins, drawing both horses down to a canter, then a trot, and finally a walk.

"One of these days you'll break that pretty neck of yours."

"Don't be silly. I've been riding almost since I could walk."

He scowled.

Oh, he was frustrating. *But he thinks my neck is pretty.* Her heart sang.

They rode in silence the rest of the way, the carriage nowhere in sight. Obviously Rand didn't want to race either. Which served her purpose well. What dear, sweet Griselda—whose eyesight was not the best and whose hearing had diminished greatly—didn't see or hear, she couldn't report to Bethany's father.

In the barnyard, Hawk swung down from the saddle and came to stand between the two horses. Without permission, his hands spanned Bethany's waist, his grip warm and firm as he lowered her to the ground in front of him.

Her lungs lost all ability to take in air. He was near enough to kiss her. Would he? She wanted him to. He must know she wanted him to.

"I've got something to show you," he said, releasing his hold.

The sting of disappointment was keen. He'd acted as if it was unpleasant to be near her, as if he were merely tolerating her. Well, she wasn't going to tolerate his toleration. She would make him enjoy her company if it killed them both.

One did not catch a man by mooning over him. That's what Eliza Carpenter had told her when they were at Miss Henderson's. Eliza must have known whereof she spoke for she had married six months later.

Hawk headed toward the barn. "Are you coming?"

"Yes."

Bethany followed Hawk into the barn, stopping in the doorway to give her eyes time to adjust. Somewhere nearby a horse stomped its hoof and snorted. The air smelled of hay and horse and dung, pungent but not altogether unpleasant.

"Over here." He stood beside a stall. With his hand, he beckoned her onward.

Curious, she moved closer to peer over the stall door.

"This is Storm. Remember him?"

The black horse bobbed his head, causing his heavy mane to sway against his neck. He stepped closer to the gate, then pawed the barn floor before stretching his head forward to nibble Hawk's hand where it rested on the stall door.

She turned her gaze from the horse to the man at her side. "I'm sorry. Why would I remember him?"

"He's the bronc I was breaking the first time you and Ingrid were here."

"That's the same horse? But he looks as gentle as a lamb."

"A steady hand ... a calm voice ... a little time." His eyes held hers captive as his hand moved from the stall to her shoulder.

She trembled at his touch. Perhaps she'd been mistaken that he merely tolerated her company. Perhaps...

"You can tame the wildest of creatures that way." His other hand rose to cup her chin. "Bethany." He tipped her head back.

She held her breath, waiting, hoping.

The first brush of his lips against hers was so light, she wasn't sure they touched. In the next instant, an explosion of sensations spiraled through her as the kiss deepened. Involuntarily, her arms rose to circle his neck.

It was everything she'd hoped their next kiss would be, and when he released her, she felt bereft, abandoned. She hadn't wanted it to end.

This must be love. What else could it be?

Hawk stepped away from her. "We'd better go outside." His voice was low and husky. "The others should get here soon."

THIRTEEN

Bethany rolled onto her back, arms on the pillow above her head. Morning sunshine warmed her face as it fell through her bedroom window. Eyes closed, she allowed a soft moan to slip between her lips.

Each time she remembered yesterday's kiss, it became longer and more breathtaking. She'd never felt like this before. It must be love. For both of them. He wouldn't have kissed her if he didn't love her. Not like that.

Throughout the night she'd thought of him, dreamed of him. As the hours passed, she forgot the cool look that could glaze his eyes. She forgot the firm set of his mouth that sometimes made him seem harsh. She saw only his wonderful, rare smile. She heard only the gentle sound of his voice when he'd spoken her name. He must love her. He must.

She opened her eyes, her heart quickening again. If only she could be with Hawk today. She wanted to throw caution to the wind and hurl herself into his arms and let him kiss her again and again and again.

But, of course, she couldn't do that. She would have to wait until he called upon her. How soon would it be? Today? Tomorrow? Next Sunday? When?

"Bethany, dear." Her mother's voice was followed by a rap on her door. "Are you awake?"

"Yes, Mother." She sat up.

Her mother opened the door. "Have you forgotten? The men start work on the church today. We need your help."

"I did forget. I'm sorry. I'll hurry."

Following a quick washing, she dressed in a white blouse and dark blue skirt, then tied her hair at the nape with a matching blue ribbon. By the time she was downstairs, her mother, Griselda, and Ingrid were making sandwiches and rolling dough for piecrusts.

"What can I do to help, Mother?"

"Eat your breakfast first."

"But I'm not hungry."

"Eat anyway, dear. It's going to be a long, busy day for everyone. You'll need your energy."

There was no point arguing with her mother at a time like this.

Thirty minutes later, she carried a tray out the back door. She placed the cups and pot of coffee on a table that had been set up in the shade of a tree. Before returning indoors, she paused to take in the activity.

The building site was located between the Silverton home and the boarding house. Stacks of lumber waited on the north side of the lot. Several men were stretching twine between pegs that had been driven into the ground. Nearby, her father stood with John Wilton and Fred Eberlie, the three of them studying the plans for the new church.

She called to him, "Papa, I've brought coffee."

"Thank you, Bethany."

There was joy in her father's eyes. His dream was coming to life. This was what he'd worked toward from the moment he felt God calling him away from the familiar and into the unknown.

How blessed her family was. They couldn't have known when they boarded that train in Philadelphia how happy they would be when they reached their final destination. Sweetwater was a place they hadn't heard of until two or three months ago. Her mother, of course, was happy wherever Papa was, and Papa was happy because he was fulfilling God's purpose and calling. Ingrid was happy because she was engaged to Rand. And Bethany? She was happy because she'd found—

"Good morning, Miss Silverton."

She whirled around, hoping she hadn't conjured his voice. Hawk Chandler stood not more than four feet away from her, his shirtsleeves rolled up above his elbows.

"I'll have some of that coffee if it's for the taking."

"I didn't know you would be here today."

His gaze held her captive as his lips curved. "Coffee?"

"Of course. I ... I'm sorry." She lifted the pot and poured the dark brew into a cup.

His fingers touched hers as he took the cup from her grasp. She felt a spark ignite between them. Had he felt it too? No, he didn't seem to.

He took a sip. "Not real hot, but it's better than what I make." He smiled briefly, then raised the cup to his lips and drank, his Adam's apple moving with each swallow.

She tried to think of something to say, anything that would keep him with her for a while, but her mind was blank. That's what being near him did to her all too often.

He held the empty cup toward her. "Thanks." He glanced behind him. "I'd better get back to work."

Don't go. Talk to me a little longer.

He stopped and looked at her again. "Your hair looks pretty in the morning light. You should wear it down like that more often."

If she died right now, it would be from pure bliss.

❧

From his vantage point atop the stack of lumber, Vince ground his teeth as he watched the brief exchange between Hawk and Bethany. Minutes before he'd heard one of the Circle Blue men mention that Miss Silverton and Miss Johnson had paid a visit to the Chandler ranch the previous day. He hadn't believed it. Hadn't thought it possible that her father would allow anything so foolish. But now it seemed the proof was right before his eyes.

By thunder, this wasn't to be borne. That young woman was destined to be his bride, whether or not she knew it. He would not see her reputation sullied by association with a worthless saddle bum who didn't know his place. If the reverend didn't have the good sense to protect her, then Vince would have to step in and show him the error of his thinking.

Hawk turned and walked back toward the building site, but Bethany didn't move. Even from here, Vince could tell she watched Hawk with longing, a longing no decent woman should feel, let alone reveal, except for her husband. One day he would teach her that lesson.

❧

It was almost sunset before Hawk rode his horse into the corral at the Circle Blue. The stretch of muscles across his upper back and shoulders ached with fatigue, but it was a welcome feeling. He was ready to drop into bed and fall asleep, ready to get that green-eyed beauty out of his mind.

Several times during the day, she'd brought trays of food and drink to the laboring men. Each time she'd sought him out with her eyes, and each time he'd felt drawn to her. The feeling angered him. Her duplicity was flawless. Why didn't she leave him alone? She'd won her bet.

Of course, he wouldn't win his own wager if she decided she didn't like him, so he supposed it was as it should be. He couldn't have it both ways.

In the dying light, he unsaddled his horse and placed the saddle and blanket over the top corral rail. He scratched the gelding beneath his mane.

"Women," he muttered.

Flame snorted and bobbed his head, as if in agreement.

"A man would be better off with just his horse, wouldn't he, fella?" He stroked the gelding's muzzle. "Just plain better off."

FOURTEEN

Bethany fingered the bolt of fabric and pondered again the gown she had in mind. If she could get her mother and Ingrid to help, she knew the dress could be finished by next week.

"Good morning, Bethany."

She looked up from the fabric. "Hello, Martha."

"That's lovely material. The finest in the store." Martha Eberlie, who worked most days in her parents' mercantile, was a born saleswoman.

Bethany nodded. "Yes."

"It'll look pretty on you. Just the right shade of rose pink." She walked around the counter to stand opposite her. "I'll bet Mr. Chandler would like seeing you in that color too."

"Do you think so?"

Martha frowned. "For a city girl, you're not very smart."

"I beg your pardon?"

"Don't you know?" the young woman whispered. "Folks have been talking about you ever since the barn dance. You and him, letting him waltz you around like that."

"But why shouldn't I? I thought everyone liked Mr. Chandler."

"Most do. But that doesn't make him a proper beau for ... for any of the *nice* girls in town. My pa says the reverend should keep you at home where you belong before you're ruined, sure and for good."

Bethany's surprise turned to anger. "Who I dance with is no one's business but my own. Mr. Chandler is a gentleman." She sent an icy glare toward Martha. "And he would never stoop to gossip about others the way you gossip about him." With that, she whirled around and walked down the aisle toward the exit, head high, hands balled into fists. Only at the last moment did she see Hawk standing in the open doorway. Had he heard the exchange?

She stopped in front of him, her way of escape blocked. His expression revealed nothing—not anger or disgust or wounded pride or anything else. He simply looked at her with that inscrutable gaze of his.

Tears sprang to her eyes. Impulsively, she touched his forearm. "It doesn't matter what anyone says. It doesn't."

Then she slipped past him and hurried toward home.

"You must try to understand, Reverend. It's your daughter's welfare I'm concerned about."

Nathaniel understood, all right, but he wished he didn't. "Mr. Richards, I'm sure you mean to be helpful, but I'm afraid I do not agree with you. I find a great deal to like and admire about Mr. Chandler."

Those weren't idle words. They were true. Nathaniel liked Hawk Chandler. The young man wasn't the talkative sort, but Nathaniel had managed to pry more details about his life from him as they'd worked together on the church this week. He'd learned that Hawk's parents had been believers, something that, as a pastor, he could build upon.

"But an afternoon alone at his ranch." Vince leaned forward on the chair. "You must see how improper—"

"She was not alone, Mr. Richards. She was accompanied by our housekeeper as well as Miss Johnson."

The man had the decency to look repentant. "You're right, of course. I apologize. I didn't mean to imply that anything inappropriate happened." He stood and picked up his hat. "Thank you for your time."

Nathaniel wasn't sorry to see him go. Still, he said, "Thank you for coming." He followed Vince from the room.

Before they reached the front door, it flew open and Bethany entered the house. Her color was high, and her eyes had a watery gleam.

"My dear, what's wrong?" Nathaniel asked.

"Nothing." She didn't even glance at Vince before hurrying toward the stairway.

Nathaniel bid a hasty farewell to his visitor, his thoughts already upstairs. Should he ask Virginia to join him? No, she was resting. He didn't want to disturb her.

When he reached his daughter's bedroom door, he rapped on it softly. "Bethany?"

"Yes, Papa."

He opened the door. "May I come in?"

She sat on the end of her bed, dabbing her eyes with a kerchief. "Of course."

"Can you tell me what's wrong?"

"Martha Eberlie is a hateful thing." She sniffed.

"Is she?" He sat next to her. "And why is that?"

"She ... she's a gossip."

"Oh?"

Bethany blew her nose. "She implied very unkind things about Mr. Chandler. They like him, but … but no good woman should befriend him."

"Oh." He understood now. Fred Eberlie's prejudice had rubbed off on his daughter, Martha. How many others in Sweetwater thought like Eberlie and Richards? He hoped not many.

"Papa, why must people be hateful toward anyone who is different?"

"Because we live in a fallen world, my girl. I'm afraid people will continue to find reasons to hate until the day Jesus returns."

Pleading eyes turned in his direction. "You don't think it's wrong of me to like Hawk, do you?"

He noticed, of course, her use of Hawk Chandler's given name, and it told him a great deal about her feelings. Not that he hadn't guessed as much already.

Give me wisdom, Lord.

He took hold of her hand. "No, it isn't wrong. I like him myself. But guard your heart, Bethany. Don't give it away too quickly. Once given, it is hard to take back. I would rest easier if you expressed interest in a man with a strong faith in God."

She turned to look out the window. "I know, Papa."

And with those three words, Nathaniel knew his warning had fallen on deaf ears.

Late in the afternoon, Rand Howard sat on the edge of the sofa in the Silverton parlor, nervously sliding his hat brim through his fingers. His eyes shifted from the carpet to the rosewood claw feet of the nearby love seat, then returned to his battered hat. He heard the methodical ticking of the great mantel clock. The room seemed stuffy. His fingers came up to loosen the stiff collar that promised to choke the life from him.

"Sorry to keep you waiting," the reverend said as he entered the room. "I was working on Sunday's sermon. Ingrid tells me you wish to have a word with me. Nothing wrong at the Circle Blue, I trust?"

Rand stood. "No, sir, Reverend."

"Please, sit down, my friend."

He obeyed.

"You seem distraught. Are you sure nothing's wrong?"

Rand cleared his throat, his gaze returning to the dusty hat brim. "Well, you see, sir, I've got this piece of land up in the mountains a ways. I've been clearin' it this past week, gettin' it ready to build a house." He drew a deep breath. "I mean to build a house fit for a wife and family. I've asked Ingrid to marry me, and she says she's willin', but that I'd need to ask you for her hand, you bein' her guardian and all."

"I see. That is news."

"I figure it'll take me a few more weeks to get it fit for Ingrid. It won't be nothin' fancy. She knows that. But I love her, and I'll be good to her. I'll love her like Paul says a man's to do in Ephesians. I'd die for her if I had to. I don't own much, but whatever I got will be hers. She won't ever go without, Reverend Silverton. Not as long as I got a breath in me. I swear it."

Nathaniel smiled. "Swearing isn't necessary. I believe you." There was a twinkle in his eyes. "Your proposal doesn't come as a surprise. I believe your intended has been dropping hints all week long. And if she is willing, I will not withhold my blessing."

"You do?" Rand hopped up from the sofa. "I can? I mean, you will?" He let out a whoop, unable to stop himself.

The reverend laughed aloud as the women of the house rushed into the parlor. He looked at Ingrid who watched, wide-eyed, from the doorway. "You'd better tell her, Mr. Howard. She looks a little frightened."

Rand crossed the room in a few strides and took hold of his betrothed's hands. "The reverend said yes. We're gettin' married, just as soon as I got us a house fit to live in. God willin', that'll be soon."

FIFTEEN

Bethany paced from the parlor to the dining room, from the dining room to the kitchen, from the kitchen to the parlor again. She stopped at the window and looked at the town. The sun hung low in the sky. Soon it would dip behind the mountains. Hawk's mountains. The mountains where Rand was building a home for Ingrid. She sighed.

She was happy for Ingrid. Really and truly. She thought it wonderful that her friend had found love and would be married. But she also felt sorry for herself. Envy was not an attractive trait. God called it sin: A sound heart is the life of the flesh: but envy the rottenness of the bones.

Again she exhaled.

She hadn't seen Hawk since she ran into him—almost literally—at the mercantile the previous week. He hadn't come to services on Sunday nor had he been back to help with work on the church building.

Why are you staying away?

She flopped onto the settee and picked up the novel she'd been reading. The pages might as well have been blank. Her thoughts returned to Hawk.

What was she to do about him? She loved him, she was sure, but if he didn't come to town more than once a week, how could she make him love her in return?

She remembered his embrace in the barn at the Circle Blue, and her face flushed. He wouldn't have kissed her like that if he didn't care for her.

She tossed the book aside and walked once more to the window. A few lights had begun to appear as evening settled over the town. The sky was darker now. Black clouds, heavy with rain, had arrived with the coming of night. Thunder rolled in the distance.

When would her parents and Ingrid return? They'd gone to pay a pastoral visit on the Mackeys, whose farm was a good distance to the south of Sweetwater. The elderly Mrs. Mackey—Martha Eberlie's maternal grandmother—was ill and thought to be dying. Bethany's father had said it might be very late before they returned home. It could be later still if a storm caught them.

Perhaps she should have gone with them. She'd claimed a headache, but the truth was she'd expected Martha and her widowed father to be at the Mackey farm as well. She wasn't feeling charitable toward either one of them at present. They'd been hateful toward Hawk, and she couldn't find it in herself to forgive them yet.

"Oh, Mr. Chandler." She leaned her forehead against the cool pane of glass. "Why do you make me feel this way?"

Her shoulders drooped as she turned from the window and lit a lamp. Then, holding it before her, she climbed the stairs.

Her bedroom window was open, and a breeze brought with it the smell of rain. She set the lamp on the table next to her bed and crossed to the window to close it. After drawing the drapes, she shed her dress and undergarments and put on her nightgown. Then she sat on the edge of her bed, loosened her hair, and began brushing it.

And all the while, the same thought repeated in her mind: *Come to see me. I miss you.*

Hawk had waited too long before deciding to ride into town. He should have known it would be too late to pay a visit to the Silvertons by the time he reached Sweetwater. And maybe that was for the best. He had no business trying to court Bethany, no matter the reason, whether it was for real or for revenge.

And it wasn't for revenge. Not anymore. It had become increasingly difficult for him to believe the girl who'd invited him to church in order to win a wager was the same young lady who'd stood up for him in the mercantile last week. In his heart, he believed the real Bethany was the one in the mercantile, the one who'd touched his arm and, with tears in her eyes, said, "It doesn't matter what anyone says."

He slowed his horse as he drew near the Plains Saloon but didn't stop. He continued down the street until he reached the livery stable. There he dismounted, his gaze on the Silverton home. There were lights burning both downstairs and up. The family must be awake. It wasn't all that late. Maybe they wouldn't mind if he called on them at this hour. He left his horse inside the livery and strode toward the preacher's house. Raindrops began to fall, sparsely at first, then harder. If he didn't get under cover quick, he would be drenched.

He was past the boardinghouse and nearing the church site when someone grabbed his arm and yanked. As he spun around, a fist crashed into his jaw, knocking him backward. He stumbled, then righted himself. But before he got his bearings, his assailant slammed into him a second time. This time Hawk took a hard hit in the solar plexus. The air whooshed out of him.

Rain fell in sheets now, getting in his eyes, making it hard to see. The earth beneath his feet turned slippery.

As he straightened, he saw the approach of a shadowy figure. He took a swing and connected, heard a grunt of pain, and snarled in satisfaction. Another shadow came at him from his left. A blow to his jaw knocked him backward a second time. His boot slipped in the mud and he fell. His head struck something hard, perhaps a stack of lumber for the church. He rolled to his side, struggling to rise.

"We got a message for you, Chandler. Stay away from the Silverton girl."

One of the assailants kicked him in the ribs. Another kick and another and another. Fingers grabbed him by the hair, pulled his head up. A fist cracked against his cheek.

The men—he thought there were three of them—backed off. Were they leaving? He rolled onto his stomach, then rose up on all fours, coughing and gasping for air. Just one deep, long breath. That's all he needed. Just one long—

The toe of a boot caught him in the gut, so hard it lifted him off the ground. Then he slammed to earth again, and everything went blessedly blank.

There was a moment as consciousness returned when Hawk felt nothing except the cold of the rain and the mud on his skin. Then he tried to get up, and pain exploded. In his head. In his chest. In his gut. It shot to the tips of his fingers and toes.

By sheer grit, he rose to his knees, dragged in more air, and got to his feet. Water and mud—or maybe it was blood—ran into his eyes. He couldn't see anything clearly, but he made out some light that didn't seem too far away. Instinct pulled him toward it. He held one arm tight against his belly as he dragged one foot, then the other forward.

He didn't know how long it took to reach the porch of the preacher's house. Minutes? Hours? Holding on to the railing, he wiped his shirtsleeve across his eyes, trying to clear his vision, before staggering forward and falling against the door. With his right hand, he knocked. Once, then again.

At that point what little strength he had left him, and he slid down the door. Unconsciousness loomed a second time. He lifted his hand as though to knock again, but his arm fell back to his side.

"God, help me," he whispered before sliding again into the black abyss.

Bethany couldn't say what drew her downstairs. She thought at first that it was her parents and Ingrid returning, but there was no sign of them. She went to Griselda's room off the kitchen and listened at the door. The housekeeper snored in a steady, undisturbed rhythm. She smiled. Griselda was the soundest of sleepers, even moreso now that her hearing was getting bad.

She returned to the parlor where she lit a second lamp before pushing the drapes aside to look out at the rainy night. The street was empty. Only a few horses could be seen outside the Plains Saloon. Even the light that spilled through the swinging doors of the drinking establishment failed to reach very far. The blackness seemed complete.

She shivered and pulled her wrapper closer about her. Then she heard something. Not a knock. More of a thump. It seemed to come from the entry.

Her pulse quickened. Was someone in the house? Someone who didn't belong?

No, of course not. She was allowing her imagination to run wild. No one was in the house except her and Griselda. And Griselda was sound asleep.

She went into the entry hall, lamp in hand. Empty, as she'd been sure it would be. But there could be someone on the porch. Although why they would not knock to announce themselves—

They could be up to no good. She had to know. She had to reassure herself. She held her breath and reached for the doorknob. *Open it and see. Then you can go back to bed.*

There was a thud as the door creaked open. With a squeal of surprise, Bethany jumped back. Heart pounding, she held the lamp out in front of her.

And there he was, a man, soaked through to the skin, covered in mud, lying on his side where he'd fallen.

"Sir." She stepped forward. "Sir, are you all right?"

First she saw the blood.

Next she saw his face.

"Hawk?" She dropped to her knees, set the lamp to one side, and pulled his head into her lap. "What happened?" She wiped mud and blood from his face with the hem of her wrapper. "Oh, Hawk. Please wake up."

A gust of wind blew through the doorway, bringing rain with it. The water hit her face, tiny shards of glass against her skin. She must get him out of the weather.

She gently lowered his head to the floor. Then, standing, she grabbed him beneath his armpits and pulled. Nothing. He didn't budge. She grunted as she threw her weight backward. To her surprise, his body followed a few inches. She lost her balance, tried to catch herself, tripped on the hem of her wrapper, and heard it rip as she sat down hard.

"I didn't know you were so heavy," she muttered as she got up.

She eyed the distance she needed to cover before she could close the door. About a foot more should do it. She positioned herself at his head but noticed the torn wrapper waited to trip her again.

That wouldn't do. She untied the belt and removed the ruined garment.

It took a few minutes, but at last she managed to drag him far enough inside that she could close the door.

"Hawk?"

Nothing.

She ran to the kitchen and pounded on the housekeeper's door. "Griselda, wake up. I need you."

She didn't wait for the woman before going in search of bandages and ointment, water and soft cloths. It seemed forever before she was back to the entry hall and kneeling beside him. With one of the cloths, she washed the mud from his face and hair. He had cuts and scratches on his cheeks and forehead, and his lower lip was split. The wound that bled the most, however, was on the back of his head. It would need stitching.

She straightened. "Griselda!" Where was that woman?

She couldn't tell what other injuries he had as long as he was covered in his mud-soaked clothes. Perhaps she should go for the doctor. No, Doc Wilton was with Mrs. Mackey. If her parents weren't back yet, neither was the doctor.

She couldn't afford to be missish. Not when Hawk needed her. She freed the buttons on his shirt and removed it without too much difficulty. Holding the lamp above him, she looked at his chest and stomach. Angry red splotches, the beginning of bruising, covered his torso. There were more on his upper arms.

"What happened?" she whispered. "Who did this to you?"

SIXTEEN

Am I dead?

When Hawk opened his eyes, he saw a bright light above him and an angel clothed in white hovering nearby. The angel had a dark reddish halo. Weren't halos supposed to be golden? That's how most artists painted them. And he hadn't expected pain in heaven either. He'd thought it a place without hurt, sorrow, or tears. Maybe the Devil had taken his soul after all.

"Hawk?"

He blinked, trying to clear his blurred vision. It didn't work, so he closed his eyes again and concentrated on ignoring the pain.

"Hawk, please look at me."

He opened his eyes a second time. She leaned over him now, her hair falling over her shoulders. Ah, not an angel after all. "Bethany."

Her smile was uncertain. "Yes."

"How ... did I ... get here?"

"I don't know." She smoothed the side of his face with her fingertips. "I found you on the porch."

He groaned, the pain in his head throbbing.

"What happened?" she asked.

Stay away from the Silverton girl. "Somebody used me for a punching bag."

"Who was it?"

He grunted. It hurt to talk, hurt to breathe. "Not sure. Too dark." He gritted his teeth and tried to sit up.

Her arm was behind his back in an instant. "You shouldn't move yet. You're hurt. You need the doctor."

"Well, I can't stay on the floor of your entry forever."

"Let me help you then."

If he'd felt better, he would have laughed. She was a little thing. How much help could she be? But to his surprise, with his right arm draped over her shoulders, her left arm around his waist, she did get him to his feet. Only then did he realize he could feel the warmth of her hand on his skin. Where was his shirt?

Which must have been what the reverend and his wife thought when they opened the door at that precise moment.

Bethany felt awash in relief when she saw her parents. She didn't notice Ingrid and Martha Eberlie right away. She only knew that help had arrived.

"Papa, you're here."

Her father turned to her mother. "Virginia, you and Ingrid see Martha home." He stepped into the house.

In the moment before the door swung closed, Bethany caught a glimpse of Martha's horrified expression. Then she was gone from view.

"What is the meaning of this?" her father demanded.

Hawk's weight pressed on her shoulders, and she glanced up at him. His eyes had that glazed look again. She feared he was about to lose consciousness.

"Mr. Chandler, unhand my daughter. Bethany Rachel, cover yourself."

Hawk lifted his head. "I'm sorry, sir." He pitched forward, taking Bethany to the floor with him.

"Is he drunk? By heaven, if he's harmed you, I'll— "

She rose to her knees, tears streaking her cheeks. "He's not drunk, Papa. He's hurt."

"Hurt?" The anger left her father's voice as he knelt on the other side of Hawk. "What happened?"

"He's been badly beaten. He needs the doctor."

"Where's Griselda?"

"I don't know. I called for her, but she never came."

Her father looked at Hawk. "I'll stay with him. You go upstairs and change out of that nightgown before your mother returns."

She lowered her gaze. Her nightgown was wet from the rain, and the fabric clung to her like a second skin. In a flash, she pictured herself and Hawk as her parents, Ingrid, and Martha had seen them when they opened the front door. The heat of embarrassment flooded her cheeks.

"Hurry, Bethany. Make yourself presentable."

She dashed up the stairs to do her father's bidding.

❧

When Hawk came to, he found himself lying on the settee in the Silvertons' parlor, his feet hanging over the armrest. Someone had covered him with a blanket. He slowly turned his head. No one else was in the room.

He tried to sit up, but pain made him think better of it. With his right hand, he touched the back of his head and found it sticky with congealed blood. The pillow beneath his head would be ruined for sure.

Raised voices reached him through the parlor doorway.

"Her reputation will be forever ruined." Virginia Silverton.

"She was helping an injured man." The reverend. "They're innocent of any wrongdoing."

"No one will care what really happened. Appearances matter. They were both in a state of undress, and Martha saw them. She'll make certain others know what she saw."

"You don't know that, my dear. She may keep it to herself. I'm sure all will blow over soon. Once Dr. Wilton gets here— "

"No, Nathaniel, it will not blow over. In this matter, I understand the nature of people much better than you. Mr. Chandler has forever compromised our daughter's good name."

The sound of knocking ended the couple's discussion.

Hawk closed his eyes, a different sort of pain pounding in his head. His presence had compromised Bethany. He'd ruined her reputation by being here.

Stay away from the Silverton girl.

The door to the parlor slid open. He rolled his head to the side and looked to see who was there. Doc Wilton was the first to enter the room, followed by Nathaniel Silverton.

"Ah, good. You're conscious." The doctor set his black bag on the floor near the settee. "Care to tell me what happened?" He lifted the blanket to have a look at Hawk's torso. "I assume you lost the fight."

He grimaced. "That's a safe bet."

The parlor door slid shut again. Hawk glanced beyond the doctor and saw that the reverend had left the room.

Doc pressed against Hawk's abdomen with the fingers of one hand. "Does that hurt?"

Breathless with pain, he answered, "Only when I'm conscious."

"Well, at least you haven't lost your sense of humor."

That's what you think.

❧

Bethany wanted to know what the doctor had found. She wanted to ask him how serious Hawk's injuries were, if he was in danger for his life. But she knew better than to leave the kitchen. Not until her mother or father summoned her.

"He was hurt," she said to Ingrid, who sat nearby. "What else could I do?"

Her parents acted as if she'd broken half of the Ten Commandments in a single night.

All I did was try to help him. Can't they see that?

SEVENTEEN

Hawk was moved that night from the Silverton parlor to a spare room in Doc Wilton's home behind the apothecary shop. The doctor refused to let him leave until it was certain he'd suffered no internal injuries.

Two days later, after word reached the Circle Blue, Rand rode into town. "Who was it, Hawk? Me and the boys will— "

"I don't know who it was. It was too dark to see their faces."

"What did they sound like? Maybe that'll place 'em."

Stay away from the Silverton girl. He tried to see the man who'd spoken those words in a soft, raspy voice, but he drew a blank. "They did their talking with fists and boots."

Finding the men who'd given him the beating wasn't his first concern. What consumed his thoughts as he lay on the bed in the doctor's house was Bethany. Folks were talking about her, demeaning her unjustly.

He'd pieced together how things had looked when they were found together. Even with his thoughts dulled by pain, he remembered that she'd worn a white nightgown with pink ribbon woven into the fabric. He remembered that her hair had been unbound, falling over her shoulders in a mass of curls. He knew she had removed his shirt to tend his wounds and, because of it, she was the object of cruel gossip.

Mr. Chandler has forever compromised our daughter's good name.

This was his fault, and he would have to fix it. Only one way he knew to do that.

"Rand, I need you to ask the reverend to come see me as soon as he can. There's something I must say to him."

"Sure, Hawk. I'll go get him now."

❧

An hour later, Nathaniel closed himself in his study, knelt on the floor, and prayed. He begged God to show him what to do. Hawk Chandler's offer had taken him by surprise. The young man had done nothing more than lose consciousness after being brutally set upon. And what better place for him to come for help than to the pastor's home? It wasn't his fault that no one was there except Bethany and a hard-of-hearing housekeeper.

Which was worse, he wondered—the gossip that had spread through town, damaging his daughter's reputation or to allow her to be unequally yoked in marriage? The young man had a measure of faith, thanks to his Christian parents—that much Nathaniel knew—but Hawk Chandler wasn't wholly surrendered to the Lord.

Father God, grant me wisdom.

And what of Bethany?

Nathaniel leaned his head against his hands, folded on the chair. She loved the Lord, this child of his, but she didn't always put God before all else. Too often she let her emotions lead the way. It seemed to him that from the first moment she met Hawk, she'd rushed toward scandal of one kind or another. Her foolish ride out to his ranch. Her boldness in asking him to dance. And then last night ...

Lord, should I allow them to marry? What's the right thing to do?

❧

Bethany stood near the window of the front parlor, staring out at the town. It was warm, the remnants of the storm forgotten. After two days of sunshine, the muddy street had hardened. Soon dust would again swirl up behind horse hooves and wagon wheels.

Her gaze turned toward Doc Wilton's house. Was Hawk still there? No one had told her, and she hadn't had the courage to ask. Not with her mother acting as if the end of the world was nigh.

"Bethany?"

At the sound of her father's voice, she turned around.

"I need to speak with you."

"Yes, Papa." Her pulse quickened with dread. She didn't know what to expect from anyone at the moment.

Her father looked at her with somber eyes.

"What is it, Papa?"

"I have been to see Mr. Chandler at Doc—"

"How is he?" *Please let him be well.*

"He is mending."

"Thank God." She pressed her hands against her stomach and breathed a sigh of relief.

"Bethany." He cleared his throat. "He has asked for your hand in marriage."

"Marriage?" she whispered.

"Daughter, I blame myself for this unhappy circumstance. You have not always behaved with proper decorum, and I have too often allowed your impulsiveness to go without correction. If I'd been less lenient—"

"He wants to marry me?" Her heart bubbled over with joy. "What did you tell him?"

Her father crossed the remaining distance between them. "I told him I would speak to you." He put his hands on her shoulders and stared into her eyes. "Do you want to marry him?"

"Oh, yes, Papa." She felt no hesitation. Hawk had asked for her hand. Proof at last that he loved her.

"You're sure? Marriage is a serious decision, Bethany. Not one to be made lightly. Mr. Chandler is not what Philadelphia society would call a gentleman. His life hasn't been easy, losing his parents at a young age, growing up among cowboys on the trail. I cannot help but admire a man who is willing to work hard to make a better life for himself, and that he has surely done. But do I— "

"So you like him." The words came out half statement and half question.

Her father didn't answer at once. When he did, his words came slowly. "Yes, I do. He seems to be a decent man and, I believe, a caring one. But it won't be me sharing his home and his life, for better or for worse, for richer, for poorer, in sickness and in health."

"I love him."

"Marrying him may not stop tongues from wagging. People may be cruel to you."

"I don't care what people say or why they say it."

Her father continued to search her face with his gaze. "You've known him such a short time."

"No less time than Ingrid has known Mr. Howard, and you gave them your blessing."

"True." He shook his head. "But Rand Howard is a man of faith. He and Ingrid are much alike. Besides, they will not be marrying this afternoon."

She ceased to breathe. "Today? We're to marry today?"

"It may help protect you from those determined to speak ill of you both. But only if it's what you want, Bethany. Perhaps we should send you to your grandmother. In time you could— "

"Oh, Papa." She threw her arms around him and hugged him for all she was worth. "I don't want to be sent away. I want to marry Hawk."

EIGHTEEN

It hurt to walk and to stand, but Hawk managed to do both in order to be at his wedding. Shortly before the appointed hour, he arrived at the reverend's home, wearing a new shirt and a pair of trousers that Doc Wilton had bought for him at the mercantile. His grim-faced future father-in-law led him into the parlor where Rand, Ingrid, and the housekeeper—the only witnesses besides Bethany's parents—awaited him.

"I will tell Bethany you are here," Ingrid said before leaving the room.

Nathaniel motioned to a chair. "Perhaps you should sit down."

"I'm all right," he answered. The need to appear strong was greater than good sense.

Drawing a slow, deep breath, he willed himself to stay upright through the next half hour. It still seemed surreal that he was about to take a bride. He hadn't given much thought to marriage. Not since he was a boy in Chicago and had believed himself in love with a girl he'd known in school. But the object of his affection had rejected him because of his mother. After that, he'd steered clear of the fairer sex.

Until Bethany...

There was no denying it was her beauty that first caught his attention, but it was something much more difficult to define that drew him to her like moth to flame. She was a mysterious mixture of girl and woman, lady and minx. He'd seen the kindness of her heart, although her headstrong nature often led her into trouble. Like the trouble they were in today. If not for her wager . . .

No, if he had to place blame, he would place it upon himself. If not for *his* wager—or more accurately, his pride—they wouldn't be here. His pride was what caused him to make his wager with Rand. If he hadn't made that wager, maybe he could have ignored his attraction to her, and if he'd ignored his attraction, maybe he wouldn't have come into town the other night, and if he hadn't come into town, those men wouldn't have delivered their message, attached to boots and fists.

The reverend cleared his throat, drawing Hawk's attention. He followed the older man's gaze to the parlor entrance. He didn't know what he'd expected, but it wasn't to see Bethany float into the room in a cloud of white satin and silk. She wore a white bonnet over her hair, and he could see little of her face behind a veil of intricate lace.

This wasn't the sort of bridal gown one threw together in an afternoon. It was one they'd brought with them from the East. Perhaps it had been her mother's dress. Perhaps mother and daughter had talked often of the day Bethany would wear it, planning and dreaming the way he'd heard mothers and daughters liked to do.

If so, he doubted this was the wedding day they'd had in mind.

It struck him how unfair this was to Bethany, to be wed to a man she didn't love, to be sent to live in a rough-hewn log cabin, far from all the niceties to which she was accustomed, far from her parents who loved and pampered her. His offer of marriage may have been well-intentioned, may have been made to repair her damaged reputation, but she couldn't be happy about it.

Virginia Silverton walked beside Bethany until they reached Hawk, then she kissed her daughter's cheek through the veil of lace and stepped back to stand with Griselda, Rand, and Ingrid.

After a moment of silence, the reverend began, "Dearly beloved ..."

Bethany hadn't looked at Hawk as she entered the room to stand at his side, but as her father spoke, she dared to glance at her groom. His face was bruised, the back of his head bandaged. Pain was written in the set of his mouth.

She tried to catch his eye, to show him the joy she felt, but he avoided her gaze. Why? Wasn't he as happy as she was?

A sudden thought came to her: What if he *wasn't* as happy? What if he resented her for accepting his proposal? She hadn't thought of that before. He'd offered marriage to save her from gossip, but she'd believed he also cared for her. Perhaps that wasn't so. Perhaps he hadn't expected she would accept.

An ache settled into her chest, replacing the elation of moments before.

"Do you, Hawk Chandler, take this woman ..."

As her father asked his questions, Hawk looked at her and all air left her lungs. It wasn't resentment she saw in his eyes. Nor was it anger or passion. For an instant, it looked like a tender wanting. And then it was gone, vanished so quickly she doubted she'd seen anything at all. Once more his expression was unreadable, the man a mystery to her. She saw only the firm set of his jaw as he looked once more at her father and answered, "I do."

Uncertainty knotted her stomach.

"Do you, Bethany Rachel Silverton, take this man ..."

She hadn't lied to her father when she told him she loved Hawk. It was true. She loved him with her whole heart. But perhaps she should have met with him first, talked to him before she pledged the rest of her life to him. She should have gone to see him at Doc Wilton's. She should have discovered if he really wanted a wife. If he wanted her. Oh, why was she so impetuous? When would she ever learn?

The ceremony continued. She knew her father spoke, and she even managed to murmur the correct responses at the appropriate times. But time passed in a blur.

"... and before God and these witnesses, I proclaim you man and wife."

No one moved. No one spoke. It was over. What now? She didn't know what to do. Then Hawk turned toward her, lifted her veil, and kissed her cheek. Her cheek, not her lips. She feared she might begin to cry. This was not at all the way it was supposed to be.

With a hand at her elbow, her new husband turned her to face their few witnesses. One by one, they came forward—her mother, her friend, Hawk's friend. As Bethany accepted their kind wishes, she felt her nerves stretching like a bowstring. Hawk stood at her side, his feelings impossible to guess. He didn't smile. He didn't speak. He was her husband, but he was a stranger.

If only he'll love me, even a little, it'll be all right.

He looked at her and said, "You'd better change. It's time we left for the ranch."

The bowstring tightened.

As soon as his bride left the parlor, Hawk sank onto the chair the reverend had offered earlier, his body thrumming with pain. Doc had warned him not to overdo on his first day out of bed, and he still had the ride to the ranch to endure.

"You all right, Hawk?"

He looked at Rand and nodded.

"You sure you shouldn't stay in town a few more days?"

"I'm sure."

Rand lowered his voice. "Guess I wouldn't want to spend my wedding night on a cot in the doctor's office either."

His wedding night. His body battered. His bride reluctant, forced to marry him because of the wagging tongues of malicious people. He closed his eyes and willed himself not to think, not to feel.

The other men must have sensed his mood, for they said nothing further, to him or to each other, as the mantel clock ticked away the seconds until Bethany returned.

In the upstairs bedroom, her mother and Ingrid helped Bethany out of the wedding gown and into a dark blue dress suitable for travel. In silence, she changed her satin shoes for a pair of riding boots and replaced the veiled wedding bonnet for a more serviceable hat. A glance in the mirror did nothing to calm the flutter of nerves in her stomach. She looked so pale.

"You look lovely," Ingrid said, as if reading her thoughts.

She turned and hugged her friend, kissing her on both cheeks, tears filling her eyes as she whispered, "Thank you."

She repeated the actions with her mother. *Oh, Mother. I'm frightened.*

Behind Virginia, the housekeeper sniffed and wiped beneath her eyes with a handkerchief.

"Stop that, Griselda," Bethany managed to say as she drew away from her mother, "or you'll have us all crying."

It was too late. Each woman's cheeks were already damp with tears.

"There was much I meant to tell you before your wedding day," her mother said softly. "You are so unprepared for marriage."

She wouldn't allow herself to agree. "I'm not a schoolgirl, Mother." She lifted her chin in a show of self-confidence.

"No, you're not. But you— "

"You can visit me at the Circle Blue. It's not as if I'm moving far away. And we'll come to church on Sundays. We'll see each other often."

"You can't cook."

"I'll learn. We'll manage."

"We never should have left Philadelphia. I never should have let your father convince me this was God's plan."

Bethany hugged her mother again, whispering near her ear, "I love Hawk. I wanted to marry him. I'll be all right." The truth of those words lessened her fears. "I'll be happy. You'll see."

After a quick glance and smile in Ingrid's direction, she hurried from her bedroom before she could give in to more tears. She found her father waiting for her at the bottom of the stairs. Her throat tightened. As difficult as it had been to say good-bye to her mother and Ingrid, it would be twice as hard to say good-bye to her papa.

When she reached him, he cupped her face with his hands and looked directly into her eyes. "I'll pray for your happiness every day."

"Thank you."

"I'll pray that you and Hawk will grow closer to God and, in doing so, grow closer to each other."

She nodded.

"I love you, my dear girl." He kissed her on the forehead.

"I love you too."

For a long while neither of them moved, but at last his hands fell away and he took a step backward. "It's time for you to go. Seek God's wisdom, Bethany. Exercise patience and compassion. I believe your husband's a good man or I wouldn't have consented to the union. Love him for who and what he is and overlook what he is not."

She nodded, unable to speak.

Her father looked beyond her. "Here is your husband, ready to leave." He turned her toward the parlor. Then he took hold of her arm and escorted her the short distance to where Hawk stood, framed in the doorway. After kissing her cheek, her father passed her hand to Hawk. "May God bless you both."

There was nothing left to do or say. She had changed out of the wedding dress and into this traveling costume. Her trunk, filled with clothes and keepsakes, had been sent ahead of them to the ranch. A borrowed carriage awaited the bride and groom by the gate of the white picket fence.

Hawk's hand settled against the small of her back, and with it, he guided her out of the house and into the afternoon sunshine. After assisting her into the carriage, he slid in beside her.

Trepidation filled her as Hawk slapped the reins against the horse's backside and the carriage moved forward. She twisted on the seat to look toward the front porch. Her parents were there, along with Griselda, Ingrid, and Rand, all of them waving in farewell.

She wanted to hurl herself from the vehicle and race back to the safety of her father's arms. She wanted to feel her mother stroking her hair. She wanted to whisper and giggle with Ingrid as they talked late into the night, staring out the window at the stars.

She turned a surreptitious glance in her groom's direction. Everything felt wrong, very wrong. This was supposed to be the happiest day of her life, and instead she felt like her heart was breaking. She was fine china shattering into a thousand pieces, and her new husband was stone.

Please, God, let me be wrong. Let him love me.

NINETEEN

Three times before her wedding day, Bethany had been to the Circle Blue, but as the carriage approached the ranch after a long, silence-filled journey, she looked at everything with different eyes. This was now her home.

There was the large and sturdy barn—where Hawk had kissed her—and the bunkhouse where the cowhands lived when they weren't on the range. The wood of the outbuildings and corral was unpainted, faded by summer suns and winter winds.

Her gaze moved to the house. It was made of logs and had glass-pane windows and a roof that looked weathertight. Nothing at all like her parents' home in Sweetwater, of course, but that didn't matter. She wasn't afraid of change. Look at how she'd taken to her new life out West. This place suited her. She would be happy here.

This is where I'll live with Hawk. This is where our children will be born. The thought made her pulse quicken.

Hawk eased back on the reins, stopping the horse near the front door. He stepped down from the seat, moving stiffly, and offered a hand to assist her to the ground. "I'm sorry there wasn't time to fix up the place and make it ready for you." He moved to the door and opened it.

She hesitated on the threshold, overcome with uncertainty.

"I'll tend to the horse. Go on in. I won't be long." Without a backward glance, he returned to the carriage and led the horse toward the barn.

Bethany stepped inside the cabin and took in her surroundings. The parlor had a stone fireplace at one end. A rag rug covered a good portion of the wood floor. Two straight-backed chairs stood on either side of the hearth, and beneath the window was a small sofa. She frowned. It couldn't be. She moved closer. It couldn't be, but it was.

Her eyes moistened. The brocade love seat had been in her parents' bedroom for many years, first in Philadelphia, finally in Sweetwater. How many times had she sat on it, holding her mother's hand, shedding tears of disappointment or sharing her dreams? Countless times. Now it was hers. Her parents had meant it as a special wedding gift, and it was.

She ran her fingers over the worn fabric on one arm of the sofa. "Thank you, Mother. Thank you, Papa."

She turned from the piece of furniture to continue her exploration. To the right of the parlor was an open doorway leading into the kitchen. She crossed the room for a better look. The middle of the kitchen was filled with a sturdy wooden table and four chairs. Pots and pans hung on nails in the wall. Firewood, neatly stacked, was next to the black iron cookstove, and beside it was an icebox, very similar to the one in her mother's kitchen. Beneath the kitchen's single window was another table, taller, longer, and narrower than the dining table, this one holding a large dishpan and two buckets. No sign of a pump or sink. Against the far wall was a round washtub, and to her right was a tall cupboard, presumably filled with dishes.

She turned from the kitchen and let her gaze stray to the two doors on the back side of the house. Bedrooms, she supposed. She would share one of those rooms with Hawk, beginning this very night.

Hating the anxious twist in her stomach, she walked across the parlor and sat on her mother's love seat, her back ramrod straight, her eyes locked on a loose thread in the center of the rug. How long before Hawk returned from the barn? How long before she understood the furtive whispers and nervous giggles of the older girls at Miss Henderson's?

As if in answer to her silent questions, the door opened and her husband stepped inside. His forehead was beaded with perspiration, and his complexion seemed the color of slate. He pressed one arm against his ribs, as if trying to hold himself together.

She rose to her feet. "Hawk?"

He looked at her, but for a moment she wasn't sure he saw her.

"Are you all right?"

"I'm sorry, but I need to lie down for a while." He moved toward the door on the left. When he reached it, he paused and glanced over his shoulder. "If you're hungry, you should be able to find something to eat in the kitchen."

She could almost hear her mother say, *I warned you, dear.* "I don't know how to cook."

He stared at her for the longest while without moving. Perhaps he was too tired or in too much pain to react to her confession. "When I get up, I'll fix dinner." He tipped his head toward the closed door of the other room. "If you want to rest, you'll find everything you need in there." Before she could respond, he went into the bedroom and closed the door behind him.

When word reached the Bar V Ranch that Bethany Silverton had married Hawk Chandler earlier that same day, Vince wanted nothing more than to smash the face of the man who'd delivered the news. Instead, he closed himself in his study, poured himself a glass of whiskey, and pondered his options as he nursed the drink, taking pleasure as it warmed his throat on the way down.

Chandler might *think* he'd won the girl just as he might *think* he would hang on to his land. Thinking didn't make it so.

If not for his political aspirations, Vince might have given in to his craving for swifter results. But even his desire to possess the lovely Bethany as his own would not make him reckless. He must be careful how he proceeded, both with how he acquired the Circle Blue and how he acquired the future widow of Hawk Chandler.

Patient. He would have to be patient.

Hawk had plenty of things to trouble his thoughts, but thankfully, none were so potent that they kept him from falling into a deep, dreamless sleep. It was hunger that awakened him. Light had begun to fade outside, which surprised him. He hadn't expected to sleep that long. It must be close to eight o'clock, judging by the light, a long while since he'd eaten breakfast at the doctor's house.

He got out of bed and, after splashing water from the washbasin onto his face, stared at his reflection in the mirror. Had he made one of the biggest blunders of his life? He'd wanted to help, to do the right thing by Bethany, but his gut told him he'd made a mistake. Their marriage might alleviate some of the gossip for now, but in the long run ... No, he had to make sure things didn't get even worse from this moment forward.

His mind made up, he straightened and turned toward the door. No sounds came from the parlor. Perhaps his bride had fallen asleep as well. That would be for the best as far as he was concerned. The less time they spent in each other's company, the better it would be for them both. When the day came that Bethany realized she shouldn't have married him, when the day came that she knew she wanted a different life than what he could give her, he wanted her to be free to go, free to have their marriage annulled without any legal or moral difficulties. He would never send her away—he'd done enough damage as it was—but he must do nothing that might force her to stay either.

Resolved to keep his distance despite the tender feelings he had for her, Hawk left the bedroom. The door to the other room was open, and Bethany was nowhere to be seen. Not in Rand's old room or in the parlor or in the kitchen.

"Bethany?" He left the house by way of the kitchen. "Bethany?"

No reply.

He walked to the barn, unsure if he should be concerned or relieved. Maybe she'd discovered her mistake and left him already.

"Bethany?"

As far as he could tell, the only horses that weren't in the proper paddocks or stalls were the ones the boys had out on the range. Even her buckskin mare was here, delivered along with her trunk and that sofa earlier today.

His eyes swept the barnyard, then moved up the skirt of the mountain. He almost missed seeing her in the dying light of day, but there she was, a patch of blue among the shadows, seated on an outcropping of rocks. Either she hadn't heard him or she'd chosen to ignore him. Either way, it seemed he would have to join her on the ridge.

He drew a deep breath, testing his rib cage. The pain wasn't quite as bad now. He hoped it stayed that way. He didn't want her to think him weak. Pride again. The very thing that had started all of this trouble.

A cool breeze whispered through the tall grass as Hawk climbed the hillside, his gaze locked on his bride. It wasn't until he was almost to her that he saw she sat with her head bent forward, her face covered with her hands.

"Bethany?"

He heard her startled intake of breath an instant before she straightened.

"What are you doing?" he asked.

"Nothing." Her voice broke over the word.

His heart pinched. She'd been crying. "Are you hungry? I was going to fix something to eat."

"Could we sit here a while longer?"

Without reply, he lowered himself onto the rocky ledge.

Nightfall had come in earnest now, but a nearly full moon, only a sliver missing from one side, threw a silver white light over the rangeland below them. Good country. His country. He wondered if Bethany saw its beauty the way he did.

From the corner of his eye, he saw her dab her cheeks with a handkerchief. Yes, she'd been crying.

"I'm sorry you were forced by circumstances to marry me." His gaze returned to the moonlit range below. "I promised your father I'll do right by you, and I meant it. No one will speak unkindly about you without having to deal with me for it."

"Thank you."

"You'll be safe while you're with me."

"I know." She sniffed.

Did she have any notion what he meant? No, probably not. She was young and naive. And the kind of safety he meant wasn't something he wanted to try to explain to her.

"I don't pretend to be a gentleman. I don't have a lot of fancy manners. I'm a cowboy. I've spent more time with cattle than with women since I left Chicago. But I'll be kind to you."

"I like you the way you are." She leaned toward him, the moonlight caressing her face.

"You barely know me." His voice was low and gruff. Not because he was making sure she kept her distance, but because her words had touched his heart. And that was a dangerous thing for him to allow.

❧

Oh, that he might have kissed her. She wanted him to. Surely he knew that.

Instead, he stood. "Come on. I'm starved. You must be hungry too."

She should be, but she wasn't. Her appetite was for his kisses. Why didn't he understand that? They were married now. He had the right to kiss her.

He offered his hand, helped her to her feet, then stepped away from her, breaking the connection. With Hawk setting the pace, they walked—side by side but without touching again—down the hillside and into the house.

"Have a seat." He lit a lamp in the center of the kitchen table. "Fried beefsteak and potatoes all right?"

"Yes. May I help?"

"I'd better do the cooking tonight."

She was happy to oblige. They were more likely to enjoy their supper that way. Besides, she took pleasure in watching him. Strange how quickly her mood could change. When she left the house for a walk and sat down on the ridge overlooking the ranch, she'd felt sorry for herself. She hadn't expected to find herself all alone on her wedding day. That's what she'd told God as she sat in the gathering darkness. And then, like an answer to prayer, Hawk had come for her.

She didn't care that he wasn't a gentleman. She loved him because he was different from the other men she'd known. He thought she didn't know him well enough. He was right. He was a stranger to her in many ways. Perhaps in most ways. And yet she'd seen enough to lose her heart to him.

Forty-five minutes later, they dined on fried steak and potatoes. Bethany enjoyed the food. She'd been hungrier than she thought. But she couldn't help noticing Hawk's reluctance to talk. She suspected he was in pain again. It showed in the hard set of his jaw and in the way he held his ribs with one arm.

Finally, he set his fork and knife on his plate and looked at her. "It's late. I'll leave the dishes until morning."

"Griselda would be horrified," she said, hoping to win a smile.

It didn't work. "Griselda isn't here."

He rose from his chair and picked up the lamp with his left hand. There seemed nothing else to do but rise and follow him out of the kitchen and into the parlor. Nerves fluttered in her belly as they moved toward the bedroom.

But he stopped in front of the wrong room and held the lamp high so that light spilled into it. "As you can see, I told your father to have the men put your trunk in here. I thought, under the circumstances, you'd prefer to have your own room."

Under the circumstances?

He stepped into the bedroom and set the lamp on a tall chest of drawers. "It isn't fancy. Rand never spent much time here. I imagine there will be things you'll want. You can make a list and next time I go to town for supplies, I can get them for you."

Her parents shared a bedroom and a bed. They always had, even when they'd lived in a much larger home than the one in Sweetwater. Wasn't that how it was supposed to be?

He doesn't want me near him.

His rejection hurt more than she would have thought possible. He'd said he was sorry that she was forced by circumstances to marry him, but he didn't seem sorry for her sake. He seemed sorrier for himself.

Hawk met her gaze for a few seconds, then shook his head as he slipped by her. "Good night, Bethany." He left the room.

He didn't want her. He didn't love her. The worry that had begun to flower in her mind moments before they spoke their vows, the fear that he might not love her or want to marry her despite his offer, had not been for nothing. It was all too true.

Swallowing bitter tears, she closed the door and hastened to shed her gown and undergarments, replacing them with a nightgown from her trunk. Then she crawled into bed and cried herself to sleep.

TWENTY

By the time Bethany awoke, sunlight had replaced the glow of the moon. It surprised her that she'd slept past sunrise. Was Hawk still asleep as well? Tears welled at the thought of her new husband. She wouldn't have thought she had any tears left in her, but there they were, burning her eyes, twisting her heart.

She rolled onto her back. He couldn't have married her only to protect her reputation. Surely not. He must care for her at least a little. Maybe he didn't know that she loved him. She hadn't told him she did, but she'd thought for certain he must know her feelings. If she told him ...

But what if he didn't love her in return? What if he resented her for accepting his proposal? What if it had been a polite gesture that he thought she or her father would decline? She couldn't bear it if that were true.

He wasn't mended yet from his beating. It could be that was the reason for the distance he'd put between them. Yes, that must be the cause. She would be patient. She would be his helpmeet. Then, as he mended, he would be ready to open up to her, to express his true feelings and devotion.

A delightful odor wafted into her room—bacon sizzling on the stove. Hawk must be cooking breakfast.

Wash your face and make yourself pretty for him. Don't let him know you've been crying.

A short while later, she left the bedroom and went straight to the kitchen. Her husband was nowhere in sight, but the table was set with plates and cups and the bacon she'd smelled cooking was now on a platter on the sideboard.

"Thanks for bringing those things." Hawk's voice drifted to her from the half-open side door. "I'll give them to Bethany when she wakes up."

"Still asleep?" That was Rand. "Late night, huh?" He sounded amused.

"Not what you think." There was no humor in Hawk's reply.

She moved across the kitchen.

"You okay, Hawk?"

"I've been better."

"We'll find out who did this to you."

"That's not what I meant. It's Bethany. If it weren't for my blasted pride, she wouldn't be stuck in a marriage neither of us wanted."

Bethany covered her mouth with one hand as she pressed her back against the wall near the door. She'd feared that he might not be the most willing of bridegrooms, but it was terrible to hear him say it. He didn't want a wife. No. Even worse than that. He didn't want *her*.

"Stuck? She married you willingly. Remember? I was there. I reckon she's in love with you."

Hawk laughed—a sound without humor. "I'm not sure she knows what she wants."

"You underestimate her." Rand cleared his throat. "And you care more than you think you do."

"Just because you've lost your head over Ingrid, don't think—"

"Tell yourself all you want that you were courtin' her to get even for that wager she made with Ingrid . . ." Rand continued to talk, but what he said next was lost on Bethany.

To get even for that wager . . . To get even for that wager . . .

Oh, that cursed wager. How had Hawk learned of it?

Her mother often said that people who listened at doors to the conversations of others were apt to hear unkind things about themselves. Bethany didn't want to hear what else Hawk said. She didn't want to hear him say he didn't love her, that he'd been trapped by circumstances into marrying her.

She eased away from the wall and hurried to her bedroom, closing the door without a sound, not wanting the men to know she was up. They mustn't know she'd heard them talking. Hawk mustn't ever know her true feelings.

She'd kissed him. Flirted with him. Fallen in love with him. But his only design was to get even because of her bet with Ingrid. He'd married her because it was the honorable thing to do—because of his pride, because of those awful circumstances that were neither his nor her fault—not because he wanted her for his wife.

"O God, why? Why can't he love me too?"

She fell onto the bed and dissolved in another pool of tears.

Hawk heard sounds from inside the house. "She must be up. Thanks again for bringing those things from town. She'll be glad to have them."

"I'll get to the chores then. You remember what the doc said. You take it easy a few more days. I'll see to things around here 'til you're back on your feet."

"What about your work on the new place?"

"The boys've been pitchin' in to help, so it's comin' along good. But it'll keep a while."

Hawk gave his friend a nod. "Thanks. I appreciate your help."

"Sure thing. Now you go see to your wife." Rand grinned. "And Hawk? It wouldn't hurt for you to spark her a little."

He didn't tell his friend, but sparking Bethany wasn't in his plans. Not if he meant to protect not only her reputation today but tomorrow too.

He reentered the kitchen through the side door just as his bride appeared at the entrance to the parlor. When she saw him, she smiled, but it was a sad, tentative one. And there was no mistaking that she'd been crying. The puffiness around her eyes declared it so.

His fault, and he hated himself for it. It took all his resolve not to draw her into his arms, hold her close, and swear he'd never make her cry again.

"I didn't mean to sleep so late," she said.

"No problem. Breakfast is ready if you are."

She nodded as her gaze moved around the room. "You did last night's dishes. I meant to wash them."

"I'm used to doing for myself."

Her voice dropped to a near-whisper. "I may not know how to cook, but I'm not entirely useless. I can wash dishes."

He remembered that girl he'd seen outside the Plains Saloon, the girl whose wager had turned his life upside down. He remembered the way she could toss her head with a confident air. He remembered her laughter and the way joy of living seemed to bubble up from inside her. But that wasn't the girl he saw before him now.

And that too was his fault.

Careful, Chandler. She'll never stay with you. She'll never be happy here. You knew that from the outset.

TWENTY-ONE

They lived together as polite strangers. Bethany rose at dawn to prepare breakfast, the results not always appetizing, but at least edible. Hawk ate whatever was put before him without complaint. Then—once his body had mended enough—he saddled his horse and rode out, returning when the day was nearly gone. After a supper most often eaten in silence, they retired for the night to their separate rooms.

Bethany tried to keep herself so busy during the days—washing clothes, sweeping and scrubbing the floors, dusting the shelves, mending clothes, rearranging the furniture—that her thoughts didn't have time to stray to her husband. Her efforts were unsuccessful. Reminders of him were everywhere. She prayed for wisdom. She searched for ways to break through the invisible wall he'd erected between them since their wedding day, but she found none.

She was lonely, but never completely alone. Hawk's hired hands had returned to the bunkhouse after giving the newlyweds two days of privacy. When her husband was away, one of them was always within shouting distance of the house, and she felt certain they were there by his instructions. She took some comfort in that knowledge. Perhaps it meant he cared, at least a little.

And so the days passed until they became one week and then two and then three. Summer arrived with its clear skies and unrelenting sun that baked the Montana range and the log house that was nestled at the foot of the mountains.

Bethany lugged a bucket of wash water toward the shade at the side of the house. Beads of perspiration dotted her forehead, and the underarms of her dress were damp. Her body ached from all the lifting she'd done today. How on earth did Griselda manage, week in and week out?

As she approached the washtub, she saw two riders cantering toward her. A smile curved her mouth when she recognized her visitors. She set the bucket at her feet and raised her hand to wave. Moments later, Ingrid and Rand trotted their horses into the yard.

"Have we come at a bad time?" Ingrid asked as Rand helped her dismount.

"Of course not. The wash will keep." She wouldn't admit how glad she was for an excuse to stop and rest.

Rand touched the brim of his Stetson in greeting. "Hawk around?"

"No. He left early this morning."

"D'you know which way he rode?"

She shook her head. "Rusty's working on something behind the barn. He will know."

"I'll go ask him." He glanced fondly at Ingrid. "You girls have yourselves a nice visit. I'll be back for you later."

Radiantly happy, Ingrid watched Rand until he disappeared around the corner of the barn. "I love him more every day."

"I can tell." Bethany hooked her arm through Ingrid's. "Come inside. Hawk brought ice from the icehouse this morning. We'll have something cool to drink, and you can tell me all the news from town. There hasn't been a moment to catch up when I've seen you at church."

"The big news is that we've had our last service in the tent. Tomorrow we will celebrate the Lord's Day in our new building."

"They've accomplished so much this week?"

Ingrid nodded. "It is good that Hawk is feeling better. He has worked very hard. They could not have finished so soon without him."

Bethany turned her back toward her friend, busying herself with glasses and tea. Hawk had gone into town to work on the church? He hadn't said a word. Why would he keep it to himself? Why hadn't he invited her to go with him? Didn't he want to share anything with her?

"Bethany?" Ingrid's hand landed lightly on her shoulder. "Are you unhappy?"

For one dreadful second, she feared she might break down. But she swallowed hard and forced a contented expression as she faced her friend. "Of course not. I'm very happy. And look!" She laughed as she waved an arm around the kitchen. "I'm even learning to cook and clean." She turned away a second time. "Now tell me. When is your wedding to be? How is Rand coming on the new house?" She set the glasses of tea on the table and sat down across from her friend.

Ingrid grinned. "That is why we came to see you. The house is finished. Rand and I are to be married next week. On Wednesday afternoon. We have come to ask you and Hawk to stand up with us. You cannot say no."

"I wouldn't think of saying no. Of course we'll be there."

Hawk wondered during the ride back to the ranch house, Rand at his side, what Bethany was telling her best friend about their marriage. He got his answer as soon as he walked into the cabin's parlor.

She rose from the sofa and came to his side, slipping her arm through his. With her eyes, she pleaded with him not to ruin the pretense. "Isn't it wonderful? Rand and Ingrid have set a date for their wedding."

"So he told me." Hawk continued to stare down into her face, caught afresh by her beauty. He'd forced himself to remain aloof these last weeks, and now he reacted like a man dying of thirst, drinking her in while the opportunity remained. He was a fool to do so, and he knew it.

From the doorway, Rand said, "Ingrid, we'd better get goin'. I promised the reverend I'd have you back before supper. He's like to skin me alive if I don't."

"Must you leave already?" Bethany asked softly.

"We will see you tomorrow." Ingrid joined Rand by the door. "Perhaps you could stay in town a little longer after the service. Your parents would like it. You hurry away so quickly each week that we have had no time to visit."

Hawk had forgotten tomorrow was Sunday. And the idea of lingering for long talks with his in-laws wasn't a welcome one. He feared they would see through their daughter's attempts to appear happy. But why it mattered was beyond him. He expected her to leave eventually. Wouldn't sooner be better than later?

Together they walked outside to see their friends off. Bethany continued the charade, her arm still locked with his. In unison, they raised their outside arms to wave farewell as Ingrid and Rand rode away. Hawk waited for her to withdraw, but she didn't.

This is how it should be. This should be us at the end of every day.

Except it wasn't the end of the day. There was still plenty of daylight, and he was already at home with Bethany. The longing to crush her to him and drink the sweetness from her lips was almost more than he could resist.

He eased from her side. "I think I'll go for a swim in the creek. I'm hot and dusty."

"May I . . . may I come too? It's too hot to bathe in the tub."

He swallowed a groan. His purpose had been to remove himself from her company. "Can you swim?"

"Yes." She smiled. "And I have my bathing costume in my trunk."

How could he refuse when she looked at him like that? "Get your things while I saddle your horse."

A short while later, they rode up the mountain slope, Hawk leading the way. The secluded pool, about a mile from the mouth of the springs, was surrounded by trees and brush. They reached it as the sun dipped behind the tallest peak, hinting at the end of day long before darkness would fall.

Hawk glanced over his shoulder at Bethany. She was clad in her bathing costume, an odd little getup complete with a matching cap over her hair. She rode astride, displaying a nice glimpse of leg between the top of her boots and the hem of the costume's short trouser legs.

"This is it," he said. "I'll take care of the horses. You go ahead and get in if you want."

"Okay." She dismounted and walked to the water's edge, where she sat on the ground and proceeded to remove her boots.

He watched her as he tied the horses to a couple of nearby pines. Despite himself, he grinned, not sure if she looked adorable or ridiculous in that outfit.

Adorable. No question about it.

She stood and dipped a toe into the water, then drew back. "It's like ice!"

"I know. That's why I don't go in slow."

To prove his point, he stripped down to his summer union suit and launched himself into the center of the pool. Surfacing, he gasped for air, the cold stealing the breath from his lungs. As his breathing began to regulate, he heard her laugh and turned just in time to see her hold her nose as she jumped into the pool, landing not far from him.

Her gasps for air mimicked his. Instinctively, he reached out to hold her above the surface of the water.

It was a mistake, of course. Better to keep his distance. Better to tell himself that she was unsuited to the life of a rancher's wife. Better to tell himself that she was too different from him for them to get along. Better to remember that she came from a wealthy family and money would help her escape a loveless marriage when the time came. Better to remember the promises he'd made to himself.

If only things were different. If only he was different.

But he wasn't.

He released his hold on her. "I'll get the soap," he said before swimming toward the place where he'd dropped his things.

He wasn't different. He wasn't the sort of man a girl like Bethany should marry. He would always be an outcast in many people's eyes. He never would be the husband she deserved.

TWENTY-TWO

Vince Richards sat in the back pew of Sweetwater's new church on the first Sunday it was in use. Not that he held much with religion. Never had. But most folks did, and it behooved a good politician to be seen in church. He was nothing if not a good politician, even though he held no public office at this time.

Besides, he hadn't failed to notice how quickly the good Reverend Silverton had become an influential member of the community. People in Sweetwater turned to Nathaniel for advice in many different matters, not merely for spiritual guidance. When the time came for Vince to run for political office in Montana, he would want the reverend's backing. He definitely didn't want him as an enemy or opponent.

His gaze shifted to the couple seated in the front pew next to Mrs. Silverton. His jaw clenched, and he had to force it to relax. It galled him beyond words to see Bethany with Hawk Chandler. Beautiful and refined, she had been—and would always be—meant for him. He'd known it from the first time she and her father visited the Bar V.

Next time his hired men would do a better job of delivering a message. Next time, Chandler wouldn't walk away.

He suppressed a sneer. By the time he returned from the East, if things went as he hoped, he would be able to make some substantial changes, regarding both Chandler's land and Chandler's bride. Three months should be ample time.

His thoughts shifted to his upcoming trip. In Washington, he meant to strengthen his ties with men of power in the nation's capital. The time was ripe. The main line of the Northern Pacific was now complete. Land was being snatched up throughout the western territories, and the population of Montana was growing. Ranchers had become rich off the cattle and sheep that roamed the range. It was time for him to make his move. When Montana became a state, he meant to be in Helena, seated at the head of its government.

His gaze moved again to the front pew, settling on Bethany. Tiny burnished curls brushed her neck and the collar of her bodice.

One day.

Vince wasn't the sort who gave up, not even when it appeared something—or someone—was out of his reach. Miss Silverton's vows to Chandler wouldn't dissuade him from making her his own. He could be patient. Didn't the Bible say good things come to those who wait?

This time he didn't bother to suppress the gloating expression that came over his face.

Hawk had enjoyed the reverend's preaching from the first, maybe because it reminded him of his father, a man whose faith ran deep, a man who would have loved to sit with Nathaniel and discuss the fine points of Scripture. Maybe if his parents had lived, Hawk's own faith would have grown stronger. He believed in God, but he didn't have a whole lot of trust in God's people. He'd been content with that until he'd come to Reverend Silverton's church. Not for the right reasons, mind you. No, his attendance at first had been for reasons more emotional than spiritual. Perhaps even more carnal.

But on this morning, something the reverend said captured his full attention: "The Scriptures tell us that we are all unclean, and all our righteousness is as filthy rags. Our good works are meaningless if we are apart from God. But the Bible also tells us that Christ will become our righteousness if we trust in him. We will become as white as snow, forever clean because of Christ's work on the cross."

It would have been hard to describe what he felt as those words sank in — a hunger, a longing, a need to experience it for himself.

Then again, the good things about him must count for something. He was an honest man. He dealt fairly with other men and was loyal to his friends. He helped others when he could. Didn't God care about those things too?

He thought of the anger and resentment that he'd harbored in his heart for years, emotions that rose to the surface at the slightest provocation. He thought of the revenge that had motivated him after learning of Bethany's wager. The bad outweighed the good.

He glanced at his wife, seated beside him. There was a sadness in her eyes, a sadness that she tried to hide from everyone — but he saw it. He'd put it there. Supposedly he'd married her to protect her. He'd promised to take care of her.

More filthy rags in God's sight.

That night, Nathaniel sat in a winged-back chair near the window of their bedroom, the Bible open on his lap. But his thoughts were not on the text. They were on his daughter and her husband.

Things were not right between the two. He could sense it. Had he been mistaken in giving his consent? He'd thought God opened that door, but he may have been wrong.

"Nathaniel, I want you to talk to Bethany when she is here for Ingrid's wedding," Virginia said, drawing his gaze toward the bed. "I can't shake the feeling that something's not right."

He put aside his reading glasses and closed his Bible. "Why do you say that, dear?" He didn't tell her he'd been thinking the same thing. He valued her opinions.

"A mother feels these things. Now you promise me you'll talk with her and try to learn what's amiss."

He turned down the lamp and rose from the chair. "Why is it that you have the feeling, but I must do the talking?" He slid his legs beneath the blankets and held out an arm to draw his wife into the pillow of his shoulder.

She nestled against him, the position a familiar one after so many years together. "She loves him."

"I believe so."

"And he loves her."

I hope so.

"Then you'll speak to her and find out what's wrong?"

"I'll speak to her, Virginia. I promise."

She lifted her head and kissed his cheek. "Thank you, dear."

As Nathaniel drifted off to sleep, it was with a silent prayer of thanks to God for his wife and another prayer for his daughter and her husband.

TWENTY-THREE

Ingrid Johnson and Rand Howard were married on the second day of July at two in the afternoon. After the ceremony in the church, the wedding party and guests moved to the Silverton home for cake and punch. The rooms soon grew uncomfortably warm, yet people seemed reluctant to leave the merry gathering.

From one side of the parlor, Hawk observed his wife as she visited with her mother and the bride. Bethany was a vision of beauty in an embroidered gold-colored gown and matching satin bonnet. It was a dress he hadn't seen her wear before, certainly not one appropriate for the ranch, but one that looked perfectly suited to her. She deserved the kind of life that required that sort of dress every day.

He'd made up his mind. He would leave here without her. He would put an end to her unhappiness.

Whoever beat him up that night back in early June must have knocked good sense clean out of his head. Otherwise he never would have thought—even for a minute—that marrying her was the answer to her mother's concerns. In the weeks since their wedding, he'd managed to make Bethany unhappier than any amount of gossip could have done.

She glanced his way, a soft smile on her lips, and he felt a catch in his chest.

He cared for her more than he should. That truth couldn't be ignored any longer. What her feelings were for him, however, he couldn't begin to unravel. She pretended so well in front of others that he couldn't be sure she didn't pretend when it was just the two of them. Sometimes he wondered if maybe . . .

No, it would be better this way. Better for her. An annulment would free her to live the life she was meant to have. She shouldn't have to pretend. She needed a husband who could give her a life of ease. She needed a man who was accepted in fine company, not one who would always be seen as "less than" by some folks.

He remembered how hard she'd worked since her arrival at the Circle Blue. She'd earned more than one blister on those pretty white hands of hers, hands that were meant for fine embroidery, not scrubbing clothes in a washbasin. No, she deserved a better life than he could give her, and the time to set her free was now. Today he would return to the ranch alone.

And though he was loath to admit it, the cabin would be a forlorn place without her in it.

"Bethany?" Ingrid's fingers closed around her forearm. "Rand wants to leave soon. Will you help me change?"

"Of course."

She glanced toward the corner where Hawk had been standing moments ago. He was no longer there. Well, no matter. He could find her when the bride and groom departed. She hooked her arm through Ingrid's, and the two young women made their way to the stairs.

Once they were in the bedroom, Bethany set about freeing the train of tiny buttons that ran along Ingrid's spine, from collar to below the waist of the pale yellow gown.

"I am glad we will live closer than we do now," Ingrid said. "It will be good to have you to come to if I need advice on marriage."

Bethany shook her head. She would be the wrong person to come to for that. "You won't need advice."

"I'm a little frightened of this first night together."

Bethany looked up, meeting Ingrid's gaze in the mirror. The bride's cheeks were stained with a blush. *Please don't ask me.* She lowered her eyes to the buttons on the back of the dress. *I have nothing to tell you.*

"Who would have imagined when we arrived in Sweetwater that we would both be married by midsummer?" Ingrid raised her arms as Bethany lifted the gown over her head. "Your mother says she will be lost without us."

"She will find others to mother. You wait and see if she doesn't."

Ingrid laughed softly. "I think you are right."

A soft rap sounded on the door. "May I come in?" Rand asked from the hallway.

"Just a moment more," Bethany answered as she lifted the blue calico dress from the bed.

When Ingrid was ready, she moved to the door and opened it, a smile lighting her face.

Rand grinned in return. "You're as pretty as a summer day, Mrs. Howard."

"Thank you, Mr. Howard." She blushed an even brighter red than before.

He kissed her cheek, then her lips. "We'd best get a move on." His gaze flicked to Bethany. "You tell Hawk I'll see him soon. I couldn't find him downstairs."

"Maybe he stepped outside to escape the heat."

"Maybe." Rand offered his arm to Ingrid. "Ready?"

"Yes. I am ready."

Bethany followed the bride and groom down the stairs. She observed the hasty farewells, then moved onto the porch to wave good-bye as the newlyweds drove away in a black buggy. The remainder of the guests dispersed soon after that.

"Oh, my." Her mother sighed as she stepped into the parlor and sagged onto the closest chair. "I'm exhausted."

Her father patted his wife's shoulder. "It was a wonderful wedding and reception, my dear." Then he turned his gaze upon Bethany. "I'm glad you haven't gone yet. I've scarcely had a chance to say hello. Where's Hawk?"

"I don't know. He was in here before I went upstairs with Ingrid, but I haven't seen him since. I thought maybe he went outside. It's so hot in the house."

"Well, sit down and wait here for him. He can't have gone far."

Something niggled in her stomach, a worry that was hard to define. As she settled onto the sofa, she thought back over the day. Hawk had seemed even more distant than usual this morning. She'd done her best to coax one of his rare smiles out of him but had failed.

Should she tell her parents how things were between them? Maybe Papa could help in some way. She'd run out of ideas of her own. She'd tried her best to tend to the house and the meals. She'd tried to be pleasant and accommodating. Yet nothing had changed between them.

Her thoughts drifted to last Saturday, to the kiss they'd shared at the swimming hole. Oh, it had filled her with so much hope. If only it could have lasted. If only he hadn't pulled away so soon. If only . . .

Griselda appeared in the parlor entrance. "I found this in the kitchen." She extended her arm, an envelope in her hand. "It's addressed to you, Miss Bethany."

She took the envelope, glanced at each of her parents, then opened it and withdrew the paper from inside.

Bethany, I think it's best that you remain with your parents. Our marriage was a mistake. I thought it would protect you, but I realize now that I was wrong. It wasn't fair to you. I'll send your things back to town. Tell your father that I will sign any necessary papers that will allow you to obtain an annulment. It should be possible since the marriage wasn't consummated.

Hawk

Her gaze rested on his name for a moment before the paper slipped from her fingers and drifted to the floor.

"Bethany?"

"He's left me, Papa."

Her father rose to his feet. "Left you?"

"Yes."

He crossed the room and picked up Hawk's note, reading it for himself. When he looked at her again, he asked, "Is this true? The marriage wasn't . . ." He didn't finish the question.

He didn't have to finish. She knew what he meant. "Yes, Papa. It's true."

Her father turned toward her mother. "I don't understand."

"It's easy enough." Bethany's throat grew tight as she tried not to cry. "He doesn't want me." She lost the battle with tears. They welled in her eyes and fell down her cheeks.

Her father drew her up from the chair and folded her into his embrace. "There, now. There, there." He patted her back. "We'll sort this out. You'll see. We'll sort it all out."

When she'd cried herself out, he led her to the sofa and sat her beside her mother, who immediately grasped Bethany's shoulders and leaned close, staring into her eyes.

"Do you love him, Bethany? You said you did when you married him."

She nodded.

"And I believe he loves you."

"You're wrong, Mother." More tears, blurring her vision. "He ... he never truly cared for me. I ... I hurt his pride. That's all." Another sob escaped her. It wasn't pleasant loving a man who didn't love her in return. It hurt, way down deep in her heart.

Her father drew a chair close to the sofa and sat upon it. Then he leaned forward, taking one of her hands in his. "My dear, this is your home if—and I emphasize, if—you need it. But I want you to think very hard about what you do next. It seems from this note that Hawk is leaving it up to you, whether or not you dissolve the marriage. It even seems to me he is suggesting it because he thinks it would be best for you. That doesn't sound like a man who doesn't care."

Her pulse skipped at her father's words. She hadn't thought about what Hawk had done in that light.

"Marriage isn't something you try out and then throw away if it isn't easy, my girl. Real love is a rare and precious thing, and it usually doesn't come about without hard work and devotion."

If only Hawk could love her, even a little.

"You've never been a quitter, Bethany Rachel." Her father paused before asking, "Have you done everything you can to make your marriage work?"

No, she hadn't done everything. She'd never told him she was sorry about the wager she'd made with Ingrid. She'd never told him that she loved him.

Her father must have seen an answer in her eyes. "You go upstairs to your old room. Stay for a few days and decide what it is you want to say to your husband. Then I'll take you home myself."

Home. Home to the Circle Blue.

The old determination returned. She wasn't beaten. She wasn't a quitter. She wouldn't give up or give in. She loved him, and she meant to tell him so.

TWENTY-FOUR

Bethany spent the next four days thinking about Hawk, pondering every moment they'd spent together, repeating in her mind everything she'd said to him and he'd said to her. The note he'd left for her was wrinkled and smudged from the many times she'd read it, studying the words, looking for meanings between the lines. She took long walks by the river and sometimes sat on the riverbank, praying, asking God what she should do and how she should do it. She asked the Lord to forgive her for her impetuous and stubborn nature. She prayed for Hawk's forgiveness too.

On the morning of the fifth day, she awoke with one thought. This was the day. It was time to go home. She tossed the light coverlet aside and slid her feet to the floor, her gaze moving to her trunk that sat in the corner. It had arrived the day after Ingrid's wedding, delivered by one of Hawk's hired hands. She hadn't opened it. Today she would take it back to the Circle Blue.

She could scarcely wait to tell her father.

Not all of her gowns were packed in that trunk. Many remained in her wardrobe, including the dress she'd worn the first day she met Hawk on the sidewalk outside the saloon. That was the dress she selected. For some reason it seemed the perfect one to wear, as if it represented a second chance to do things the right way.

"Miss Bethany!" Griselda's frantic cry from the hallway startled her.

She dropped the gown on the floor and hurried to the door.

"It's your mother. The reverend says to come at once."

Bethany hurried toward her parents' bedroom. When she entered, she found her father holding her mother as she violently emptied her stomach into the washbasin.

"Papa?"

Her father eased her mother back onto her pillow. "Get Doc Wilton."

"What—?"

"Hurry!"

She spun around and raced back to her room, slipping into the dress she'd dropped a few moments before. She didn't bother with stockings or shoes. Then, skirts held high, she ran as she hadn't since she was a child, down the stairs, out the door, and through the street to the apothecary.

"Mr. Wilton," she cried as she burst into the shop. "Where's the doctor?"

"Eberlie's. Called down there in the night and hasn't been back."

She was gone before he could say anything more.

Her pulse pounded in her ears as she took the stairs at the side of the mercantile two at a time. She knocked on the door and then called, "Mr. Eberlie. Martha. It's Bethany Chandler. I'm looking for Doc Wilton. Is he here?" She knocked again, harder this time.

It was Doc Wilton himself who opened the door. "Who's ill, Mrs. Chandler?"

"It's Mother. Please, come quick."

"What's wrong with her?"

"I . . . I don't know. She was vomiting when I went to her room. My father sent me for you."

His shoulders sagged. "I'll be there directly. Go back home. Give her plenty to drink. Make her drink even if she doesn't want to. Wait!" he called after her as she turned to descend the steps. "Boil all your drinking water first."

What Doc Wilton hadn't said frightened her more than what he had. Something in his eyes spoke of defeat. It couldn't be as bad as that. Could it?

Hiking up her skirts, she raced for home again.

Nathaniel rolled his wife onto her back and covered her with a sheet. Then he stooped to pick up the soiled bedding and carried it from the bedroom. His head ached and he felt feverish, but he couldn't allow himself to rest. Not while Virginia needed him.

"Father, help me," he prayed as he descended the stairs and turned toward the kitchen. "Griselda?" He received no reply, but he hadn't the time or the energy to look for her. He carried the soiled linens outside and dropped them in a heap beside the step. They could be washed later.

As he turned, a violent stomach cramp doubled him over. Beads of sweat broke out on his forehead. He stepped inside and grabbed for the back of a nearby chair, holding on until the pain passed. A sour taste of bile rose in his throat. He drew a deep, determined breath and moved on. He was reaching for the banister when the front door flew open.

"Papa!" Bethany came to a halt in the doorway. "The doctor says he'll be here directly. How's Mother?"

The reverend shook his head, unable to speak.

"Doc Wilton says she's to drink lots of water, but I'm to boil it first. I'll do it now. Is Griselda in the kitchen?"

"I don't know where she is."

His daughter frowned. "Papa, are you all right?"

He nodded, though it was a lie. "Boil the water, Bethany. I must get back to your mother."

"It's cholera," the doctor said in a soft voice.

"Cholera?" Bethany echoed.

"And your father's ill too."

"Papa too?" A chill passed through her. She knew little about the disease except that it was feared and usually fatal.

"The Eberlies have it too. Both Fred and his daughter."

"But—"

"Burn the sheets. Handle any of their soiled things carefully. Destroy them. Wash your hands often and especially before touching any food. Cook all fruits and vegetables, and boil your drinking water. You must make your parents drink as much as possible. We must stop the dehydration if we can."

"But, Doc, I don't know how—"

"Then you're going to learn," he snapped. "We may have an epidemic on our hands."

She pressed the knuckles of one hand against her mouth. Those were her parents in there. They couldn't have cholera. They couldn't die.

"Find that housekeeper of yours. You're going to need plenty of help." His voice softened a little as he touched her shoulder. "You must be strong. We haven't time for hysterics."

Bethany drew a deep breath. "I'm fine. I'll get Griselda."

She went downstairs, calling the woman's name. When the housekeeper didn't answer, she rapped on her bedroom door and opened it. Griselda was in bed, and the room smelled of sickness.

The horse picked its way along a narrow trail on the side of a mountain. Hawk didn't push the gelding. Without a particular destination in mind, he wasn't concerned how long it took him to get there. He glanced up, gauging the trek of the sun across the sky. Just about noon, he'd guess.

He wondered if Bethany was sitting down to eat with her parents. It was easy to picture her in his mind. His thoughts had been full of little else during his five days on the trail. She was with him all the time. Maybe he would never be free of her. Maybe he couldn't ride far enough or fast enough to escape her. When he bedded down at night, he sometimes thought he could smell her cologne on the breeze. When the trees swayed overhead, he thought he could hear her laughter. And when he slept, he dreamed he held her in his arms. He imagined he could taste the sweetness of her kisses.

But it didn't matter if thoughts of her tortured him. He'd done the right thing, leaving her with her parents, setting her free from a marriage that never should have taken place. He was sure of it.

He rode for another hour, stopping when he came upon a meadow. There was plenty of grass for the horse and a brook for them both to drink from. He'd eat some of the dried jerky and let the gelding rest a while.

As the horse grazed, Hawk leaned his back against a tree and opened the Bible he'd brought along. He wasn't sure why he'd thrown it in with the other supplies as he'd readied to leave the Circle Blue. It wasn't as if he'd spent much time reading the Good Book in the years since his mother and father died. Still, he'd found it a good companion.

Today, he opened to the book of Romans, the twelfth chapter. Somewhere along mid-morning, he'd remembered something his father once said. Something about this chapter being a guide on how a man should live. Hawk figured it was time he found out what his father had meant.

Within hours of learning of the outbreak of cholera, the Silverton home became a hospital, not only for Bethany's parents but for others too. Fred and Martha Eberlie were the first to sicken, but they weren't among the first to die. That distinction fell to the miller and his wife, followed by John Wilton's youngest son, one of the girls from the Plains Saloon, and Griselda.

Water boiled in kitchens in every home within easy reach of Sweetwater. Disinfectant fires filled the air with smoke. It lingered over the town like a shroud for those who had passed on and those who were soon to die.

It was past ten o'clock at night when Bethany sat beside the bed and pressed a cup of water against her mother's lips. "Please, Mother. Please swallow just a little more water."

Weariness dragged at Bethany's arms, and her eyes felt as dry as sandpaper. She'd been awake for more than thirty-six hours, but her weariness was more than physical. Her spirit felt crushed, her heart broken. As much as she longed to deny it, her mother would be gone before midnight. How was it possible that Bethany had learned the signs of impending death in such a short amount of time?

She swallowed a lump in her throat as she looked at the woman in the bed. She was nearly unrecognizable as Virginia Silverton. Her eyes were sunken, her cheeks hollow. When Bethany touched her, her mother's skin felt cold, covered with a clammy sweat. The watery diarrhea persisted, but thankfully the cramps had lessened somewhat in the past hour.

"Your father? How is he?" Her mother's voice was hoarse and weak.

"He's better," Bethany lied as she leaned closer. "He'll be in to see you soon."

"You must take care of him for me."

"Papa likes it ever so much better when you take care of him."

"I won't be here."

"Oh, Mama. Of course you will." Tears streaked her cheeks.

Her mother's eyes drifted closed. "I was so hoping to get to hold my grandchildren before I went to be with the Lord." The words were barely audible.

"Mama, please."

"Stay close to God ... Bethany."

She bit her lower lip. It wouldn't be much longer now.

The bedroom door opened, admitting the doctor. "You'd better go in to your father. I'll stay here."

She raised her mother's limp hand to her lips. "Good-bye, Mama," she whispered. "I love you." Then she lowered the hand to her mother's side and rose from her chair.

The walk across the hall seemed a mile long.

She paused inside the doorway and stared at her father's still form on the bed. His appearance was much the same as his wife's, his face blue and pinched from the dehydration and accompanying poor circulation, the skin of his hands drawn and puckered.

"Bethany?"

She forced a smile as she moved to his bedside. "Yes, Papa."

"Your mother?"

She couldn't lie to her father the way she had her mother. "She's nearly gone." Oh, how her soul ached saying those words.

She knelt on the floor and took one of her father's hands between both of hers. He felt so cold. She lifted the withered fingers to her tear-dampened cheek. "Papa ... I'm so afraid. Please get better."

"We needn't fear death, my girl. Not if we belong to Christ. I do not regret leaving this world to live with him in paradise."

"I know, but I'll be so alone."

He gave her the slightest of smiles. "Jesus will never leave you nor forsake you. You won't be alone."

Please, God. Please don't take Papa too. I cannot bear to lose them both.

Her father closed his eyes. "I will miss you, Bethany, but your mother and I will see you again. In heaven." His voice was whispery thin.

"I'm not a very good Christian. I've done so many things wrong." Even as she spoke, she saw him slipping away from her. "I need you, Papa."

He rallied for a moment, his eyes opening to meet her gaze. His voice seemed stronger when he spoke. "Put your trust in the Lord. Others will fail you, but Christ never will."

Papa, please don't go.

Breath eased through his parted lips, and then all that remained of her wonderful father was his emaciated shell. Her papa had gone home to his Master.

TWENTY-FIVE

Ten days later, Bethany stood on the back stoop, clad in a black dress that was a size too big for her. Rand Howard sat astride his horse some distance away. Although there hadn't been any new cases of cholera in the past two days, the town remained under quarantine—which Rand had broken by coming to see her.

"Hawk's not at the Circle Blue," he said. "The men told me he rode out the day after our wedding. Said he might not be back before the first snow. I was mighty surprised when I heard it. I thought you must've known or I would've come sooner."

She hadn't thought it possible that her heart could hurt more than it did already. She was wrong. It could hurt more. Much more. It was as if in that moment her many losses crushed her, physically pushing her to the ground. She slumped to the steps and willed herself to stop the words that circled in her mind.

Ingrid isn't here ... Mama is dead ... Papa too ... And Hawk ... Hawk left me ... He left me here alone. He's gone away. How will I ever bear this on my own?

She couldn't hold in the single, aching sob that wrenched her body.

Rand was obviously frustrated he couldn't comfort her. "He would have been here if he'd known about the cholera, Bethany. He'd have been right here with you."

Raising her head, she gave him a weak smile. It was pointless to disagree with him, and besides, she hadn't the energy. Let Rand think what he would about his friend. She knew that Hawk wanted to get as far away from her as possible.

Hawk, how could you leave me now?

"As soon as Doc gives the all clear, Ingrid says she's comin' to town to take care of you for a spell."

At that, something inside her snapped. She couldn't bear the thought of staying in this place one moment more. "I won't be here, Rand. I'm returning to Philadelphia. I just ... I can't." It was the only thing she could do. There was no reason to stay in Sweetwater. There was nothing to hold her here. Her best friend was married, her parents were dead, and her husband didn't want her. She would go back East where she still had family. She would go to her grandmother and wait for her heart to mend—if it ever would.

"Bethany, surely you don't—" The look in her eye stopped him. He paused, cleared his throat, then nodded. "Well, Ingrid will be mighty sorry to hear you're leavin'." He removed his hat and wiped the sweat from his forehead. "Mighty sorry. She was settin' store in the two of you livin' close to each other."

"I will write to her often."

"You wantin' to leave soon?"

"Yes," she answered softly, a great heaviness weighing on her chest. "As soon as I can make the arrangements."

"Is there anything you want me to tell Hawk when he gets back?"

She shook her head. "No." She turned and went inside without saying good-bye. The word would have choked her. There'd been too many farewells in recent days. Too many to bear.

In the kitchen, she removed the pot of boiled water from the stove and replaced it with a second pot. Doc Wilton had told her not to stop boiling her water too soon. At least not until the last of the recovering patients—only two of them now—were sent back to their homes.

So few had recovered. So few.

Her eyes filled as she leaned against the table, head drooping forward. Because of the dangers of the cholera epidemic spreading, the dead had been burned. None had received a proper burial, not even her mother and father. Bethany hadn't had time to mourn their passing. Not really. She'd been too busy helping the doctor tend to the ill.

She'd wondered more than once why she hadn't fallen sick too. Why had she been spared when others died? It made no sense to her. No sense at all. And there were times when her heart hurt so much she wished she had been taken. Even now she wished ...

"There you are." Doc Wilton stepped into the kitchen.

"Were you calling for me?" She forced herself to straighten. "I'm sorry. I didn't hear you. Am I needed upstairs?"

"No. The patients are resting peacefully, so I'm going to my office to see to a few things." His eyes narrowed. "And you need to get yourself something to eat. You've been running yourself ragged, and it shows. You've lost far too much weight."

"I'm fine, Dr. Wilton. I haven't been hungry. That's all."

"Your appetite isn't my concern, Bethany, but your health is. I'm going straight over to the restaurant and order a meal for you. I'll deliver it myself."

"That isn't—"

"Don't argue with me, young woman. As your physician, I expect you to follow my orders."

She gave him a tired look. "As you wish."

In the days since the outbreak began, she'd come to admire the doctor a great deal. He was tender and compassionate. Because he genuinely cared about his patients, the many deaths were written in the creases on his face.

"You need to rest yourself," she said.

He nodded. "I will. If there are no more reports of illness by tomorrow evening, I believe we can lift the quarantine. And the last of our patients will go home in the morning. You'll have the house to yourself again."

The house to herself. That didn't sound all that inviting.

She thought of Hawk, remembered him holding her and kissing her. If only he were here to hold her now. Perhaps then she might not be so afraid of the future.

But that wasn't going to happen.

Hawk was somewhere near the Idaho border when God finally got through to him. By then he'd read through the gospel of John and all of Paul's epistles, including the book of Romans twice. He was camped out under a clear July sky, a million stars looking close enough to reach up and touch, when he realized that it wasn't enough to believe in God. He needed to know him. He needed to follow him.

He used to say he could trust God but not God's people. But then he began to remember the believers he could trust. His parents. Rand. Reverend Silverton.

And Bethany. He could trust Bethany.

He hadn't trusted her, but why not? Because she'd wanted to get him to come to her father's church? Was that such an awful thing?

Maybe that wager of hers was God's way of getting his attention. Like Romans said, all things worked together for good to them that loved God. Maybe God had used Bethany's wager to get through his thick skull.

Other verses from Romans came to mind as he lay on the ground, a blanket rolled up for a pillow beneath his head. There was the one about blessing those who persecute you, bless and do not curse. There was the one about living peaceably with all men. There was the one about not avenging yourself, but leaving that to God. There was even one about feeding your enemies and giving them something to drink. Be not overcome of evil, but overcome evil with good, the Bible said.

Would God want him to forgive those men who'd given him that beating? Yes, it seemed that he would. Not just forgive them but also feed them. That was asking a lot.

He remembered the sermon he'd heard his father-in-law give. The one about his righteousness being nothing but filthy rags. He thought he'd done a lot of good things, but they didn't count for much in God's eyes because he'd done them for the wrong reasons. And then there were the things he'd done that were wrong. Plain and clear wrong. Like marrying Bethany so he wouldn't feel guilty. Like ignoring the fact he'd promised before not only her family but God that he would love and care for her. Like running out on her the way he had instead of facing her like a man. He'd told himself that he'd done it for her benefit, but that wasn't true. He needed to go back. He needed to tell her he was sorry. And he needed to honor his commitment to her, if she'd give him a second chance.

There it was. That's what he wanted most of all. A second chance with Bethany.

TWENTY-SIX

"I should have canceled the ball as soon as you arrived. Whatever will people think of me?"

Bethany stared out the bedroom window at the expanse of green lawn and elaborate gardens behind the Worthington home. "It's all right, Cousin Beatrice. No one will think ill of you. My parents have been gone a month now."

Beatrice Worthington came to stand beside her. "I wish there was something I could say or do for you. It breaks my heart to see you this way."

Bethany looked at her father's cousin and offered a sad smile. "Please stop worrying about me. Your guests will arrive soon, and you're not dressed for the evening."

"Gracious, you're right. Harvey says I would lose my head if it weren't attached. I'd best dash."

Alone once more in the bedroom, Bethany exhaled a long sigh. She'd forgotten how wearing Beatrice could be. She rarely ceased moving or talking. And her husband, Harvard Worthington, was cut from the same cloth. The pair were pillars of Philadelphia society, always in the midst of every social function of note. When Bethany was a girl, she'd loved her visits with the Worthington cousins. But now . . .

It wasn't as if she'd had much choice where to stay when she arrived in Philadelphia nine days earlier. Her grandmother was traveling abroad and wouldn't return from the Continent for another month. And so she had come to Cousin Beatrice.

Oh, but such thoughts seemed ungrateful. Her cousins had good hearts, and they genuinely cared for her and grieved the loss of her parents with her. They had done their best to make her feel at home.

She allowed her gaze to move around the large bedroom that was now hers. It was too large. Not at all like her small bedroom in the two-story house in Sweetwater. Not at all like the even smaller one in that log cabin to the west of town.

She tried to swallow past the tightness in her throat as once again tears blurred her eyes. She missed Montana. She missed her parents.

She missed Hawk.

But she didn't want to think about him. She didn't want to think about anything that had happened in recent months.

Pushing away the memories, she walked to the dressing table, sat on the stool, and stared at her reflection in the mirror. Her cheeks looked pale and hollow. She'd lost more weight since leaving Sweetwater. Beatrice claimed she would soon waste away to nothing if she didn't start eating more.

I don't care if I waste away.

If only she could go home. If only ...

She hardened her heart against the memories of Hawk that tried to resurface. She couldn't bear to think about him. Not today. Her pain was already too great.

Perhaps she should go downstairs. Beatrice had said she could if she wished. No one would ask her to dance since she was in mourning—nor would she want to dance—but she could observe the festivities for a while. It might be diverting.

She rose and walked to the wardrobe. Among the dozen mourning gowns, she found something suitable—a black satin dress with soft lines, simply cut but fine enough for a ball. She would eschew jewelry except for the broach that had been her mother's and the ring she still wore on her left hand.

One more reminder of Hawk.

Vince Richards stepped into the brightly lit entry hall of the Worthington home. Every inch, every detail of the splendid mansion spoke of generations of wealth and influence.

"Senator," their hostess said to his companion. "How wonderful to see you. We were afraid you wouldn't make it up from Washington."

"And miss your annual ball, Beatrice? Perish the thought." Senator Wright bowed toward the woman, his long white mustache brushing her hand before his lips did the same. When he straightened, he motioned to Vince. "I've brought a friend with me. Vince Richards, may I present our hostess, Beatrice Worthington, and her husband, Harvard."

Vince acknowledged the introductions while recalling bits of information the senator had told him about the Worthingtons. Despite Harvard's unassuming looks and stature, the rotund man before him—known to one and all as Harvey—was esteemed by men in places of power. Vince hoped to be counted among his friends one day.

Following the senator, he moved into the house. The strains of a waltz floated to them from the ballroom. As they walked in that direction, the senator introduced Vince to other guests and, between introductions, filled in helpful details about those he met.

Half an hour later, the ballroom was a swirling mass of dancers. Vince was engaged in conversation with a Philadelphia banker, the two of them standing near the patio doors that had been opened to catch the evening breeze. When the music ended, he let his gaze wander toward the doorway of the ballroom.

It was then she appeared, gliding through the entrance like an angel. Bethany Silverton. Here. In Philadelphia. His stomach tightened in shock.

Surely it wasn't her. She was back in Sweetwater ... in the arms of ... It must be someone who resembled her.

But no. There couldn't be another young woman as beautiful as she. He knew that face, that hair. That figure. He'd coveted them for several long months.

"Please excuse me," he said to the banker in midsentence. Leaving the other man speechless, he moved toward the ballroom entrance, all the while keeping her in his sight.

She wore a gown of glossy black, a color without relief save for the pale broach worn near her throat. But she was as beautiful in black as she'd been in the pastels she seemed to favor in Sweetwater.

Black. By George! Was she in mourning?

He couldn't stop the smile that twisted his mouth. So Chandler was dead. Better news he couldn't hear.

Hawk stood in the parlor of the Silverton home, the light in the room growing dim as the sun settled in the west. Sadness lurked in every corner. Sorrow tinged the silence.

The reverend and his wife dead. Bethany gone back to Philadelphia.

He stared at the toes of his boots and forced himself to breathe while his fingers traveled the brim of his hat, held between both hands.

If he'd pushed himself a little harder on his return from the Idaho border. If he'd slept one or two fewer hours each night. If his horse hadn't pulled up lame outside of Butte. If he'd known about the cholera, he would have bought another horse. He would have done anything to get here as fast as he could. But he hadn't known, and so he'd taken his time, giving his gelding lots of rest.

Why hadn't he sensed there was trouble? Why hadn't he known Bethany needed him? Why hadn't God told him to hurry?

He was in Sweetwater now, but he was too late. Bethany was gone. He'd lost her. Because of his pride, he'd lost the woman he loved.

Bethany found it difficult to breathe. She'd thought coming down to join her cousin's guests would distract her thoughts. Instead the merriment overwhelmed her. So many people crowded into one place. So many voices. So much laughter.

Nonetheless, she was determined to stay. At least for a short while.

She allowed her gaze to roam the massive ballroom. Opposite walls had gilded mirrors that reached from the glistening tile floor to the high ceiling above. The near wall—the one through which she'd entered—was painted with life-size figures of waltzing couples. The far wall had two sets of French doors that opened onto a stone patio surrounded on three sides with tall evergreens. Beyond those evergreens were the gardens of Worthington Manor.

"Bethany, dear. You came down after all. I'm so glad." Beatrice, a sparkling tiara in her silver gray hair, stepped to Bethany's side and hooked arms with her. "Look, Harvey. Bethany felt up to joining us."

Her cousin's welcome was so effusive that she couldn't help but warm to her.

Beatrice drew her toward a cluster of guests. "Look, everyone. My young cousin has come down to join us. Peter, you remember Bethany, don't you?"

For a brief time, Bethany forgot the loneliness that had driven her from her bedroom. For a time, she didn't think about the loss of her parents. For a time, she forgot Hawk and the way she ached for him. But all too soon, the old feelings returned. The crush of people, the music, the bright conversation all overwhelmed her, and she longed for wide-open spaces and the vast blue skies of Montana. She wanted peace and simplicity and silence. She wanted a small house and a cozy bed and . . . Hawk.

She slipped away from those around her and worked her way through the crowd toward the French doors and the dark solitude of the August night. But the lights from the ballroom spilled through the doors onto the patio, and the noise spilled with it. Almost in flight now, she hurried down the steps, following the pathway into the gardens until she reached the fountain at its center. There she sank onto a stone bench and closed her eyes, breathing deeply until the rapid pace of her pulse began to slow. Feeling calmer, she raised her eyes toward the starry heavens.

Was Hawk looking up at this same sky?

She squeezed her eyes shut. "Forget him," she scolded in a whisper. "It's over. Put him behind you."

"Good evening, Mrs. Chandler."

She turned toward the sound of the male voice and felt her eyes widen. "Mr. Richards?" The last person she expected—or wanted—to see here in Philadelphia.

"You are surprised, I see. No more, I trust, than I was to see you."

"I heard you were in Washington."

"I was, but fate brought me here tonight." Another waltz began to play inside the house. "Would you dance with me?" He motioned toward the ballroom.

She stood and stepped back, putting some distance between them. "I'm not dancing tonight, sir. As you can plainly see, I'm in mourning."

"I do apologize. You look so beautiful, I didn't notice you wore black, and I hadn't heard of your loss. Tragic to be widowed so soon after your wedding."

Bethany felt a tiny sting in her heart. "Hawk is alive and well—" *to the best of my knowledge*— "It's my parents who died. Along with many others in Sweetwater. There was an outbreak of cholera."

"Cholera?" The information seemed to shake him. Apparently no one had sent him that news either.

"I couldn't bear to remain in Sweetwater, so I came to stay with my cousin."

He glanced toward the ballroom. "Do I know your cousin?"

"I'm sure you must. She's your hostess."

"Beatrice Worthington is your cousin?"

Sadness swept over with a suddenness that momentarily prevented speech. An unbearable weight of loss and despair. Perhaps it was seeing someone from Sweetwater, even someone she disliked. It brought back too many memories. More than she could bear. "If you'll excuse me, I must say good night. I hope you have a pleasant trip back to Washington."

Without waiting for his response, she turned and retreated to the safety of her bedroom.

TWENTY-SEVEN

Hawk stopped his horse and eased out of the saddle. Hunkering down, he ran his fingers over the ground. The man—a lone rider—had left a clear trail. Either he wasn't smart or he was leading Hawk into a trap. Better to prepare for the latter and hope for the former.

He lifted his gaze and scanned the range to the east, then looked toward the mountainside to the west. He'd been losing cattle here and there all summer. Not many, but enough to concern him. Funny thing was, most rustlers didn't stop with a few cows every now and then. This felt different, like it wasn't about the cattle.

He and his men had tried to track down who was responsible without success. But this time the troublemaker had gone too far. He'd shot one of the Circle Blue cowboys. It was a miracle Westy hadn't been killed. Hawk wasn't letting him get away this time.

He stood and reached for his canteen. With several quick swallows, he slaked his thirst, then hung the canteen from the pommel and swung into the saddle again. He wiped an arm across his forehead before pulling his hat brim lower to shade his eyes from the glaring sun.

Don't let me lose track of him, Lord. I want answers.

Bethany had been staring out the sitting room window for over an hour. In her right hand, she held a fan that she waved in front of her face, trying to dispel the thick heat of the afternoon.

"Excuse me, Mrs. Chandler. There's a Mr. Richards to see you."

"I'm sorry." Drawn from her reverie, she looked at the housemaid. "What did you say?"

"A Mr. Richards, ma'am. He says he's a friend of yours from Montana."

She was about to tell Chloris to send him away when he stepped into view behind the maid.

"I'm sorry to intrude, Bethany, but I wanted to see you before the senator and I return to Washington."

She didn't want to see Vince Richards, of all people, but she saw no polite way to be rid of him now. The maid, however, looked as if she would gladly toss him out on his ear.

"It's all right, Chloris," she said softly.

"Yes, ma'am." The maid tossed a scowl in Vince's direction before leaving the room.

Bethany closed her fan and motioned with it. "Do sit down, Mr. Richards."

"Thank you." He settled onto the chair nearest her. "You look beautiful, as always."

She didn't reply. Better to let him say whatever he wished—no matter how inappropriate—so she could be rid of him.

"I was stunned by the news about your parents, and I fear I failed to properly express my condolences. Your father was a fine man and an important member of the community. I came to respect him a great deal in the short while you were all in Sweetwater."

"Thank you, Mr. Richards."

"I wish you would call me Vince."

And I wish you would stop calling me by my given name. She gave her head a slow shake.

His gaze seemed to harden as he waited for her to speak.

She didn't oblige.

He smiled, but it was forced. "Let me be frank. I never believed your father should have forced you to marry Chandler after that ... *unfortunate* incident earlier this summer. I know, whatever the gossips say, that you were completely innocent. Surely everyone knows it cannot be a happy union, coming about as it did. Isn't that why you are here? With your parents deceased, who is there to make you stay with such a man?"

She stiffened. How dare he presume to say such things to her?

"Bethany, I would be pleased to help in any way possible. I know many excellent lawyers. I'm sure the union could be dissolved quickly and quietly. Divorce needn't be a stigma if it's handled properly."

At last she found her voice. "No one *forced* me to marry Hawk. Not my parents or anyone else. I married him of my own free will. Be assured of that, Mr. Richards. But then, it is really none of your concern."

"You're wrong." He leaned toward her. "I care for you. I am your friend, and one day, I want us to be more than friends."

She rose from the sofa. "I'm sorry for any misunderstandings, sir, but we shall never be more than acquaintances." She lifted her chin in defiance. "And I have no need of a lawyer. I will not seek a divorce. Not now. Not ever."

It felt good to say those words aloud, and she felt stronger because of them. Even a little hopeful.

"I'm afraid you've—"

"I want you to leave."

He stood. "But I—"

"Now, Mr. Richards. Please go and don't return."

Vince placed his hat on his head. "Good day, Bethany." He bowed, then turned and strode from the room.

Chloris appeared in the doorway seconds later. "Are you all right, Mrs. Chandler?"

She drew a deep breath. "I'm fine, now that he's gone." She sank onto the sofa. "Please inform the rest of the staff never to let that man into this house again. Not to see me, at any rate."

"Not a chance of that. I didn't like the look of him. Not one little bit."

"Neither do I," Bethany whispered, her gaze returning to the window, her thoughts returning to Montana—to the place and to the man who held her heart.

Vince Richards stood on the sidewalk outside the Worthington mansion, fighting to get his anger under control. For the second time in a matter of days Bethany had rebuffed him. It would not happen again. Hawk Chandler might not be dead now, but that would change. And soon. Perhaps it had even come to pass this very day.

Whatever it took, Bethany would be his. He would not long be denied.

With that thought in mind, he strode away.

Hawk hit the ground and rolled into the brush, drawing his Colt from the holster as he came to rest. He touched his temple with his free hand. Warm blood trickled down the side of his face from the place where the bullet had grazed him.

He didn't believe the gunman was a poor shot. Either God or dumb luck had saved his life—and he didn't believe in luck anymore. If he hadn't felt the saddle slip, if he hadn't leaned forward to check the latigo and cinch, he would be lying dead beside his horse right now.

He drew back into the thicket beside the mountain stream, listening for any sound that didn't belong, for any hint the gunman approached. Except for the gurgling creek behind him, the forest was silent. No birds sang, no squirrels chattered.

He eyed the mountainside. The shot must have come from the thick grove of trees above him. It would give the gunman an advantage. If he wanted, he could keep Hawk pinned down a long while. But night was coming fast, and then the advantage would be his. He knew this area as well by night as he did by day. It was doubtful his assailant could say the same.

He settled in to wait, watching, wary. When he fingered the wound again, he saw the flow of blood had stopped. Good. It wasn't serious.

The faint snap of a twig was his only warning. He rolled and fired, instinct rather than sight guiding his aim. The gunman—a stranger—looked at him in surprise, the gun in his hand wavering before falling to the ground. A ragged gasp rattled in the man's throat before he toppled face down into the stream.

Hawk jumped to his feet and scrambled through the water to pull the man out. He'd wanted to take him alive. He'd wanted answers. Maybe it wasn't too late.

He dragged the gunman onto the bank and rolled him over. Blank eyes stared up at the sky. Dead. There'd be no answers today.

Bethany rose from the sofa and walked across the sitting room to the window that faced the street. Tall trees shaded the front of the house, creating a leafy canopy. Her gaze moved up the avenue, pausing to study the homes that belonged to the elegant members of society who lived in them.

Once she had belonged here. Once she had been one of them. When her father had taken her away from Philadelphia, she'd been certain she would always long to return. But no more. She belonged in Montana. She belonged with Hawk.

"I want to go home."

Impetuous, her father had often called her, and it was true. She knew her faults. Impetuous and willful and headstrong and stubborn and a host of other less-than-admirable qualities. But she wasn't stupid. She needn't stay where she didn't want to be. With God's help, she would go home to Sweetwater and do everything in her power to win the heart of the man she loved.

Of course, she'd thought and said that before in the two months since she and Hawk stood before her father, repeating their vows. But this time, she wouldn't let anything or anyone get in her way.

She was going home. She would make Hawk love her. It wouldn't be easy. She would make mistakes. She might stumble over her own pride a time or two. But it would be okay. God would help her right the wrongs. She would trust him, as her father had told her to do.

She turned from the window, wondering how she would tell her cousin she would be leaving soon. As if summoned, Beatrice entered the sitting room.

"There you are. Chloris told me you had a visitor who upset you. Are you all right?"

"I'm fine, Cousin Beatrice, but there's something I must tell you."

"It sounds serious, child."

"I've decided to go home to Montana."

Instead of the argument Bethany expected, Beatrice said, "I wondered when you would come to your senses. You belong with your husband, and anyone with eyes and ears can tell it's what you've wanted all along."

Bethany stared at her cousin, not sure what to say in response.

"It's clear you've been mourning more than the loss of your beloved parents." Beatrice paused and raised her brows. "So tell me. When do we leave?"

Bethany blinked. "We?"

"Of course, we. I would love to see what drew your father west. Virginia always wrote such wonderful letters about the land and about the people. I want to see it for myself. Besides, I can't allow you to travel alone across the country a second time." She took hold of Bethany's hand. "You won't mind me coming, will you, dear?"

"Of course I don't mind. I would like your company very much."

"Then it's settled. We'll make plans for our departure at once."

TWENTY-EIGHT

Hawk sat across from Sheriff Cook, wondering if the man would ever be his old self again. Since losing his wife and son in the epidemic, Chuck Cook had become intimate friends with the whiskey bottle he kept in the bottom right drawer of his desk. It was midmorning, and the sheriff's eyes already had a glazed look.

"It's been two weeks," Hawk said. "You must have learned something about him by now."

"Sorry. There's nothing I can tell you. No one around Sweetwater had seen him before. He wasn't carrying anything to help us identify him. I've been through all the wanted notices too. Nothing."

"Somebody must have hired him to make trouble at the Circle Blue." Hawk's first thought, as always, was that Vince Richards was behind it. Trouble was, the man was careful, always maintaining his veneer of respectability, never letting most folks see the blackness of his heart. Besides, he'd been gone for close to two months now. It wasn't likely he'd hired a gunman while in Washington.

Hawk could at least be thankful the sheriff hadn't arrested him. There were a few folks in town—the ones who didn't care for a man of mixed race living and working among them—who would have been happy to see him accused of murder. But Cook had accepted Hawk's report of what happened on the day of the shoot-out. Yes, he was thankful, but he still wanted answers.

He stood and put his hat back on his head. "You'll let me know if you find out anything."

"Sure, Hawk. I'll get word to you if anything comes up. But I'm thinkin' he was just some drifter. Or maybe he was on the run from the law." The sheriff chuckled. "Maybe he thought you was me and that's why he fired on you."

Sheriff Cook had it all wrong. The gunman had meant to kill Hawk. Only divine providence had saved his life.

With a nod in the sheriff's direction, he left the office, pausing on the boardwalk to look left, then right. His gaze settled on the white church with its tall steeple. It was sad, remembering how the townsfolk had pitched in to build it. Now it stood empty. The day would come when another preacher would take his place in the pulpit, but he wouldn't be another Nathaniel Silverton. Couldn't be.

Hawk wished he'd appreciated the good reverend more when he was alive. He had a lot of questions that it sure would be nice to ask his father-in-law. Like, what did God think of him for killing a man, even if it was in self-defense?

His thoughts shifted to Bethany, and that familiar dull ache returned to his chest. How was she faring in Philadelphia? Had she seen an attorney yet? Was she still his wife or had their marriage been swept away, as if it never happened?

Tugging on the brim of his hat, he stepped off the boardwalk and untied his horse from the hitching post. Time to get back to the Circle Blue. Maybe, if he was lucky, he could go more than an hour or two without picturing Bethany in his mind. Maybe he could get on with the business of living and running a ranch and not wish he could have the last few months to do over again so he could get it right.

❧

"My good man," Beatrice shouted, "you must slow those horses at once. I'm sure there are other men willing to drive my carriage should you prove too reckless to ensure the safety of your passengers."

"Sure, lady." He motioned at the countryside—not a town, not a sign of civilization anywhere. "And where you gonna find 'em?"

Beatrice impaled him with a cold glare. "I shall drive it myself if I must, and you can walk back to Miles City."

"All right. All right. I'll slow 'em down. Don't get your knickers in a twist."

"I beg your pardon." Beatrice looked at Bethany, her face flushed. "Did he say what I think he did? Why, I never ..."

Bethany stifled a grin. "At least it's a comfortable ride, cousin. If we'd come by stagecoach, you would know what I mean."

"I won't put up with impudence. Not when I'm paying him a good wage."

Bethany had enjoyed her cousin's company since leaving Philadelphia, much to her surprise. And the journey had certainly been made more comfortable than the last time.

Take the matter of the Worthington carriage, for instance. Beatrice had insisted on shipping it—along with a matched pair of chestnut horses—by rail from Philadelphia. When the carriage was unloaded and reassembled in Miles City, it had been the talk of the town. Bethany had thought it an unnecessary extravagance, but she was glad for it now. She remembered the uncomfortable—if much faster—passage by stage. This well-sprung vehicle, with its softly padded seats and backs, was by far a more pleasant way to travel, and their frequent stops to stretch their legs was a welcome relief.

"I don't know what you find so appealing about this country," her cousin muttered as she smoothed her dust-covered skirt.

"Don't you, indeed!" Bethany laughed. "You're a dreadful liar. You've enjoyed every moment of this trip."

Beatrice harrumphed. "Perhaps it has been interesting at times."

Still smiling, Bethany turned her gaze to the passing range. How different the scenery was from the street outside the Worthington home. Instead of tall brick and stone mansions and the spreading tree limbs that obscured the sky from view, she could see for miles in every direction, the gently rolling range a mixture of gold and green and brown.

"We might be able to see Hawk's mountains when we make camp tonight."

"We're that close?"

"We'll reach Sweetwater tomorrow."

"Thank heaven. One more night under the stars is as much as I can bear. It will be wonderful to sleep in a real bed again. Harvey tried to warn me, you know. I should have insisted that he join us. He would have loved it. I remember the time he ..."

Bethany listened with only half an ear as her cousin spun story after story. It didn't matter if she replied. Beatrice was capable of carrying on an entire conversation by herself.

She leaned toward the carriage window, hoping to catch a glimpse of the mountain range. Home. She would be home tomorrow.

Hawk sat astride his horse and gazed down at the pool, remembering the day he and Bethany had gone there to bathe, remembering the moment he'd held her and kissed her, water lapping around them.

He never should have left her at her parents' home after Ingrid and Rand were married. If he hadn't . . .

He considered leaving the Circle Blue again, only this time going farther away. Rand and the men could handle the place fine without him. Since his encounter with the gunman, there hadn't been any more trouble on the ranch. No more missing or injured cattle. And if trouble came up again, Rand could handle it.

Yes, leaving was a tempting idea. He could head for Texas. Or maybe California. He could stay away until an entire day passed, maybe even a week at a time, without him thinking of Bethany.

Again he saw her in his mind. Laughing. Crying. Angry. Sad. Cooking breakfast. Racing her horse. Falling into the river. He wanted to kiss her. He wanted to protect her. He wanted to crush her to him and keep her there forever.

But Bethany was gone, and there was no way he knew of that he could bring her back again. While the Bible said the Lord would turn everything to good in the life of a believer, it didn't say God would change the past. Hawk would have to live with the mistakes he'd made and the consequences that had followed. He'd just have to keep on praying that the Lord would heal that ache in his heart.

Make it hurt just a little less, Lord. Just a little less than it hurt yesterday.

He pulled the gelding's head around and started him down the side of the mountain toward the ranch house.

❧

The August sky clouded over as the Worthington carriage approached Sweetwater the next afternoon. The rain followed soon after, just as they rolled to a stop in front of the Silverton home.

Bethany didn't wait for the hired driver to get down and open the carriage door for her. She stepped to the ground, ignoring the rain, her eyes fixed on the white two-story house. Home. She was home again. Or at least as close to home as any place could be that didn't include Hawk.

She hurried up the walk to the front porch, pausing there a moment before reaching forward and opening the door. Silence greeted her as she stepped into the entry. She felt the absence of her parents as a sharp sting in her chest.

"Bethany, the house is charming. No wonder you missed it."

As she turned, she noticed the gentle rain had become a cloudburst.

Beatrice said, "I sent the driver to find the livery. He'll deliver our things after the storm passes."

Bethany loosened her bonnet and pulled it from her head. "Welcome to Sweetwater, Cousin Beatrice. Welcome to Reverend Silverton's home." Tears threatened as she spoke those words, but she blinked them back.

Her cousin moved into the parlor. "Let's get these dust covers off the furniture so we can sit down in comfort. Just think. A seat that isn't moving. How heavenly."

Watching her cousin bustle about the small parlor, pulling covers off the furniture and opening the drapes, did much to lighten Bethany's spirits. Beatrice had often surprised her during their journey. Here was a woman who rarely poured her own cup of tea, and yet she'd slept under the stars and endured the carriage ride from Miles City to Sweetwater without serious complaint.

"I'll check the kitchen and see if there's anything in the pantry, but I suspect we'll need to dine at Mrs. Jenkins's Restaurant tonight. We can pick up supplies at Eberlie's Mercantile tomorrow." She felt the sting of loss again. "I wonder who's running the mercantile. Mr. Eberlie and his daughter died in the epidemic." Her gaze moved toward the stairs and the dark second story.

Beatrice's arm went around her shoulders. "You needn't be strong all the time, my dear."

Bethany felt her throat thicken with suppressed emotions. "I'd like to go over to the church, Cousin Beatrice. Will you go with me?"

"Shouldn't we wait until the rain stops?"

"No. I'd like to go now. I need to go. Will you come?"

Beatrice patted her shoulder. "Of course I'll come. Let's find some wraps."

Ten minutes later, Bethany stood at the rear of her father's church, running her fingers over the smooth wooden back of a pew. Someone had crafted it with loving care. Someone who had helped her father build this church earlier in the summer.

She lifted her eyes toward the altar area. Above it, muted light filtered through a stained glass window. That glass had come with them from Philadelphia. Her father had taken great care over hundreds of miles so it could one day grace a church in the West.

She swallowed hard and started down the narrow aisle.

A white altar cloth, lovingly stitched and embroidered by her mother, fell in gentle waves almost to the floor. At the back of the altar was a tall gold cross, and at its base lay an open Bible.

She stepped onto the riser, pausing to let her hand rest on the pulpit. It seemed so unfair, after all he'd been through, that her father had only preached two Sundays here. All that waiting, all that work, all those dreams, and he only got to be in this building, in this pulpit, for two Sundays.

If only she could hear his voice again. If only she could ask him for advice. If only she could see her mother's smile. She missed them both so much.

She turned away, awash with sorrow. A ray of sunlight broke free of the clouds and fell through the window to caress the open pages of the Bible. Bethany stepped closer to the altar and touched the open book.

"Jesus said unto her, I am the resurrection, and the life: he that believeth in me, though he were dead, yet shall he live: And whosoever liveth and believeth in me shall never die. Believest thou this?"

Peace covered her aching heart like a soothing balm. "Yes," she whispered. "I believeth this."

Her father's dying words replayed in her mind. "Jesus will never leave you or forsake you. You won't be alone."

She smiled sadly at the memory. Even in death, her father had pointed others toward Jesus.

Please, God. Help me be the kind of daughter who would make Papa proud.

She wiped the moisture from her cheeks with her knuckles and then turned toward Beatrice, who waited for her at the back of the church. "I'm finished here. Let's go home. There's work to be done."

TWENTY-NINE

The forge was white hot, and sweat ran down Hawk's back and chest as he worked nearby. He set the iron shoe, red and glowing, onto the anvil and tapped it a few more times, then lifted it with tongs and dropped it into the waiting bucket. A protesting hiss rose with the steam as the metal cooled.

With a hand in the small of his back, he straightened slowly. Of all the chores that made up a rancher's life, he liked this one the least. Even on a cool, cloudy day like today, working beside the forge was like working in Hades. The heat never let up.

He pulled the shoe from the bucket and moved to the waiting horse. With a slight tug, he lifted the animal's foreleg and placed the shoe against the hoof. A perfect fit.

"Hey, Hawk." Westy entered through the front of the barn. "Somebody here to see you."

"Who is it?"

"Some woman. Never seen her before. I showed her into the house."

Hawk lowered the horse's hoof. A man he would have asked to come to the barn so he could keep working. A woman was another matter. He reached for his shirt and put it on as he headed for the door.

As he walked out of the barn, he saw the carriage, intricate scrolling on its sides. A pair of chestnut geldings was tethered to a nearby post. His caller wasn't from Sweetwater. Nothing like that carriage around these parts. Long strides carried him across the yard, his curiosity piqued. When he entered the house moments later, he found a plump, gray-haired woman seated on Bethany's sofa.

The woman looked at him, her eyes rounding as they trailed from face to boots and back again. "My goodness."

"I'm Hawk Chandler. Westy said you wanted to see me. Have we met, Mrs. . . ."

"No, Mr. Chandler. We have not met." She smiled. "But I feel as if we have." She paused, then added, "Though you are not at all what I expected."

"I'm afraid you have me at a disadvantage, ma'am."

"Oh, my. You have no idea who I am. No reason why you should. We only arrived from Philadelphia a few days ago."

Philadelphia? His heart quickened.

"Bethany has been quite busy or I'm sure she would have called upon you already. It's been difficult for her, dealing with the memories in that house. But she's told me so much about you that I wanted to see you for myself."

Hawk sat in the nearest chair.

"And I still haven't introduced myself, have I? Harvey, my husband, says I'm a chatterbox. I say that's nonsense. I'm merely making conversation." She laughed. "But there I go again. I'm Beatrice Worthington, Bethany's first cousin, once removed."

"Bethany's in Sweetwater?" He wasn't sure what he felt—hope, dread, both.

"She couldn't very well stay in Philadelphia when she wanted to be here, and when I learned she meant to return, I insisted that

I come too. I didn't want her making that long journey alone a second time."

"When did you arrive, Mrs. Worthington?"

"On Tuesday last. Quite the trip, I must say. But here we are. Now my young cousin is trying to decide what to do with herself. I've suggested she reopen the bakery. It's been closed, as you must know, since the baker passed away. Bethany seems taken with the idea."

"The bakery?" He almost laughed. "She can't even cook."

"You might be surprised what she can do when she puts her mind to it. And since she's a woman living alone, she must do something."

His humor evaporated. "She doesn't have to be alone. She has a husband. Me." *Unless she got that annulment and no one told me.*

"I'm aware of that. But you're out here and she's in Sweetwater, so her marital status is rather a moot point. Isn't it? A woman alone is a woman alone." She rose from the sofa. "Now, I must return to town." She moved to stand before him, offering her hand. "It may be belated, Mr. Chandler, but welcome to the family. I shall like getting to know you better. I hope we meet again soon."

Bethany opened the door and let out a squeal. "Ingrid!" She pulled her friend into a tight hug. "Oh, I've missed you so."

"I will not forgive you," Ingrid said when she was finally released. "To be in Sweetwater for four days and not send for me. I had to hear the news from the grocer."

Bethany took hold of her friend's hand and led her into the parlor. They sat, side by side, on the settee. "I'm sorry, but I needed some time to be alone with my memories." Her smile vanished. "It hasn't been easy, being back in this house again."

"Is that why you came back? Because of the house?"

"No." She shook her head. "I returned because this is my home."

There must have been something in her voice, something in her expression that Ingrid understood. "I knew you wouldn't stay away long. You could not stay away when you love Hawk."

Bethany sighed. "Why can you see it and he can't?"

"He is a man. You must tell him what you feel. He cannot read your mind."

Hawk watched the carriage pull away.

What had brought Bethany back to Sweetwater? The desire to open a bakery? Hardly. Maybe the inheritance from her parents was nothing more than the house. Maybe that's what brought her back. But that didn't make sense. The house could have been sold for her.

A bakery? He chuckled, envisioning his bride in a kitchen baking bread. Her cooking had improved some in the time she was with him at the ranch, but he couldn't imagine anyone paying for the experience.

Something told him she wouldn't welcome his opinion in that regard.

THIRTY

Bethany took her time getting to the Circle Blue. She wanted to savor every moment of the ride. She wanted to drink it all in. Everything was the same, yet seemed different too. Late summer had darkened the blue of the sky, deepened the browns of the earth. Although the days remained warm, September had arrived with cool nights. Soon the willows and aspens would exchange their verdant robes for ones of scarlet, mandarin, and gold.

She'd known when she awoke that morning that this was the day to see Hawk. He'd had two days to think about her return. Of course, she'd hoped he would come to town, but he hadn't. So now it was up to her to make the first move.

I hope Cousin Beatrice is right. I hope he's missed me.

"You mark my words, Bethany," Beatrice had said. "I took his measure. I saw that look in his eyes. He cares more than you know. Maybe more than he knows. So let him think you don't need him. Then he'll come around."

"Isn't that dishonest?" she'd asked.

But Beatrice had insisted this was the better way, and so Bethany had agreed not to rush any declarations of love. She would subdue her impetuosity.

At least she would have something to do while she waited for Hawk to fall in love with her. She'd rented the building that housed the bakery, a business that had been abandoned since the epidemic. The sign in the window now read, Bethany's Bakery. Not very original, but hers.

She grinned. She hadn't anticipated that she would enjoy the idea of being a businesswoman. It was rather exciting, making plans, estimating costs. Even her baking had improved in the short while she'd been back in Sweetwater. Her parents would have been surprised—and pleased, she liked to think.

Cresting a shallow gully, she reined in and feasted her eyes on the house and outbuildings of the Circle Blue.

"Home."

Hawk had wondered if she would come today. He'd stayed close to the ranch house, just in case. When he saw her riding into the yard, he ran his fingers through his shaggy hair and then stepped out the front door to await her.

She wore a black riding habit and bonnet, a reminder of her loss. But even in mourning attire, he thought her beautiful. As she drew closer, he reacquainted himself with each delicate feature—her slightly upturned nose, her heart-shaped mouth, the green of her eyes, and those dark sable lashes that framed them.

The emotion the sight of her stirred inside him was a powerful thing. Love so strong it could knock him off his feet. It left him feeling off balance and unsure of himself. He knew what he wanted—her, in his life, in his arms. He wanted her back, but he wanted it to be her decision, her choice. Instinct told him to move carefully, lest she bolt like an untrained filly.

"Hello, Hawk." She drew her mare to a halt.

"Bethany."

"Are you well?"

"Well enough. And you?"

"I'm well too. And glad to be back."

"Care to come in?"

She gave him a small smile. "Yes, I would. Thank you."

He stepped forward and placed his hands at her waist, lifting her from the sidesaddle and lowering her to the ground. He caught a wisp of fragrance, fresh and sweet. It was all he could do not to pull her to him and kiss her breathless.

He cleared his throat as he released her and motioned for her to precede him inside. Once there, she sat on the love seat beneath the window. Sadness filled her eyes as she ran her fingertips over the fabric of the sofa.

He swallowed the urge to sit beside her. Instead, he stood by the fireplace, his shoulder leaned against the mantel. "I didn't know what to do with that after I learned you'd gone back East. I should have sent it with your trunk."

She didn't reply.

"I'm sorry about your parents, Bethany. If I'd known ..." He let his words trail into silence.

He saw the quiver of her chin, the glitter of tears in her eyes, and it broke his heart.

"Where did you go, Hawk? After Rand and Ingrid's wedding. Where did you go?"

"No place special. I just rode west." He moved to a chair and sat on it. "I rode until God got my attention."

She didn't ask what he meant, and he didn't offer, not sure he could put it into words. Instead he asked, "What brought you back?"

"Philadelphia wasn't home anymore. I wanted to be here, in Sweetwater."

He nodded, hoping this was a good sign. Missing the town might mean she missed him too.

"I have the house and the money Papa left me. And I believe Cousin Beatrice told you that I'm reopening the bakery."

He couldn't suppress a grin. "An odd choice, isn't it? You and baking."

She sat a little straighter, her eyes flashing. "You know, Hawk, I don't need your blessing on this. I've had to do a lot of growing up the past few months. I had to nurse people while they died horrible deaths. Had to—" Her voice trembled but she firmed her mouth— "say good-bye to my parents, learn to live without them ... and ... and learn to stand on my own. If I want to open a bakery, I will." She stood to leave.

"You're right. I'm sorry. Don't be angry with me." He stood too. "I'm your husband, and I care what happens to you. I don't want you to be hurt."

An odd expression flickered across her face and was gone—too soon for him to understand what it meant.

"I'd like us to at least be friends," he added.

"Friends," she echoed softly. "Yes, I suppose we can be friends." Then she walked toward the door, not waiting for him to open it for her.

Ingrid placed the plate of hot food on the table and sat on the bench beside her husband. "We must do something."

"Best thing we can do is stay out of it." Rand cut a slice of beef and speared it with his fork.

"But they are our friends. They need our help."

"I'm tellin' you, Ingrid, we'd best keep our noses out of their business."

She sighed and pushed her food around the plate with her fork. It didn't seem right that she should be so happy and her friend so miserable. The Silvertons had been good to her. If they hadn't taken her in after her father died, if they hadn't brought her to Sweetwater, she never would have met and married Rand. It was up to her to help Hawk and Bethany.

"You're up to somethin'." Rand shook his head. "Don't do it."

She offered an innocent smile. "Bethany has never seen our home. I think it is time we had her come to dinner."

"Alone?"

She shrugged. "Unless someone else happens by."

THIRTY-ONE

Bethany looked around the shop front. The bakery wasn't meant to be a restaurant, but she had decided to place two tables near the large window for customers who might prefer to eat their desserts upon purchase. She'd covered the tables with floral-print tablecloths and set two wooden chairs at each one. A tall glass case at the rear of the room would display the breads, pies, and pastries. The kitchen, with its large oven and long worktable, was behind a wide door that swung on hinges in either direction. Everything looked in order for next week's opening.

"Are you ready to go home?" Beatrice asked. "I'm completely exhausted."

Bethany turned. "Yes, I'm ready. There's nothing more to do until we begin baking. And we wouldn't be ready for that without your help. I so appreciate you, Cousin Beatrice."

"My goodness, I've enjoyed this more than I can say. I know that sounds strange, but it's true. I've loved getting my hands dirty while we readied this place. I may have even lost a bit of weight. Harvey won't know me." Beatrice patted Bethany's shoulder. "The bakery will be a great success."

"I hope so."

It simply had to succeed. She had something to prove, not to herself but to Hawk. He'd laughed at the idea of her running the bakery. Well, not laughed exactly but almost. It was important that she prove him wrong. Sometimes she wondered if that had become more important to her than winning his love.

No, his love was more important. She wanted Hawk more than ever, but he didn't seem to want her. At best he wanted to be her friend.

Swallowing the hurt that thought brought with it, Bethany snuffed the lamps one by one, then slipped into her wrap and followed her cousin out the front door. A chill wind whistled down Main Street, carrying with it the brassy tinkle of piano music from the saloon.

"Evening, Mrs. Worthington."

Bethany caught her breath at the sound of Hawk's voice. He'd come at last!

"Evening, Mrs. Chandler."

She turned toward him. It was too dark to see his face, yet she sensed his gaze upon her. Her heart beat a funny rhythm in her chest.

"I hear Monday's the opening of the bakery. You ready?"

"We will be."

"Good." He nodded. "I wish you lots of luck with it."

"Thank you. Will you be at the opening?" She sounded too eager but couldn't help it. She wanted him there.

"Can't say. I'll have to see."

His reply hurt, but she wouldn't give up. He was here now. She would be glad of that.

"It's turned cold early this year." He motioned with his head toward the street where a saddle horse awaited him. "I'll be half frozen before I get back to the ranch. But I'd like to walk you ladies home before I go. If that's all right with you."

"Thank you, Mr. Chandler," Beatrice answered. "We would appreciate your company."

Hawk offered an arm to her cousin, and she took it. Then he looked at Bethany and offered the other arm.

Maybe if she could see his face, maybe if she could read his expression, she would know what to say to him. Maybe then she could find the words that would change things between them. She wanted so much more than to hold his arm while he walked her home.

I don't want to be your friend. I want you to love me.

But she couldn't see him. She had no words. And so, in silence, she slipped her arm into his.

They followed the boardwalk past the mercantile, Mrs. Jenkins Restaurant, and the Delaney Boarding House. The noise of the saloon faded behind them, swallowed by the wind. Before them, the dark silhouette of the church steeple stood against the star-studded sky.

How do I make him want me for his wife?

She longed to be able to talk to her mother and father. Her papa would have told her what she needed to do, what was right not just in his eyes but in God's eyes. She loved her cousin and Ingrid and knew they wanted the best for her. But were either of them right about Hawk's feelings or how she could heal the rift between them? If only God were as quick to answer her prayers as others were to offer advice.

Please, Lord. Please show me the way.

Hawk wasn't sure what he'd hoped to accomplish when he rode into town earlier. All he'd known was that he needed to see her again. So now he was here, walking beside her, and his mind was a blank. He didn't even have a good excuse for being in town this late.

He could ask her why she hadn't gotten the annulment. Didn't she want it or was it that the loss of her parents had shoved the matter aside? It might be good to know. But he didn't have the courage to ask. Not yet.

Beatrice broke the silence. "We must all be tired. We've not a one of us said a word this whole way." She released her hold on his arm.

Hawk glanced toward the house and then opened the gate with his free hand.

Bethany slipped away from him too. "Thank you for walking us home."

"It was my pleasure."

"Would you like to come in? I could make some coffee to warm you for the ride home."

It was tempting. He wanted to be with her, but he was afraid he would remain silent and tongue-tied, like a schoolboy. He wasn't used to feeling unsure of himself. He'd told Bethany on their wedding day that he was more used to being around cows than women, but he wasn't a complete greenhorn. He should at least know how to sweet-talk the woman he loved. But how did a man go about courting his own wife?

"I'm sorry, Hawk. You said you needed to hurry back to the ranch." She stepped away. "I won't keep you. Good night."

He watched as the two women moved up the walk and onto the porch. In the dark he couldn't tell if she looked back before entering the house, but he liked to think she did.

Next time he would have something to say. Next time he wouldn't let her get away before he could say it.

THIRTY-TWO

"You'll come for dinner tonight. Ingrid won't take no for an answer."

Hawk nodded. "Told you I'd be there."

Rand swung into the saddle. With both hands, he lifted the collar of his coat as his gaze swept the lead gray sky. "Looks like we're in for a bit of weather. Might snow."

"Kind of early for snow."

"We've seen it in the high country this early before." Rand massaged a shoulder. "And my bones tell me it's comin'. Hope it doesn't keep me from takin' Ingrid to town for the opening of Bethany's bakery. You goin'?"

"Haven't decided yet."

"Well, you can tell us tonight. If you're goin', we can ride in together."

Hawk stayed outdoors until his friend disappeared from view, then turned and went inside. Feeling the chill, he crossed the parlor and tossed another log on the fire, sending sparks flurrying up the chimney. The cabin was quiet except for the crackle of burning wood and the wind whistling around the corner of the house.

Too quiet.

He missed Bethany.

Four months. Four months was all he'd known her, and she'd turned his life upside down. He'd had his friends—cowboys like himself—and his ranch and his cattle. He'd been on friendly terms with most of the folks in town. He'd been content. Now look at him. Lonely. Trouble sleeping. And to make it worse, winter was coming. Winter, when he'd be cooped up with little to do but think about her and want her with him.

He never expected that loving a woman could cause a man so much grief. Bethany seemed an expert at it.

He grinned as he stared into the fire, replaying memories of her. The sound of her laughter. The spark in her eyes when she was angry. The tilt of her chin. He could have had her love and trust. He'd come to understand that. She'd cared for him, but he'd let pride blind him to the truth. Now he would have to start all over again.

And with the Lord's help, he wouldn't let her get away a second time.

"You didn't need to come into town for me," Bethany said to Rand as the buggy sped along the road.

"Glad to do it. This way I'll get no argument when it comes time to take you home again." He slapped the reins against the horse's rump. "How're things comin' at the bakery?"

A groan escaped her. "Everything is in turmoil. Mr. Grant, the baker I hired, has been at odds with Cousin Beatrice since he arrived from Denver."

"You gonna like running a business?"

"I think so, yes. I've learned a lot from Mr. Grant already. Only—" she looked at Rand—"I wouldn't want to do it forever."

"Yeah. I understand."

She thought he probably did.

The two of them chatted amiably about many things, and before they knew it, they arrived at the Howard cabin.

"I am so glad you have come." Ingrid gave Bethany a tight hug as soon as she was inside. "Sit by the hearth. You are cold. I can feel it in your cheeks." She placed another log on the fire. "I hope you are hungry."

"Very. It smells delicious."

"I have prepared a venison stew. I hope you will like it."

The door opened, another burst of cold air swirling into the cabin. Rand entered with the wind. "Look who's here." Hawk stepped through the doorway behind him.

While host and hostess pretended surprise, Bethany found herself captured by Hawk's gaze. She wasn't fooled by the charade. They'd planned this meeting. Had he known she would be here?

"Hello, Hawk."

"Bethany."

"I didn't expect to see you."

He glanced sideways at his friend before removing his hat and placing it on a peg near the door. "I wasn't expecting it either."

"Take off your coat and join Bethany by the fire," Ingrid said. "I will have our supper on the table soon."

She felt a strange shortness of breath as she watched him shrug out of his sheepskin jacket. She longed to rise and go to him, to hang his coat beside his hat, to run her fingers through his hair, to—

"You look tired." He sat in a nearby chair. "Are things going well?"

"Yes, but the days are long."

"Everyone's glad to know Sweetwater will have a bakery again."

Was there an apology hidden in those words? As was too often true, she couldn't read his expression. "I hope so. I want it to do well."

Before either could say more, they were summoned to the kitchen.

Hawk held out his hand to Bethany, and without hesitation she placed her fingers in the center of it, loving the feel of his grasp. As he led her to the table, she wished he would look at her again. She wished he would smile. She wished she could tell him she missed him. She wished—

Rand cleared his throat. "Before we eat, Ingrid and I've got somethin' we want to tell you both. I guess now's as good a time as any." He gave his wife a loving glance. "We're gonna have a baby."

"A baby?" Bethany pressed a hand to her heart. "Really? A baby?"

Her friend nodded, her face flushed with joy.

"That's wonderful." She hurried around the table to embrace Ingrid. "Why didn't you tell me sooner? When is the baby due?"

"I could not tell you. I was not sure until I saw the doctor."

Rand answered her second question. "Doc says the baby'll be here come April."

"Congratulations." Hawk slapped Rand's shoulder. "I'm happy for you both."

"Thanks. We're mighty pleased about it ourselves."

Bethany turned to look at Hawk. Was it possible they might have a child together one day?

The hours spent with Rand, Ingrid, and Bethany were pleasant and passed too quickly as far as Hawk was concerned. When it came time to leave, he volunteered to see Bethany back to Sweetwater and took it as a good sign when she didn't object.

"You'd best hurry," Rand said from the doorway. "Feels like that snow's comin'."

Hawk replied, "That's what you said this morning."

But Rand's words proved prophetic. They were barely down the mountainside when the first sporadic flakes—large and lazy—began to fall, floating through the air like giant white butterflies.

"How pretty." Bethany held out a hand to capture some.

He smiled as he watched her. She looked young and carefree. Like when she first arrived in Sweetwater with her parents.

But the idyllic scene didn't last. In a short while, the snowflakes turned to sleet. The wind rose, driving the freezing rain at them like shards of glass.

"I'm heading for the ranch!" he shouted above the storm.

In no time, his fingers felt frozen around the leather reins. The sleet stung his forehead and cheeks. He glanced at Bethany. Her face had nearly disappeared inside the collar of her coat as she leaned forward into the tempest. Icy crystals clung to her hat and hair.

As if knowing he watched her, she looked up and gave him a brave smile.

"We'll be there soon," he said, hoping he told the truth.

Bethany had never seen anything as welcome as the cabin at the Circle Blue. Hawk stopped the horse near the front door, then lifted her from the buggy seat and carried her inside. Near the fireplace, he lowered her to her feet.

"Better give me your hat and coat," he said.

She obliged.

"You're wet clean through. You need to change into something dry while I put the horse in the barn."

"I haven't any clothes here."

"Put on one of my shirts and then wrap up in a blanket." He brushed wet tendrils from her forehead.

A quiver ran through her that had nothing to do with the cold.

"Go on." He offered a teasing grin. "You're dripping all over the floor. I'll build the fire up so you can get warm."

Her pulse quickened as she hurried into Hawk's bedroom, closing the door behind her. Little light came through the window, but there was enough for her to find her way to the bureau. After removing a folded shirt from a drawer, she began struggling with the buttons on her dress, her cold fingers refusing to make it easy. But soon enough she shed the wet garments and donned the shirt. It almost reached to her knees. She paused a moment to rub her cheek against the fabric.

Hawk has worn this shirt.

Warmth spread through her as she reached for the blanket at the foot of the bed.

Hawk has slept under this blanket.

She wrapped herself in it.

A rap sounded at the door. "Are you decent?"

"Yes." Her heart fluttered. "You may come in."

The door opened, and she turned toward it.

He stood for a long moment in the doorway, looking at her. Even in the dim light, she read something in his eyes that she didn't quite understand. Did he feel as unsettled as she?

"You'd better go sit by the fire, Bethany, while I get changed."

She nodded, unable to speak. Moving toward him, she resisted the desire to cast off the blanket and throw her arms around him.

That was always her problem, doing or saying things without thinking them through first. She had pursued him before and made a mess of things. She mustn't make that mistake again. Not with Hawk. She must be patient.

In the parlor, she stood by the fireplace while awaiting his return. The room had grown ever darker, despite the flickering firelight. Outside the wind whistled and moaned, and the sleet continued to batter the cabin's walls and windows.

"You warmer now?" he asked as he stepped into the parlor, her dress over his arm.

She felt her stomach knotting in anticipation. She wanted him to hold and kiss her. Would he?

"We won't be going to town tonight. Not in this weather." He crossed to the fireplace where he draped her wet gown over a chair.

"Cousin Beatrice will worry."

He stood before her now, his face trapped in shadows. "She'll think you stayed with Ingrid."

"I suppose you're right."

"Bethany ..." His voice trailed off.

"Yes?"

His mouth descended toward hers. She longed to rise on tiptoe, to begin the kiss more quickly. But she waited, anticipation growing. A tiny tremor moved through her when their lips met. His kiss was light, tender, and dizzying. Her hands released their grip on the blanket and rose to clasp around his neck. It was either that or collapse into the fireplace. The blanket puddled at her feet.

I love you, Hawk. I love you so much.

He pulled her closer, the kiss deepening.

Tell me you love me. Please tell me.

He lifted his head, breaking the kiss. "I want you to come back. I want you to come live with me and be my wife. In fact, not name only."

"Why?"

"I promised your parents and God that I'd take care of you. Let me keep that promise."

Her heart broke a little over his reply. His answer was all wrong. "No."

"Do you want an annulment?"

"No."

He frowned as he took a step back from her. "I don't understand you."

"I know you don't."

"I want you here, with me."

"Wanting isn't enough." She picked up the blanket and wrapped herself in it again as she turned to face the fire. How she wished she were wrong. How she wished wanting was enough. But it wasn't, and she couldn't come back. Not if he didn't love her.

"I'll take you home at first light. You know where the bedroom is."

She heard him walk away, heard the sound of the door close.

Never had she felt so alone as she did now.

THIRTY-THREE

The cold snap held the area in its grip for a week. It rained. It hailed. It snowed. The wind rattled windows and shook houses. It felt like the middle of winter even though the calendar still read September.

But it didn't last. After seven days of cold came the return of clear blue skies and a sun that promised real warmth again.

"After we eat, I'm going for a ride," Bethany told her cousin as they walked home from the bakery a little before noon. "If I don't get out in the open air for a while, I'll turn into a lump of dough."

It wasn't as if the bakery required her presence every moment. Mr. Grant disliked anyone in his kitchen, and Beatrice could manage the customers for an hour or two.

And so, immediately after lunch, Bethany rode out of Sweetwater on Buttercup. As soon as they were a good half mile outside of town, she loosed the reins, lifted her arms and face toward the cornflower blue sky, and shouted, "It's a beautiful world, Lord. Thank you!" She laughed as she took the reins in hand again, her gaze trained on the mountains that rose like proud soldiers, guarding the range below.

The sun was warm upon her face, and the air smelled wonderful, clean and fresh. Her mother would scold her for being careless with her complexion if she could see her now. The thought dampened her spirits a little.

Only this wasn't a time for sad thoughts. This was a time to enjoy being out for a ride, to revel in Montana's beauty, to sing and to laugh. Tomorrow would have trouble of its own. Today she would take pleasure in riding her horse through the wide-open spaces.

She eased her hold on the reins and allowed the mare to break into a jog, mindless of the mud clods thrown up behind the trotting hooves. Oh, it was so beautiful out here. She loved it. She loved everything about it. Just look at those mountains.

Hawk's mountains.

She hadn't seen him since the morning after the ice storm. They'd said little to each other when he'd delivered her to the house in town, and he hadn't returned since.

I miss him.

Just as that thought came to her, Buttercup stumbled and fell to her knees. Almost before she realized what was happening, Bethany flew forward, then landed with a splat in the middle of the road. The air whooshed from her lungs, and pain exploded in her head. She rolled onto her back, dragging in gulps of air as she wiped her face. After giving her breathing time to steady, she rose to her feet, her mud-sodden skirts pulling at her.

"Look at me," she muttered, shaking her hands to fling away the clinging sludge.

She turned toward her horse and forgot her complaints. The mare's head hung low and she held her right front hoof off the ground.

"Oh, Buttercup. You're hurt."

The earth sucked at her boots as she moved toward the injured animal. She ran her hand over the knee, cannon, and fetlock. Nothing appeared to be broken. She was thankful for that.

"We need to get you back to the livery, girl."

Bethany picked up the dragging reins and tried to coax the horse forward. Buttercup refused to budge.

"You win. I'll go for help." She slipped the bridle off the horse's head as she spoke. "I guess you'll be all right until I get back."

What a sight Bethany made, trudging and slipping her way toward town, her dress burdened with the clinging wet soil. Hawk had found her horse a little ways back and was concerned until he saw her. Now that he could tell she wasn't hurt, he relaxed.

His mouth twitched. While in prayer that morning, he'd realized why Bethany refused to stay with him when he'd asked her. It was as if God opened his eyes, everything made clear. He had to throw pride to the wind and tell her he loved her. Whether or not she loved him in return.

She must have heard something, for she stopped and turned. Her cheeks were smudged with dried mud and her hat was askew.

"Nice day for a walk." He grinned.

"My horse took a spill."

"I know. I found her." He nudged his gelding forward. "Need a ride?" There was still a trace of humor in his voice.

"No, thank you. It isn't much farther to town."

"Far enough."

She turned and resumed walking.

"I've told you before you shouldn't ride alone."

"I know."

"So why don't you listen to me?"

"Because you never say anything I want to hear."

He swallowed a laugh. It wasn't fair of him to tease her right now. She'd taken a fall and was covered with mud. That would put anyone in a bad mood. He was about to apologize when he saw her stagger to one side and then crumple to the ground. He vaulted from the saddle and ran to her side.

She'd never seen anything more exciting. Hawk rode the black stallion, his right arm flung high as the horse bucked and twisted beneath him. They were wild and wonderful, the two of them, fighting to see who would conquer and who would be conquered. She wanted to be a part of it. She wanted to—

"Bethany?"

"Mmm?"

Fingers tapped her cheek. "Bethany?"

She opened her eyes. It really was him. Had she been at the ranch? Was he breaking that horse again?

Concern furrowed his brow. "You dropped like a rock."

"I what?"

"You fainted." He stood, lifting her with him. "I'm taking you to see the doctor. You must've hit your head when your horse threw you."

Her thoughts began to clear. "Buttercup didn't throw me. She stumbled and fell."

"Well, whatever the cause, you fainted just now."

"Don't be silly. I don't need Doc Wilton."

"You're going to see him anyway."

"Hawk— "

"We're not arguing about this." His gaze was uncompromising. "You're going to do what I say this time."

Funny. She couldn't keep arguing even if she wanted to. All the fight had gone out of her.

He carried her to his horse and stepped into the saddle, still cradling her in his arms. Once settled, he commanded her to put her arms around his neck. "Hold on to me. I don't want you taking another tumble."

Again she obeyed, this time quite happily.

As far as Bethany was concerned, they were much too close to town. Once they arrived at the house, she would have to move her head from Hawk's shoulder and unclasp her hands from around his neck. She didn't want to let go. She wanted to hold on to him forever.

If she weren't so stubborn, she could be with him all the time. He'd asked her to stay a week ago, and she'd refused. But he hadn't wanted her to stay for the right reasons.

"How does it feel to be in love, Mother?" She remembered the night she'd asked that question, and she could still hear her mother's reply: *"Quite wonderful, Bethany. And sometimes quite awful."*

Yes, it was. Wonderful and awful.

Hawk pulled his horse to a stop in front of the white picket fence.

Bethany raised her head. "We're back?"

"Yeah. You think you can stand?"

"Yes."

He slid her to the ground, his hands under her arms until he was certain she was steady, and then he dismounted. Before she could offer any protest, he swept her back off her feet and carried her up the walkway to the front porch.

Beatrice appeared from the back of the house as the door closed behind them. "Good heavens. What happened?"

"It's nothing, Cousin Beatrice."

"That's not true," Hawk countered. "She needs the doctor. Will you see she gets into bed, Mrs. Worthington, while I go for him?"

"Of course. Of course. Look at her. Oh dear. Oh dear."

He carried her up the stairs, her cousin close on his heels. "Which room is yours?"

Bethany pointed. "That one."

He opened the door, crossed the room, and set her gently on the bed.

"I'm all muddy, Hawk."

"It'll wash." He turned around. "I'll go for the doc. See that she stays put."

At the door, he glanced back one more time. He'd been all set to make things right between them, but now it would have to wait. And if there was anything really wrong with Bethany—

No, it didn't bear thinking about.

Bethany watched as Doc Wilton turned from the washbasin, drying his hands on a towel. When he was done, he rolled the sleeves of his white shirt down from his elbows, straightened his tie, and adjusted his eyeglasses on the bridge of his nose.

"Well, my girl. I don't find anything wrong with you that a good rest won't cure. You've got quite a lump on your head, but that's the worst of it."

She'd known as much before he'd come to see her.

"You'd best not do any riding for a while, just in case. It's possible you could be in the early stages of pregnancy. Many women are prone to dizziness and fainting when expecting."

She felt her cheeks flush. "I'm not expecting."

"Maybe not. But it could be too early to tell. Better to be cautious."

Her heart constricted. She could promise the doctor that she wasn't with child. She might not know much about the intimacies of marriage, but she knew she couldn't get pregnant on her own.

"I'll be going now. You stay in bed a day or two. I'll check on you tomorrow."

She nodded, unable to answer over the lump in her throat.

The door closed behind the doctor. It opened again a moment later and Hawk looked in. "How're you feeling? Doc said you're going to be fine."

"I got a bump on the head is all."

"You had me worried." He sat on a chair near the bed. "Bethany ..." He paused and his gaze dropped to his boots.

"Yes?"

"There's something I've been needing to say to you. We've made ... No, I've made a lot of mistakes. I don't want to keep on making them."

Apprehensive, she gave her head a slow shake, not wanting to hear what might hurt. Maybe he was leaving Montana. Maybe he wanted that annulment. Maybe he never wanted to see her again.

"When you were at the Circle Blue last week, I should have told you. I meant to tell you, only ... only I got angry and acted like a fool again."

Don't say anything bad. I couldn't bear it.

"I love you, Bethany."

The lightheadedness returned. The room began to spin.

"I know it's a lot to ask, after the way I've treated you, but I'd like you to come home. I'd like us to start over, you and me. Not because of the promise I made to your parents, but because of the promise I made to God, that I would love and cherish you for the rest of my days. I didn't know how much I loved you when I made that promise, and I didn't really know the God I made the promise to. But I . . . I want to keep it. Do you think you could learn to love me?"

The smile began in her heart, then appeared on her lips. "You *are* a fool." She took hold of his hand. "I've loved you from the start."

They sat in silence, staring at each other. And then she was in his arms, her face buried against his neck as he whispered again his words of love. She clung to him, not out of desperation, but with a thrill for the joy she had found with him.

She kissed the underside of his jaw, then worked her way up to his mouth. Gently, tenderly, she sought to acquaint herself once again with the sweetness of his kisses.

When at last they drew apart, he looked into her eyes. "Will you come back to the Circle Blue with me today?"

"Yes," came her breathless reply. "It's where I belong."

"What about the bakery?"

"Mr. Grant doesn't need my help. Maybe he'll want to buy it from me." She smiled. "We can worry about that later. For now, I just want to go home."

THIRTY-FOUR

Marriage, Bethany decided in the weeks that followed their reconciliation, was a profoundly wonderful institution. At least that was true when a woman was fortunate enough to love her husband and be loved by him in return.

A favorite part of her days was when she learned something new about Hawk. For instance, his facial expressions were not as inscrutable as she'd once thought. When he was impatient, his right eyebrow developed a tick. When he teased her, the slightest of smirks tugged the corners of his mouth; she couldn't help but wonder how often she'd missed that.

She'd also learned that Hawk knew about many things besides cattle and ranching. His interests were wide and varied. His parents had seen to it that their son received a good education. They seemed, from the things he told her about them, much the same as her parents—loving, kind, patient, and devoted to God. And though his loss had happened thirteen years earlier, he understood those moments when she missed her parents beyond words.

As she lay in bed one morning in mid-October, waiting for the dawn, she thought how right her mother had been about love. What Bethany had felt for Hawk five months earlier hadn't had deep roots. What she had called love had been more about her getting what she wanted, about pleasing herself, not about caring for another person. It wasn't a pleasant revelation. Thankfully, she and Hawk were learning about love—the deep-rooted kind—together. An answer to her parents' prayers.

She rolled onto her side. Her husband was little more than a darker shadow in the still-dark bedroom.

"You're awake early," he said in a morning-gruff voice.

She moved closer, laying her head on his shoulder. "I don't think it's all that early."

"You're right. We'll need to leave for town soon. Your cousin wants to get an early start."

"I'm going to miss her."

"Mr. Grant won't."

Bethany laughed softly, picturing the rotund baker. "No, he won't. Those two are like oil and water."

"I'm surprised Beatrice stayed in Sweetwater as long as she did. Once you came back to the Circle Blue—" he kissed her forehead—"there wasn't much to keep her there. Except maybe to give Mr. Grant more grief. I think she's enjoyed that a lot."

She heard his smile even though she couldn't see it.

He kissed her again, this time on the lips, one of those long, slow kisses that stole her breath away. But at last he released her and rolled to sit at the side of the bed. "I'll build up the fire in the kitchen."

She swallowed a sigh, thinking how nice it would be to stay in bed—the both of them—and snuggle another hour or two. But he was right. They had to hurry.

Her cousin Beatrice, Bethany decided as she watched the hired driver load trunks onto the back of the carriage, would have made a formidable drill instructor in the army.

"You be careful with that, young man. That trunk holds items that can never be replaced. Memories of my cousin and his wife."

"I'm being careful," the fellow snapped in reply. "If you'd leave me be, it'd get done faster."

Beatrice, her face grown pink with indignation, turned toward Bethany. "I shall be so glad to return to civilization where people exhibit a few more manners."

Bethany couldn't hold back a smile. "You don't fool me, cousin. You'll miss being here."

She knew her words were true. Her cousin had enjoyed her mornings in the bakery—irritating Mr. Grant, waiting on customers, training a girl to take over her job. She'd enjoyed her afternoons even more when she'd entertained the womenfolk of Sweetwater, holding court as only Beatrice Worthington could.

"All your new friends will miss you too."

"As I shall miss them. But as much fun as it's been, I'm looking forward to being home and surrounded with my own things. Heaven knows, the house will be at sixes and sevens under Harvey's supervision. I love that man to distraction, but he has no understanding of what it takes to run our household."

"Few would." Bethany smiled, thinking of the four-room cabin she called home and how thankful she was not to have the complications of maids, housekeeper, butler, underbutler, cooks, livery boys, gardeners, and who-knew-how-many-other servants it took to maintain the Worthington estate.

Beatrice checked the watch pinned to her bodice. "Where is that husband of yours? If he doesn't come soon, I shall miss telling him good-bye."

"He said he wouldn't be long." She glanced toward the sheriff's office. "Look. There he comes now."

Hawk strode down the boardwalk, his long gait eating up the distance. When he saw both women looking in his direction, he raised a hand in a wave.

"Oh, my. I hope I won't begin to cry." Her cousin sniffed as she pulled a handkerchief from the pocket of her traveling gown. "I've grown so fond of you both."

"You promised to come again and bring Harvey with you."

"Indeed we shall. Perhaps by the time we do so, there will be a new little Chandler for me to fuss over. That would be a delight." She raised her voice. "Hawk, you almost missed my departure."

"Not a chance, Cousin Beatrice." He stepped through the open gate. "Is everything loaded in the carriage?"

"Everything but the bag your beautiful bride is holding."

He took the satchel from Bethany's hand. "I'll take care of it for you. I imagine you want it with you."

"Indeed, I do."

As Hawk moved toward the carriage, Beatrice turned to Bethany and embraced her. "God bless you, my dear girl."

"He has."

"I know. I know. That's why I can leave without regret." She kissed Bethany's cheek. "Do keep me apprised of what happens with the bakery. I feel quite certain Mr. Grant will buy it before the year is out."

Hawk returned in time to receive a tight squeeze and a kiss on the cheek from Beatrice. "You'll write to us," he said when she released him.

"Of course. And I'll expect regular correspondence from you both." She dabbed at her eyes with her handkerchief. "Now I shall be off. Take care of each other." She bustled toward the carriage, not waiting for Hawk or the driver to help her inside. Once settled, she waved her handkerchief at them. "Good-bye, my dears."

Hawk put his arm around Bethany's shoulders. "You'll be in our prayers." Moments later, they watched as the Worthington carriage drove out of Sweetwater, remaining near the gate until the vehicle disappeared from view.

"Even this house will miss her," Bethany said softly.

Her husband's arm tightened, drawing her close against his side. "This house needs a family living in it."

She knew he meant she should sell it. She even agreed with him. But it would be difficult to let go. This was where her parents had wanted to spend their latter years. This was where they had died. Selling it would feel a little like losing them all over again.

"When you're ready, Bethany. You don't have to make any decisions until you want to."

"I know." She drew in a deep breath. "Let's go home."

A chilly October breeze rose as they made their way to the horses tied at the side of the house. Hawk helped her mount Buttercup, and then swung into the saddle of his gelding. Wordlessly, they rode down the main street of town. As they passed the bakery, several women, seated at the tables inside, waved to them. She returned the wave, and her heart lifted a little. Who would have guessed, when she was staying with her cousin in Philadelphia, heartbroken and lonely, that she would soon find her marriage restored and herself the owner of a bakery in this small Montana town.

Life certainly had a way of surprising a person.

As they rode toward the ranch, Hawk said a silent thanks to God for turning the mistakes he'd made with Bethany into something good. But his words of thanks were forgotten the instant he saw the buggy, pulled by a palomino, approaching them at a good clip.

Vince Richards.

He hadn't known he was back, and he wasn't glad to see him.

The buggy slowed as it neared them. "Chandler." Vince drew the buggy horse to a halt.

Hawk reined in.

"Good day, Beth— I mean, Mrs. Chandler. I trust you are well. You were quite distressed when I saw you in Philadelphia."

Hawk looked at Bethany. Vince had seen her in Philadelphia?

"Chandler, I heard you had a bit of trouble while I was away. Have they learned the identity of the man you shot?"

"Not yet."

"A pity."

"Yes." His suspicions about Vince returned. Had he been involved in some way with that gunman? If there were only some evidence …

"I won't keep you. I have business in town." Vince nodded, his gaze on Bethany. "I look forward to seeing you again."

Hawk resisted the urge to vault from his horse and wipe that suggestive smile off Vince's face.

The buggy pulled away.

Hawk and Bethany spoke at the same time: "There was a shooting?" "You saw him in Philadelphia?"

She answered first. "He came to a ball at Cousin Beatrice's home. He didn't know I was there or that she was related to me. Our meeting was quite by chance." A cloud passed over her face. "When he learned I was in mourning, he thought it was for you. He hadn't heard about the cholera outbreak."

"He must have been disappointed when he heard I wasn't among the dead. He'd like to see that."

She glanced over her shoulder at the departing buggy.

Hawk continued, "Richards wants the Circle Blue. He wants to control the water rights that go with it so he can drive off other ranchers. He's made several offers to buy me out and is none too happy that I won't sell."

"I don't like him." She shuddered.

Something eased inside him. "Then we're in agreement."

"What did he mean about a shooting?"

Hawk clucked at his gelding, and the two horses moved forward. "We've had trouble over the summer with rustling and other mischief. We hadn't had much luck finding the rustlers, but a while back, I found tracks and followed them. Guess the man I was following didn't like it. He fired at me, and I fired back." He touched the spot near his temple where the bullet had grazed him. "He missed. I didn't."

"You killed him?"

"Afraid so. I didn't want to, God knows, but it was him or me. There was nothing else I could do. Truly, Bethany." He spoke with a mixture of regret and resignation.

Her voice quavered as she asked, "He tried to kill you?"

"Yeah, he tried."

"And you think Vince Richards was behind it?"

"I think there's a good chance of it, yes."

She looked at him, a glimmer of fear in her eyes. "Be careful, Hawk. I don't want to wear black again. Not until I'm an old, old woman."

Thirty-Five

The wind whistled beyond the cabin walls, a sad, lonely sound. But inside, all was cozy. A fire snapped and crackled on the hearth, its light dancing across the floor, casting shadows into the corners. Bethany sat on the sofa, mending one of her husband's shirts. Every so often, her gaze strayed to the door. She had expected Hawk before nightfall and wondered what had kept him.

As if summoned by her thoughts, the door opened, banging against the wall as a gust of wind swept him into the house. He turned at once and pushed the door closed. "Snow's coming hard."

She rose and went to him. "I'm glad you're back." She took his hat and hung it on a peg.

"Me too. It's bad out there. I think you're about to get your first taste of a Montana winter. This snow will be around a while." He bent down and kissed the tip of her nose.

She smiled in response. "Supper's on the stove. Are you hungry?"

"Starved." He shrugged out of his knee-length fur-lined overcoat.

"Hawk, your clothes are wet. What happened?"

"I fell through some ice. I thought it was thick enough to hold me, but I was wrong." He shivered. "I'll tell you about it later. I'm going to change into something dry."

"You're going to do more than change," Bethany replied in a firm tone. "I'm heating a bath for you. You go sit in front of the fire until it's ready."

He grinned. "Yes, ma'am. Whatever you say."

The blizzard lasted for five days. The world outside the cabin was a flurry of white, keeping Hawk and Bethany prisoners within the log walls. Willing prisoners. For nearly a week, they forgot everything except each other. It was a delightful interlude.

It was the silence that awakened Bethany on the sixth day. The wind wasn't howling. Snow didn't sting the windowpanes. The tall pine that stood outside their bedroom wasn't whipping its branches against the log walls. It was as if the earth held its breath.

"Storm's over," Hawk said.

Sensing their seclusion was nearing its end, she snuggled closer.

"I'll be going out with the boys to check on the cattle. I could be gone several days."

"Will many cows be lost?"

He kissed the top of her head. "Cattle aren't any too smart. They've got a tendency to just stand and let the snow bury them instead of finding a windbreak. I've seen them freeze in their tracks. But the Circle Blue's been through worse storms. I expect we'll come through this one okay."

They dressed quickly in the icy morning air. When he looked at her, his eyes speaking his love, she felt a quickening in her heart, and she wished the storm had continued so she could keep him to herself a little longer.

He headed for the bedroom door. "I'll bring in more wood so you won't run out while I'm gone."

Fastening the last button on her bodice, she followed him out of the bedroom and went to the kitchen where she took an iron skillet from its nail on the wall and placed it on the stove, ready to begin another day.

After four days alone, Bethany lost track of how many times she'd found herself staring out the window, willing Hawk to ride into the yard. It felt as if the walls of the cabin were closing in on her. If her husband hadn't given her strict instructions not to leave the ranch, she would have saddled her buckskin mare and ridden up to see Ingrid. She needed the sound of another human's voice.

She was standing at the window again when someone rode into the yard at last. Only it wasn't Hawk or one of his hired hands. It was a man who was less than welcome on the Circle Blue. She considered not answering the door when he knocked on it. Except that her need to talk to someone—anyone—was momentarily greater than her dislike of Vince Richards.

"Good afternoon, Bethany." He removed his hat. "Hope you don't mind my coming by. I knew Hawk would be out checking on the herd after the storm, and I wanted to make sure that you're all right." He patted his gloved hands against his upper arms, as if warding off the cold. "May I come in?"

Hawk wouldn't like him being here, but now that she'd opened the door, she didn't know how to refuse his request. She stepped to the side and opened the door a little wider.

He moved into the parlor. "What a change this is. You've made the place into a home."

"Thank you." Regret washed over her as Vince sat on a chair near the fireplace. She wished she could undo the last few minutes.

It made her nervous, having him in the house. She should tell him to leave, the way she had three months earlier in the sitting room of the Worthington home.

"You're looking pale," Vince said, intruding on her thoughts. "Are you unwell?"

"No." She tilted her chin. "But I think you should go. You can see that I'm fine. Besides, my husband—" she stressed the word—"will return soon."

His eyes narrowed as he stood. "It seems you are always asking me to leave. I wish you understood my deep regard for you."

Without a word, she opened the door, letting in the cold.

He moved to stand before her. "I am not a patient man. I set my mind on what I want, and then I move heaven and earth to get it."

"Please go. I have things to do."

He stepped onto the stoop, then looked back at her. "This is a harsh land. All kinds of things can happen. A man falls from a horse and breaks his neck. He gets mauled by a bear. Renegades shoot him. A man can get caught in a blizzard and freeze to death and nobody finds his body until spring." He pulled on his gloves. "I'll be here to look after you should anything like that happen to Hawk. You can count on me."

She closed the door. Only then did she realize she was shaking. His words felt like a threat. Were they? Or was she reading too much into them?

I'll never open the door to him again. Not ever.

She returned to the sofa and picked up her mending, deciding as she did that she wouldn't tell Hawk about her unwelcome visitor. Better to put the matter behind her and never think of it again.

THIRTY-SIX

Winters in Montana were long, with little for cowboys to do beyond the lonely, cold task of line riding, checking to make sure the cattle weren't starving or freezing to death. Most of the men looked forward to spring and the roundups and trail drives that followed.

Not Hawk. Not this year. He'd taken a fancy to winter all of a sudden. He was content to hole up with his wife inside their cabin and saw no reason to go out as long as there was wood to burn and food to eat.

At least he was content until she started having nightmares. The first one happened in early November, not long after the season's first major snowstorm. It was her moans that woke him. He was about to reach for her to see what was wrong when she screamed and bolted upright in bed.

He took her in his arms. "Hey. What is it?"

"Stay with me, Hawk." She clung to him. "Don't go away again."

"I'm here. I'm not going anywhere."

"I thought something happened to you. You were hurt and I couldn't find you. I was so afraid."

"It was just a bad dream. Nothing's happened to me."

She began to sob.

Never in his life had he felt as helpless as he did then. He didn't know what to say to reassure her, other than repeating the same words over and over again. "Nothing's happened to me, Bethany. I'm fine. Don't be afraid. Shh. It's okay."

But it wasn't okay. The nightmares continued. Not every night, but often enough. And those bad dreams spilled into the days, changing her, slowly but surely. When she smiled or laughed, uncertainty remained in her eyes. She didn't have the same vibrancy, the same spunk that he had come to love about her. She was quiet, too quiet.

Oh, she pretended that nothing was wrong. She told him not to worry about her. But he wasn't fooled. Something *was* wrong. And when he realized how thin she'd grown, he decided to do something about it. If she wouldn't talk to him, he'd get her to talk to someone else.

"We're going to town," he announced at the breakfast table one morning. "I need to pick up supplies." He stood. "You get ready while I hitch the horses to the sleigh. Bundle up good."

He followed his own advice, donning coat, hat, and gloves before heading outside. Even so, the cold bit into him as he made his way to the barn. He almost welcomed it, hoping it would clear his head.

"Lord, something's eating her up inside, and I'm feeling helpless." He stopped and looked heavenward. "And if you could help me find a way to get her to see Doc Wilton without her getting angry at me, I'd be thankful for it."

Vince sized up the man who stood across the desk from him, hat in hand. He was young, early twenties more than likely, with the look of someone eager to prove his prowess with a gun. McDermott, the Bar V foreman and Vince's trusted ally, seemed to think Rick Saunders could do the job. He'd better be right. Vince was tired of waiting. Tired of failed attempts. He wanted Chandler out of the picture soon.

He rose from his chair and offered Saunders his hand. "It's agreed then. You get rid of Hawk Chandler, and you'll be paid five hundred dollars for your trouble. And until the job's done, you stay clear of the Bar V and any of my men. I want no connection to you in any way. Get yourself hired on at one of the other ranches. Better yet, get hired on at the Circle Blue, if you can. Blend in until you get your chance. But once Chandler's dead and you've got your money, I want you gone from Montana. Understood?"

"Understood." There was a hard glint in the cowboy's eyes as he shook Vince's hand. "I've got no reason to stay."

Vince held the man's hand a moment longer. "Do the job right."

Saunders nodded.

A movement beyond the study caught Vince's eye. He looked and saw Hutchens hurrying away from the open door. Had he overheard? He must have. Vince swore beneath his breath as he led Saunders to the back door where McDermott waited with Saunders' horse.

"See him off the Bar V, and don't let any of our men see you with him."

McDermott nodded.

Vince closed the door and immediately went in search of Hutchens. He found him in the butler's pantry, polishing silverware.

"I don't like servants listening at doorways, Hutchens. You've been with me long enough to know that."

"I wasn't listening, sir," Hutchens protested—but his eyes said something different.

"Just know this. The same thing could happen to you that is going to happen to Chandler. You wouldn't even be missed."

Hutchens blanched.

Good. Message delivered and understood.

Bethany was surprised to find her spirits lifting as the sleigh skimmed over the snow, bells jingling on the harness. She'd allowed fear to hold her captive for so long that she'd begun to think it would always be so. It was awful to be afraid of the unknown, of the future. She wasn't a fearful sort of person by nature—or at least she hadn't been.

But maybe her nightmares weren't premonitions of bad things to come. Perhaps they were nothing more than indigestion. She'd had plenty of that lately.

She slipped her arm through Hawk's. "If the weather holds, could we pay a visit to Ingrid in the next day or two?"

He leaned his head close to hers. "Of course we can, if it would please you."

"It would." She returned his smile. "It feels good to be out. Thank you for bringing me along."

When they arrived in Sweetwater, Hawk stopped the horse in front of the bakery. "Let's sample Mr. Grant's fare, shall we?"

"If you like." She wasn't hungry, but it wouldn't hurt to see how the baker was getting along since her cousin left town.

The air inside the shop, warmed by heat from the ovens, felt wonderful. It wrapped around Bethany like a blanket.

Myrtle, the girl Beatrice had trained as her replacement, greeted them, then said, "Mr. Grant was saying just yesterday that we might not see you again until spring."

"I've thought that a time or two myself," Bethany answered. "But we're here now. Is Mr. Grant in the kitchen?"

"Yes, ma'am. Do you want me to get him?"

"No. I'll go on back." She motioned toward Hawk. "You can help Mr. Chandler decide what he wants to eat."

She unbuttoned her coat as she moved toward the swinging door that led into the kitchen. When she pushed it open, she found the baker rolling piecrust on the large flour-covered worktable.

"Hello, Mr. Grant."

He looked up, grunted, and returned to his work.

"I trust you are well."

"Well enough."

Mr. Grant—who didn't seem to have a first name, at least not one he'd shared with her—was a big man, both in height and weight, with a ruddy complexion and a thin mustache that looked as if it had been drawn on his face. His manner was prickly at the best of times, but he was a master at his craft. Even now, Bethany found it hard to believe he'd been enticed to come to Sweetwater.

"Have you given any more thought to my offer to sell you the bakery?"

"I have at that."

"And?"

He set aside the rolling pin and straightened. "I like Sweetwater, Mrs. Chandler, and I think the bakery will do well here. But I'm not sure I can raise the capital I would need to buy you out. Not anytime soon."

"Have the receipts been good? It's been weeks since I last spoke with you."

"They've been good."

"Because of you."

He shrugged.

"And Myrtle is working out well?"

"She's a good girl. A hard worker."

"Cousin Beatrice will be pleased to hear so."

Mr. Grant scowled. "Will she now?"

"Yes, she will."

With another grunt, he returned his attention to the piecrust.

He wanted to buy the bakery, and she wanted to sell it to him. There must be some way they could find a satisfactory arrangement. But right now she couldn't think what it might be. She was feeling overheated, standing in the kitchen in her warm winter coat.

"I'll leave you to your work, Mr. Grant. Good day to you."

"And you."

Perspiration beaded her forehead as she left the kitchen. Queasiness churned in her stomach. She looked in Hawk's direction—he was still trying to decide on a sweet from the display—and motioned toward the door. "I need a little air," she said, hoping she wasn't about to lose her breakfast in public.

Hawk caught up with her before she reached the sidewalk. "What's wrong?"

"The kitchen was hot. I should have removed my coat. It made me feel a little woozy."

He cocked an eyebrow. "I think those supplies I wanted to buy can wait a while. Let's you and me go see Doc Wilton."

"I don't need a doctor. I only need to cool off."

"Remember the last time you said you didn't need a doctor? You'd passed out in the road."

"And all that was wrong with me was a little bump on the head. Doc Wilton didn't do anything for me except tell me to rest and charge us for the visit."

Hawk put an arm around her back and propelled her forward with gentle strength. "No harm in having him tell us that you're all right once again."

Hawk stood the instant Doc Wilton stepped out of the examination room. "How is she?"

"She's fine, Hawk."

"What about her nightmares and her lack of appetite? Like I told you, she hasn't been herself for weeks now. You should have seen her over at the bakery. Pale as death, all of a sudden."

The doctor motioned to the chairs in the waiting room and took a seat on one of them, saying nothing until Hawk sat on the other. "I should imagine she will regain her appetite in a few more weeks."

Wasn't the doctor taking Bethany's symptoms too lightly? It sure seemed so to Hawk, and he wasn't happy about it. Something was wrong with his wife. He wanted answers.

"Many women in her condition experience similar things."

Her condition? What did he mean, her condition? That didn't tell him anything. What was wrong with her? Why didn't—

His eyes widened as understanding dawned.

Doc Wilton nodded, then tipped his head toward the closed door. "She's waiting for you now."

He was out of the chair in a flash. When he entered the examination room, Bethany was standing near the table, her hands folded before her waist. A slow smile curved her mouth as he drew near.

"Doc told you?" she asked softly.

"A baby?"

Her eyes glittered with happy tears. "Yes."

"When?"

"In late June, more than likely."

He gathered her into his arms. "And everything's all right?"

"Yes." The word came out on a laugh. "Everything's perfect."

THIRTY-SEVEN

Bethany's nightmares didn't go away, but they occurred with less frequency. And in the light of day, it was easier to push aside the fear the dreams stirred in her heart. Instead, she thought of the baby. Hawk's baby. She wanted winter to speed by. She longed for June to arrive, for the day she would hold the baby in her arms and see what their love had created.

But winter hadn't any notion of going away just because she wished it so. It held Montana in its white, frigid grip for weeks on end.

❧

Rusty Andrews—a tall, lanky man with shaggy hair and leathered skin—stood just inside the front door of the cabin, his hat in hand. He acknowledged Bethany with a polite nod, then spoke to Hawk. "We found another fresh kill yesterday morning. That's the fifth one in about a week. And the Circle Blue's not the only one."

"Cows are easy pickings." Hawk raked the fingers of one hand through his hair. "Spread the word that we'll leave from here first thing in the morning."

Rusty set his hat on his head. "I'll do it, boss." He glanced toward Bethany a second time. "Good day to you, Miz Chandler."

She acknowledged him, but there was disquiet in her heart. As soon as the door closed behind the cowboy, she rose from the sofa. "What was that about?"

"Wolves. A hard winter makes wild game scarce, so they go for the cattle. We've got to hunt them down before they pick off too many."

"Must you go?"

He shook his head. "It's my ranch, Bethany. Of course I have to go." There was a hint of frustration in his voice.

She imagined a pack of wolves circling their prey, teeth bared, growls rumbling in their throats. Only it wasn't a cow they circled in her mind's eye. It was Hawk. Words rose in her throat—pleading words, begging him to stay at home, imploring him to let the hired men go without him—but she swallowed them back. She couldn't ask it of him, and he wouldn't oblige even if she did.

"We have to kill a few wolves every winter." He crossed the room to stand before her. "You won't be alone. Ingrid will come down with Rand. Last time I saw him, he promised he would bring her to see you. He won't forget."

She struggled to appear calm. "I'm being silly, aren't I?"

"Yes." He kissed the tip of her nose. "You are." He kissed her on the lips.

I don't want to be afraid. I don't mean to be a coward. She drew a quick breath. *Please God. Keep him safe.*

The eastern sky was stained pink by the rising sun as Rand guided the sleigh along the snow-covered trail. Ingrid nestled against his side. His saddle horse brought up the rear. He looked forward to the hunt. He'd let himself get lazy this winter, and his wife's good cooking had added pounds to his girth. If he wasn't careful, his belly would be as round as hers.

He glanced her way. Her cheeks and nose were red from the cold, and he thought how pretty she looked, covered up to her chin with blankets. Every day he seemed to love her more. He wouldn't ever stop thanking God for bringing her to Sweetwater. He reckoned Hawk felt the same about Bethany.

"It will be good to see them again," Ingrid said, as if reading his thoughts. "Bethany has been on my mind often since she told us they're having a baby too."

He wondered if Bethany had shared about her nightmares, but he couldn't ask. Hawk had told him only because he wanted Rand to pray for her. That was a confidence he wouldn't break, not even to his wife.

Arriving at their destination, Rand stopped the sleigh in front of the Chandler cabin. A number of horses were tied to the corral fence, and he saw several men milling around inside the barn.

The cabin door opened and Bethany stepped outside, a shawl around her shoulders. "You came. Hawk said you would, but I wasn't sure."

Rand helped Ingrid from the sleigh, and the two women hugged each other.

"I'm so glad you're here. The day won't seem so long with your company."

"Where's Hawk?" Rand asked.

"He's in the barn with the other men." Bethany stepped toward him, touching his arm as she met his gaze. "Please keep an eye on him for me. I've had a terrible feeling all night that something will go wrong."

"Nothin' is gonna go—"

Her fingers tightened. "Don't try to reassure me with words. Just stay close to him. Promise me."

"Okay. I promise."

"And don't tell him I said anything to you." She offered him a wan smile. "I don't want him knowing."

Rand nodded. "Don't worry. I'll stick to him like bugs to flypaper."

The hunting party, made up of men from four different ranches, found fresh tracks by late morning. As they followed the predators, low clouds blew in from over the mountains. The temperature warmed as it began to snow.

It was then they saw the wolf pack. Westy fired the first shot. The predators took off, and men and horses gave chase. It wasn't long before Hawk saw a large black wolf separate from the pack. He leaned low over the saddle horn and urged more speed from his gelding, his rifle in his right hand.

The wolf darted around trees and brush as it climbed the mountainside. For a while, Hawk's horse kept an even pace with it. That soon changed. The snowfall increased, becoming a thick curtain of white, and the wolf disappeared into its midst.

He reined in, muttering, "You were lucky this time. But we'll meet again." He slipped the rifle into its scabbard and patted the gelding's neck. "We'll take it slower this time, fella."

As the wind rose, driving the snow before it, he turned the horse around, hunching forward in the saddle, his hat deflecting the stinging flakes. He hoped the rest of the hunting party had the good sense to head for cover as well.

From the corner of his eye, he saw a movement. As he straightened in the saddle and turned to see what it was, he was knocked from the saddle. He scrambled to his feet, reaching for the knife in his belt, not sure what had attacked him. A cougar would have growled. The wolf would have gone for his throat. Before another thought could form, something hard slammed into the back of his head, and the world around him turned from white to black.

The first thing he noticed was the whistling wind; the next was the pain in his head. Hawk opened his eyes. Sky and earth had become a world of white with no up or down, right or left.

How long had he been out? Seconds? Minutes? He couldn't be sure. One thing he was sure of, this being knocked unconscious was getting tiresome.

He sat up and looked around, head throbbing. He didn't know what hit him, but whatever it was, it had left its mark. He pushed to his feet, hoping he would see his horse, but the snow was falling so hard the gelding could have been two feet away and he wouldn't have seen him. The whiteness was almost blinding. Maybe if he closed his eyes he could feel the incline of the mountain beneath his feet. He tried it, but sensed no difference.

"Hey!" he shouted. "Anybody there?"

No answer. Only the sound of the wind. If he had his rifle, he could fire a few shots, but the Winchester was in the saddle scabbard, and he hadn't brought along his Colt. Well, he couldn't stay where he was. He had to find cover from the storm.

A humorless chuckle escaped him. Bethany would read him the riot act when he got home. He'd told her he would be fine, and now look at him.

He started walking. The going was hard, his feet sinking deep in the snow with each step he took. Cold seeped into his bones. He might have been walking for half an hour or more when he stumbled upon a shallow cave in a wall of rock. A smile crossed his chapped lips. He knew where he was. All he needed was a break in the storm, and he could find his way home.

He took shelter in the cave, where he scooped pine needles into a heap with chilled fingers. Then he used a match to set the needles on fire. The flame sputtered and nearly died, then caught and began to burn.

It was a meager fire by any measure but better than nothing. He glanced around for some kindling, anything that might burn a bit hotter. There were a few branches behind him, out of reach of the blowing snow. Hopefully they would last longer than the storm.

Vince stared into space as he heard the front door of the house close behind McDermott. It had taken Saunders several weeks, but at last the job was done.

He rose from the chair and crossed to the window. Gray clouds roiled across the sky. The temperature was below freezing again. Snow had stopped falling an hour ago. All he could see beyond the Bar V outbuildings was a sea of white. Fence posts rose mere inches above the blanket of snow, and trees bent beneath their heavy burden.

Men would be looking for both Chandler and Rick Saunders by now. Chandler's body they would eventually find. The other one? Well, Saunders might not ever be found. McDermott would make sure the young gunslinger never made it out of the territory.

He frowned. He supposed McDermott would have to take care of Hutchens before too long. Too bad. He'd been a good manservant these many years. Vince would hate training someone else to fill that position, but it couldn't be helped. Hutchens knew too much.

Vince gave his head a slow shake. He didn't want to think about that now. He would rather savor the news that Hawk Chandler, at last, was dead. Pleasure washed over him as he wondered how much time he should let pass before he called on the grieving widow.

Hawk left the cave as soon as the storm let up, but the going was slow. He figured he'd covered about a mile when he heard someone—it sounded like Rusty—call his name.

"Here!" he hollered back.

The next voice he heard belonged to Bethany. "Hawk?"

What was she doing out here? "Over this way!"

Below him and off to his left he heard the firing of a rifle. Once, twice, three times—the signal that he'd been found, no doubt. He wondered how many men searched for him. He felt like a fool, getting knocked off his horse and lost in that storm. Especially now that he knew his pregnant wife had been searching for him too.

She rode into view, using her boot heels to drive the big dun through deep drifts. Rand and Rusty were right behind her.

"You all right?" Rand called.

"I'm fine." He moved toward them as fast as he could. "Lost my horse in the storm. Did you find him?"

"Not yet."

"I'd sure hate to lose him. Not to mention my best rifle and saddle."

Rand asked, "Where's Rick Saunders, that new kid from the Connelly ranch?"

Hawk shook his head, trying to remember which cowboy was Saunders. He drew a blank.

"He got lost in the storm too. We thought he was with you."

"No, he wasn't with me. I never saw anybody after I gave chase to that wolf." He touched the back of his head. Did Saunders have something to do with his being knocked from his horse? But that didn't make any sense. He didn't even know him.

Bethany slid from the saddle and hurried the last few steps to reach him. "Are you sure you aren't hurt? I was so scared when they told me you got separated from the others."

"I'm fine, and you shouldn't have come out here." He lowered his voice. "You've got a baby to think of."

Rand said, "I tried to stop her, but she's stubborn."

"Tell me about it." He pulled her against him. "She has a mind of her own, this one."

She held him tight. "I kept remembering what I was told about a man getting caught in a storm and freezing and not being found until spring. I was terrified that those words were coming true."

"Who said that to you?"

She drew back and looked up at him, fear still in her eyes. After a lengthy silence, she answered, "Mr. Richards."

Anger sparked in his chest. He would know more about what Vince said to his wife, but now was not the time to press for an explanation. "Let's get home."

THIRTY-EIGHT

As soon as they were alone in their cabin, Hawk asked, "When did Richards say those things to you?"

Bethany was relieved to know that her husband was safe, but she didn't look forward to this conversation. "I'm not sure." She walked into the kitchen. "Not long after the first big storm."

"You mean he came here, to the Circle Blue?"

"Yes." She reached for the bread. "Sit down, Hawk, while I fix you something to eat. You've got to be hungry."

He ignored her request, instead joining her at the side table. "Where was I?"

"Checking the cattle." She glanced at him. "He didn't stay long. He said he came to make sure I was all right after the storm. I told him I was fine and sent him away." It was true, what she said, only there were things she could add, things she didn't want to add, words that might spur him to anger and recklessness.

His eyes turned stormy. "There's nothing altruistic about Richards. He had another purpose in coming to see you. You can bet on it."

"Let it go, Hawk." A frisson of fear ran along her spine, a feeling she'd had all too frequently in recent weeks. "It isn't his fault that I let his words go to my head." Try as she might, she didn't believe that—Vince had meant to frighten her—and she was quite sure Hawk didn't believe it either.

He studied her a while longer, then gave a slow nod. "All right. We won't talk about it anymore."

Tension drained from her shoulders, and she gave him a grateful look. "Go warm yourself by the fire while I prepare your meal. It won't take long."

Again he nodded, then turned and left the kitchen.

Bethany let out a breath of air as she pressed her palms on the table. She really had no reason to be afraid. Vince Richards had never harmed her. She might find the things he said unpleasant or unwelcome, but could she call them threatening? Besides, he wasn't responsible for the weather.

God had looked out for Hawk today, guiding him to a place of shelter, keeping him warm and dry. The snowstorm hadn't lasted long. It could have gone on for days, and instead it was over in a few hours. The worst that had happened was the loss of his horse and rifle, and hopefully the animal would be found unharmed.

Let not your heart be troubled, neither let it be afraid.

Her mother had taught her that verse when she was a little girl of six or seven. She'd suffered from nightmares then too. So each night, her mother would take Bethany onto her lap and whisper Jesus' words in her ear until she had memorized them. And eventually the nightmares and the fear that came with them went away.

Let not your heart be troubled, neither let it be afraid.

She promised herself that she would repeat those words every day until her current fears vanished as well.

❧

Hawk stared into the fire. The anger in his chest felt as hot as the flames licking at the logs in the grate. He didn't know what Vince had intended when he came to see Bethany, but he meant to make certain it never happened again. The man wasn't welcome on the Circle Blue at any time, but especially when Hawk was away.

He looked over his shoulder toward the kitchen, wondering what else Vince had said to Bethany. There was more. He felt it in his gut.

Vince waited until he was alone before he swept the top of the table clean, his curses mingling with the sounds of breaking glass and china.

Hutchens appeared in the dining room doorway in seconds. "Sir?"

He swore at his servant and told him to get out. Hutchens was smart enough to obey without hesitation.

Alone again, he kicked over the chair behind him. Saunders. That thieving, lying, no-good gunslinger had told him Chandler was dead. He'd even brought back the pearl-handled knife as proof the job was done. Vince had paid him well for it. Not that he'd had time to spend any of the money before McDermott killed him. Vince didn't like loose ends, and he didn't take chances with men he didn't know well.

He muttered another string of curses as he paced the length of the dining room. He'd told Bethany that he wasn't a patient man, and what little patience he had was now used up. He would get rid of Chandler once and for all, and this time he would do it himself.

He stopped pacing as a sneer crept slowly onto his face. Maybe he'd gone about the matter the wrong way. He just might know what to do. Yes, by George, he just might.

He left the dining room and went into his study, where he pulled open the top drawer of his desk. There it was: Chandler's knife, supposed proof that he was dead. Chandler always had this knife in a sheath fastened to his belt. Even in church. He was often without his gun but never without his knife. Vince knew it, and so did everyone else in Sweetwater.

Perhaps Saunders hadn't been a complete failure.

"Hutchens!"

His manservant was as quick to appear as he had been to disappear moments before. "Sir?"

"Tell McDermott I need to see him right away."

"Yes, sir."

Vince stroked the pearl handle of the knife, his smile growing. Then he closed the drawer and sat in his chair to await McDermott.

Hawk lay awake late into the night. The house was blanketed in silence, but his thoughts wouldn't let him sleep. Vince was up to no good. But what? He was probably behind the cattle rustling, most likely the beating Hawk had taken last summer, perhaps the gunman too. But what did he want with Bethany?

Hawk turned his head on the pillow and looked at his wife. The moonlight coming through the window provided pale illumination. She slept on her side, her back to him, her breathing soft and steady. No nightmares tonight. No sign of unrest. He rolled onto his side, spooning his body to hers, his arm draped over her waist.

Whatever else was going on, he had to protect Bethany. He would die before he let harm come to her.

Thirty-Nine

Men had continued to search for Rick Saunders until nightfall on the day of the hunt, and they were back at it the next morning. Hawk joined them, despite Bethany's objections.

"You'd want others to keep looking if I hadn't been found yet," he'd said to her. "Don't worry. The skies are clear. We won't get caught by the weather a second time."

His prediction proved correct. It didn't cloud over or snow that day. But a storm of another kind came in its stead. Midmorning, they found Saunders' body. Hawk's pearl-handled knife—the one that had belonged to his father—was sticking out of the cowboy's chest.

Hawk dismounted to get a better look. "It's mine, all right." He looked over his shoulder at the rest of the search party. "I lost it yesterday after I was knocked from my horse."

He saw a couple of Connelly cowboys exchange glances. He didn't blame them.

"Rusty, you'd better go for Sheriff Cook. Tell him we'll take the body to the Circle Blue. It's the closest."

Rusty gave him a grim nod, then turned his horse and started down the mountain as fast as the snow-covered ground would allow.

Hawk turned back to the body.

Westy joined him. "Better take out the knife, boss, before we put him over a saddle."

"Yeah, I guess you're right." He narrowed his eyes and lowered his voice. "This doesn't feel right, Westy."

"Whatcha mean?"

"I'm not sure." He raised his eyes and studied the landscape. "How did he end up here?"

"When we took after that wolf pack, you two disappeared about the same time. Hard to tell which way he went because of the storm. We figured the two of you were together."

"If he was behind me, I didn't know it."

Hawk replayed the events of the previous day in his mind. He remembered following the black wolf, but he didn't know how long the chase had lasted. He remembered the moment when he knew he wouldn't get a shot off. He'd stopped his horse, letting the animal rest a short while, then turned him down the mountain. The snow had come harder by then. He remembered thinking he saw something from the corner of his eye. Had something moved? Could it have been another rider? He remembered being knocked from the saddle and pulling his knife. After that it was blank until the moment he came to on the ground.

Could he have stabbed a man and not remembered it?

No. He gave his head a slow shake. He would know.

Westy reached down and pulled the knife from the young cowboy's body. He turned it in his hand and held the handle toward Hawk.

He shook his head. "You'd better keep it for now, Westy."

"Sure thing, boss."

Bethany couldn't believe what was happening before her eyes. Sheriff Cook was taking her husband to the jail. "Sheriff, you know Hawk. You know he wouldn't kill a man."

"That's just it, Mrs. Chandler. He shot and killed a man last fall. I let that go, seein' as he had that head wound where the bullet grazed him. Looked like self-defense to me. But I can't let this go. They were out in that storm together, and Saunders was killed with Hawk's knife. There's talk that he and Saunders exchanged heated words a while back."

Hawk said, "I never met the man before yesterday."

"That's what you say. Others say different."

"Who?"

The sheriff shook his head. "Enough talkin'. I need you to come along quietlike. Don't make me put the cuffs on you."

"But why would he help them find the body if he was guilty?" Bethany took hold of Hawk's arm, as if she could hold him there.

"That'll be up to a judge and jury to decide." The sheriff cocked his head toward the waiting horses. "Let's go."

Panic swirled through her veins.

"It'll be all right," Hawk said softly. "Let Rand know what's happened. And don't stay here alone. Do you hear me? Make sure someone is with you all the time."

She nodded, still clutching his arm.

He kissed her on the forehead. "It'll be okay." Then he turned and walked toward the horses, the sheriff at his side.

As the tears flowed, she blinked furiously, desperate to keep sight of him. She watched him mount his horse, saw him look back and nod at her. Then he and Sheriff Cook rode out of the yard.

No one spoke for a long while. A horse snorted, another stomped its foot, another nickered softly.

Rusty stepped toward Bethany. "What do you want us to do, Mrs. Chandler?"

She drew a deep breath to calm her screaming nerves. "I need someone to ride up to the Howard place. Rand must know what's happened. I'm going to ride into town to stay in my parents' house until Hawk is free again."

"He said you weren't to be alone, ma'am."

"Westy can come with me." She looked toward the cowboy in question. "Is that all right with you?"

"Anything you want, Miz Chandler. But I'm thinking you'd best have another woman there too."

She shook her head in exasperation; it seemed she was determined to ruin her own reputation, and others were forever trying to rescue her from it.

"Hopefully Hawk will be free by tonight." She looked at Rusty again. "Please ask Mrs. Howard to come and stay with me in town." Drawing another deep breath, she looked at the remaining cowhands. "I'll need you to look out for the place until Hawk and I return."

She received a series of nods and murmurs of agreement.

"Westy, if you wouldn't mind, please saddle Buttercup while I put a few things together."

"Yes, ma'am. We'll be ready when you are."

"He murdered a man in cold blood. You ought to string him up now."

Hawk wasn't sure who said that, but the voice seemed familiar.

"Nobody's hanging anybody," Sheriff Cook answered. "I'll hold Chandler until the circuit judge comes through. He'll get a fair trial, like anybody else."

Hawk turned his back toward the doorway and leaned against the iron bars of his cell. Someone was out to get him, and he wasn't sure he'd get a fair trial. But at least the sheriff was sober these days. Hawk was thankful for that. There wouldn't be any lynching by a mob. His fate would be decided by a court of law and not some angry mob. Sheriff Cook would make sure of it.

He remembered the frightened look on Bethany's face when the sheriff had taken him away. She'd tried hard to be brave for his sake, but she'd been plenty scared. Just last night he'd sworn he wouldn't let harm come to her. He'd promised himself that he would die first. Trouble with that was, if he was dead, he couldn't protect her.

And something down deep inside told him that she might be in as much danger as he was.

He closed his eyes and said a silent prayer for God's protection for all of them—for his wife and their unborn child and for him.

Bethany went to the jail as soon as she got to town. Seeing Hawk in that small cell stirred the fear in her heart. The cot mattress looked lumpy, the blanket worn and none too clean.

"Are you all right?" She reached through the bars and took his hand in hers.

"I'm fine."

He was lying. He wasn't fine. She saw it in his eyes. He was worried. Why had she ever thought his gaze enigmatic? It seemed to her now that she could read his mind.

"But what are you doing here, Bethany? I told you—"

"I'm not alone. Westy is with me. I'm going to stay in town until the sheriff releases you." She squeezed his fingers. "I've asked

Ingrid to stay with me too. I'm sure she and Rand will be here shortly."

Hawk nodded. "Good."

She leaned closer to the bars, lowering her voice. "Who would do this? Someone set you up. They used your knife so you would be accused of the murder."

"I've thought the same thing. I just can't figure out how my knife fell into his hands."

His hands, Hawk had said. He had someone in mind. And then she knew. "Vince Richards?" A shiver passed through her. "But he wasn't involved in the hunt. Nor were any of his ranch hands."

"I know. It doesn't make sense, but I'm sure he's behind it somehow. Maybe Rand will have some ideas when he gets here."

"Sorry, Mrs. Chandler," the sheriff said from the doorway. "You'll have to leave now. You can come back in the morning."

It felt as if someone were tearing out her heart when Hawk let go of her hand. She didn't want to leave him in this horrible, cold, drafty place. He didn't belong here. He belonged with her. He was innocent. How could anyone think him guilty?

"It'll be okay, Bethany. God will look after us."

FORTY

Sleepless and aware of every creak and moan the house made in the deep of night, Bethany slipped her arms into the sleeves of her robe, then left the bedroom, careful not to make a sound. Ingrid and Rand had retired several hours before and were surely sound asleep.

After reaching the ground floor, she went to her father's study, where she lit the lamp before settling into the comfortable chair behind the desk. It was here that her father had written his sermons, here that he had prayed for her and for others.

She laid her cheek against the desk, eyes closed, heart aching. If her father were here, he would know what to do. "What would you tell me to do, Papa?" she whispered.

"I'm not sure about your father," a voice said from the corner of the room, "but I have a suggestion."

Startled, she straightened.

"I advise you not to scream, my dear." Vince Richards moved into the light of the lamp. "If you do, you'll never hear my offer to help your husband."

She looked behind his shoulder to the closed study door. The room felt as small as Hawk's jail cell.

"Please, hear me out." He sat opposite her. "I have a proposition for you."

"A proposition?"

"Yes. You come with me to the Bar V. You leave a note saying that you have left of your own accord. You agree to marry me once you are legally free of Hawk Chandler. You do these things, and I will provide proof that another man killed Saunders."

"I don't believe you."

"I'm a man of my word. Haven't I made it clear from the start that I meant for you to be my wife? I will keep this promise as well."

"You must be mad."

His eyes narrowed as his mouth curved into a one-sided smile.

She shuddered. He was insane—and evil.

"Well, my dear. What is your answer? It's late, and we should be going."

"No one would believe I left of my own accord. They know I love Hawk."

"What they know is that you left him once before. It should be easy enough for them to see that his current troubles were the last straw." He stood. "And if you want to save his life, you'll be sure they believe it."

If she screamed for Rand's help, Hawk might not be freed. He might hang for something he didn't do. And then there was the way Vince looked at her. An odd light that warned he would do her harm if she called for help. If she was the only one in danger, she would take a chance, but there was the baby to think about. There was Hawk to think about. What choice did she have?

Ingrid hastened along the boardwalk, her pulse racing, her breath forming in white clouds before her. When she entered the sheriff's office, she found the deputy pouring himself a cup of coffee.

"Mr. Delaney, I need to see Sheriff Cook."

He gave her a quick glance, then set the pot back atop the black iron stove. "Sorry, Miz Howard. He ain't here. He's over havin' himself breakfast at the restaurant."

Ingrid knew that, of course. Sheriff Cook was a man of routine and ingrained habits. He ate breakfast at Mrs. Jenkins's Restaurant at the same time every morning.

"Then you may help me," she said. "I need to see your prisoner."

Delaney cocked an eyebrow.

"I have come on behalf of his wife. She ... she could not come this morning. She is so upset about what has happened she has made herself unwell. But she has a message for him which I promised to deliver."

"Well, I suppose it won't hurt nothin' for you to have a minute or two. But that's all you'll get."

She nodded.

The deputy crossed the room, took the ring of keys from the nail in the wall beside the jamb, unlocked the door, and opened it wide. "Two minutes. That's all."

When Hawk saw her in the doorway, he rose from the cot. Ingrid held up a hand in front of her round belly, motioning for him to be silent. Then she glanced over her shoulder. The deputy had moved to the window, where he stood, staring outside, sipping his coffee. She held her breath, reached out, and slipped the key ring from the nail. Somehow she did it all without the keys jingling a warning. When she looked at Hawk again, she saw him watching her with a puzzled expression. She shook her head, again pleading for him not to say a word.

Reaching the cell, she slipped the key ring from her hand to his. "Bethany is in trouble," she whispered. "Rand is waiting for you by the river. He's got your horse. I will take care of the deputy." She leaned closer. "And be careful, both of you."

Her heart hammering in her ears, she hurried back into the office. "Deputy!" she cried, at the same moment hugging her belly. "Oh, help me." She bent forward at the waist.

"Miz Howard, what is it?"

"Something is wrong. The baby. It is the baby. Please, get me to the doctor."

"Well, I—"

"Ooooh! Please. Help me. I cannot make it on my own."

"Okay. Okay." His left arm went around her back. His right hand grabbed her by the right elbow. "Don't worry. We'll git you there."

As Deputy Delaney helped Ingrid down the street, she wondered if she and Rand would find themselves in the cell next to Hawk's before this was over. But the dangers of that mattered little compared to needing Bethany to be safe. The only people she trusted to make that happen were Hawk and Rand, so she prayed for God's speed for them both.

Even as Rand gave Hawk a quick rundown of events, they swung into their saddles and turned their horses toward the Bar V. They rode hard. Ingrid would keep the deputy with her as long as possible, but all too soon either the sheriff or the deputy would discover the cell was empty.

Hawk supposed a jailbreak wouldn't go far in convincing people of his innocence, but he would worry about that after Bethany was away from Vince and the Bar V.

He pictured his wife in the hands of his enemy. The man was dangerous—he would obviously do whatever it took to accomplish his goals. That thought twisted his gut. If anything should happen to Bethany and the child she carried, he'd never forgive himself.

"Maybe you should ride to the ranch and get more help," he called to Rand above the sound of galloping hooves.

"I'm stickin' with you. I broke my promise to Bethany the last time. It ain't happenin' again."

Hawk wasn't sure what his friend meant, but he didn't argue. There might not be time to get more men. Who knew what Vince planned for Bethany? Did the man know she was pregnant? What would he do if he did?

Hawk should have had things out with Richards long before this, long before the Silvertons ever came to Sweetwater.

Bethany stood at the dining room window, staring at the snowy landscape.

"Soon this house will be yours, my dear."

She glanced over her shoulder. Vince sat at the large table, eating his breakfast. Another plate had been set on the table to his right. Her plate. She'd refused to eat.

Ingrid and Rand would have found her note by now. They would have told Hawk about it. She pictured him, trapped behind those bars. He would want to come after her. He would want to demand an explanation, one she couldn't give him. Not yet. Not until he was proven innocent of the murder of Rick Saunders.

"Bethany." Vince's voice had sharpened. "I've had enough of this. Come to the table and sit down."

She placed a protective hand on her stomach, reminding herself why she hadn't fought him while still in her father's study.

She wouldn't allow harm to come to this baby. Help would come. She believed that with all of her heart.

"Didn't you hear me?" Vince's hand landed on her shoulder, and he turned her toward him. "I said, sit down and eat."

She bit back the fear that rose in her throat. "I'm not hungry."

He stared at her a long while. Then his eyes widened with surprise. "You think he's coming for you."

She pressed her lips together, refusing to answer.

"Despite my warnings of what I can and will do, you still think he'll be free. You still think you'll be reunited with him. You are quite naive, my dear. Quite naive."

She tilted her chin higher and forced her gaze to remain steady. She would not let him see that she was afraid.

He took her by the elbow and propelled her to the table, forcing her to sit with a none-too-gentle pressure on her shoulder.

"Perhaps you're right," he said, more to himself than to her. "It might not hurt to prepare for visitors." He left the dining room but returned within moments. He had a thick, silky cord in his left hand. "I'm sorry to do this, my dear, but it is probably for the best."

She didn't understand his intent until it was too late. His grip was strong, and although she struggled once she realized what he meant to do, he had no trouble binding her wrists together and then tying her to the chair.

"Now I shall finish my breakfast while we wait to see if your husband has managed to escape the last trap I laid for him."

Bethany grew still. "You killed Saunders, didn't you?"

He smirked.

That was answer enough.

FORTY-ONE

"All right, little lady." Sheriff Cook stared down at Ingrid. "I don't cotton to putting a pregnant woman in jail, but I'll do it if you don't tell me where to find Chandler. And don't think that you're not in trouble. Bustin' a man out of jail is no small matter. Now where did he go? Has he got a place to hide?"

"He is not hiding, Sheriff." She hoped this was the right time to say what she must. "He went to the Bar V. Mr. Richards has taken Bethany, and Hawk went to bring her home."

The sheriff muttered a curse beneath his breath, then caught her reaction. "Sorry." He turned toward his deputy. "Get a few men together. We're going to the Richards ranch to bring Chandler back." He looked at Ingrid again. "You stay here with Doc Wilton. Don't you budge an inch. You hear me?"

She nodded.

"Doc, you make sure she doesn't go anywhere."

Riding right up to the main house wasn't much of a plan, but Hawk didn't see how to do it any other way. There were too many Bar V ranch hands and no cover to hide behind. It seemed best to use the bold approach and hope the sheriff and his posse would be close behind them.

He and Rand trotted their horses into the yard and dismounted. A quick glance told him that two men were right inside the barn, another couple outside the bunkhouse. No telling who or how many might be inside.

As they stepped onto the veranda, Hawk noticed that Rand had his hand close to the gun in his holster. His own fingers itched to be holding his Colt.

"Keep Bethany safe, Lord," he whispered.

He knocked on the door. No one answered right away, so he knocked again. This time, the door opened, revealing a fellow Hawk didn't know. Judging by his clothes, he was a servant.

"I'm Hawk Chandler. I've come for my wife."

The man looked uncertain. "She's in the dining room." He stepped back, allowing Hawk and Rand to enter, and motioned toward the room to the right of the entry.

Hawk stopped in the doorway of the dining room. Bethany sat at the table, her hands in her lap and her lap covered with a blanket. Vince stood beside the chair, one hand on her shoulder.

Hawk's response was a powerful combination of relief and fury. His wife and baby were safe, but currently within the grasp of a criminal. He saw red.

"Bethany expected you," Vince said. "But it was a mistake to come. Surely you know that."

"I don't want trouble with you, Richards. I just came for my wife."

"She's left you. Haven't you heard?"

Hawk took two more strides into the room. "I heard. But she didn't write that note of her own accord."

"Are you so sure? She and I spent time together in Philadelphia. We formed an attachment that she couldn't forget. Surely she told you."

Hawk heard something behind him and turned in time to see Rand go down, thanks to the butt of a revolver cracking against his skull.

"I'll take your gun, Chandler." McDermott, the Bar V foreman, stepped over Rand.

He had little choice but to comply.

"What do you want me to do with them, boss?"

"Take Howard out to the barn and tie him up. I'll deal with Chandler myself." Vince raised the gun that had been in his free hand all the time. "He won't be any trouble while we wait for the sheriff." He motioned with the business end of the gun. "I think you should sit down over there."

Eyes on Bethany, Hawk moved toward the indicated chair. She was afraid. He saw that. But she wasn't afraid for herself. Her fears were for him. He hoped she could read his feelings as easily as he could hers.

"Do you know what I have on my desk, Chandler? Plans for the new Bar V. A bigger Bar V once I've married the Widow Chandler and her property becomes mine."

He forced himself not to react. "Aren't you jumping the gun? I'm not dead yet."

"You will be after you're found guilty of the murder of that young fellow Saunders."

Bethany paled. "You said—"

Hawk saw Vince's fingers tighten on her shoulder, cutting off her words. It was all he could do not to vault across the table. Only he knew he'd be shot dead trying, and that wouldn't help his family. "Why are you so sure I'll be found guilty?"

"Because I own more than land in this territory. I own people too. That's something you couldn't begin to understand."

"I take it you were behind the rustling?"

Vince chuckled.

"And the gunman who tried to kill me?"

"Yes, I hired him. He was supposed to be a good shot, but as it turned out, I'm glad you killed him instead. It makes you look guiltier of Saunders's murder."

Vince left Bethany's side and walked around the table, motioning with his gun again, warming to his story. "You should have taken the money I offered you. Now you'll end up with nothing. You'll end up at the end of a hangman's noose."

Hawk looked at Bethany. "What makes you think she'll marry you, even if I'm dead?"

The barrel of the gun pressed against his head behind his left ear. "Because she's going to do what I say from now on. Because if she doesn't promise, she can watch me shoot you right now."

"Please don't," she whispered.

It was Bethany's plea that distracted Vince, giving Hawk the chance he needed. He grabbed him by the wrist and slammed his hand against the table. Once, twice. The third time, the revolver spun away from them. Hawk bolted from the chair, grappling Vince. They hit the floor and rolled toward the window, then back again. As Hawk slammed against the overturned chair, he managed to get his hands around his enemy's throat. Fury tightened his grip.

He knew the moment the fight was his.

It would be easy to kill Vince, to choke the life from him. It would take only seconds to have his revenge for the stolen cattle, for the shooting, for Saunders, for Bethany, for the danger this man had put his unborn child in.

Vengeance is mine; I will repay, saith the Lord. Romans, chapter twelve.

He wished he hadn't read that chapter of the Bible so many times. Right now, he wanted to do things his way.

But he couldn't. He loosened his hands and pushed Vince away from him. His enemy lay still, gasping for air, his own hands now at his throat. Hawk rose and hurried around the table to Bethany, grabbing for the revolver on his way. When she didn't get up to meet him, he yanked the blanket from her lap, revealing the cords that kept her bound, confirming his suspicions. It made him want to strangle Vince all over again.

He tried to keep both the doorway and the man on the floor in sight as he freed Bethany.

"You can't stay here, Hawk. You must run. You must hide until we find some way to prove your innocence."

He gathered her to him with one arm, still watching for other signs of danger. He hoped the sheriff would arrive soon. It's what he and Rand were counting on when they rode in here.

"I'm not running, Bethany. We're going to have to trust God to work this out."

In a scratchy whisper, Vince said, "God can't help you. You'll hang."

"Only if he wills it, and I'm trusting that he won't."

Sounds from the entry hall drew Hawk's attention toward the dining room entrance. He moved Bethany to stand behind him, the revolver ready. When he saw the sheriff, he put the gun on the table and raised his hands in a sign of surrender.

Vince got to his feet. "About time you got here, Cook. Chandler just tried to kill me."

"Only after you threatened me and my wife. And if I'd wanted to kill you, you'd be dead right now."

The sheriff looked from Vince to Hawk.

Bethany stepped from behind him. "Hawk's telling you the truth, Sheriff."

Sheriff Cook nodded, his expression grim. "Maybe we'd all best go into town so I can sort things out."

"Wait." The manservant who had opened the door for Hawk and Rand appeared in the entry hall. "Sheriff, I can tell you what's been happening around here."

"Hutchens," Vince said, the name sounding like a growl, "none of this concerns you."

For an instant, it looked as if Vince's threatening tone had done its job. But then Hutchens drew himself up, saying, "I've kept quiet long enough. When you tie a woman to a chair and lay in wait for her husband with a gun, it concerns me. When you order a man killed and then attempt to put the blame on someone else, it's my concern." He looked at the sheriff again. "I can tell you what you need to know about Mr. Chandler and the death of the man called Saunders. And you'll find proof about more illegal dealings in Mr. Richards' office."

"Hutchens!"

"Shut up, Richards." Sheriff Cook looked at his deputy. "Keep an eye on all of them." He turned to Hutchens. "Now, why don't you take me to that office so I can have a look-see for myself."

Silence prevailed in the dining room for several moments after Hutchens and the sheriff disappeared from view. Then Bethany looked up at Hawk. "It's over."

He pulled her into his arms and buried his face in her hair. Holding her, some of the dread he'd felt when he learned Vince had taken her began to drain away.

"I'm unharmed, Hawk. So is the baby."

He drew back and cradled her face between his hands. "If I'd lost you . . ." He let the sentiment go unfinished.

"But you didn't. I'm right here." She glanced toward Vince. "He can't hurt us again. It's over."

Of all the ways Hawk might have imagined God would bring truth into the open and set him free, what had just happened wasn't one of them. Apparently the book of Romans was right. It was better to leave vengeance to God. And instead embrace the miracle that was his wife and child.

Epilogue

Nine months later

Bethany looked in the direction of the springs even as the orange sun slipped behind the highest peak. She could see the skeleton of their new home rising against the darkening mountainside. The sounds of hammering had faded as daylight waned. Hawk would be here soon.

She glanced at the infant in her arms, and then lowered her lips to brush them against the baby's downy head. Everything about this child amazed and delighted her. That their love could create something so perfect, so precious was a miracle beyond all else.

When the baby girl arrived on a hot July night, they'd named her Phoebe because she was so like her father—dark eyed, black hair, firm chin. The daughter, Phoebe, a small bird. The father, Hawk, swift and strong.

Thank you, Father. Thank you for them both.

Phoebe wriggled. Her lips sucked at the air and a frown wrinkled her forehead.

"Are you hungry, little bird?"

Bethany turned with a contented sigh and went into the house, leaving the door open to catch the evening breeze. She sat on the sofa beneath the parlor window, unbuttoned her bodice, and brought Phoebe to her breast. The baby suckled noisily.

"You'll not stay small very long with such an appetite." She stroked the baby's cheek with her index finger.

As often happened when she was alone with Phoebe, her thoughts began to wander, settling on one thing one moment, moving to another the next.

Ingrid and Rand's little boy, RJ, would soon be crawling. It amazed her how quickly babies grew and changed. Yesterday, Ingrid had told her that she would have another baby come next spring.

Bethany smiled. Rand should have built a bigger cabin.

A new pastor, the Reverend Talbot, had arrived in Sweetwater before Phoebe was born. Bethany liked him, although she missed the Sunday mornings when she and Hawk had read the Bible to one another and shared what God had laid on their hearts. She imagined at times that her father was looking down from heaven and nodding his approval. He would be pleased with the man her husband had become. She hoped he would be pleased with the changes that had taken place in her as well.

In the spring, Bethany had struck a deal with Mr. Grant. The bakery was no longer hers, but to her surprise, he didn't change the name. "People like you," he'd said when she asked about it. So Bethany's Bakery it remained.

She thought then about Jasper Hutchens. He had left Sweetwater after the trial of Vince Richards was over, but Bethany would never forget him nor would she cease to pray for God to bless him for clearing her husband's name and putting her fears to an end.

So many things to be thankful for.

The room was bathed in shadows by the time Hawk stepped through the doorway. He paused a moment and smiled at her. Even in the dim light, she could read the love in his eyes. Love for her. Love for Phoebe.

He crossed to the sofa and leaned down to kiss the crown of her head, repeating the action with the baby. Knowing what he wanted before he asked, Bethany lifted the sleepy infant into his waiting arms.

"Look at you," he said as he straightened. "You're the prettiest little girl in the world." He rocked from side to side. "Maybe we'll get you a kitten or a puppy for your first birthday. What would you think of that? And when you're older, we'll get you a pony, and we'll go riding every day."

Bethany laughed. "You're going to spoil her, aren't you?"

"Only as much as your father spoiled you."

"Mercy. She'll be a handful if that's true."

"I'm sure of it." He pulled her up from the sofa with his free arm and drew her to his side.

Was it possible to be too happy? Bethany wondered. Could a heart burst from an overabundance of joy?

As she looked at her husband, she remembered how unreadable she'd once thought his eyes. But that had all changed. Love had made the difference. She had become a part of him as he had become a part of her.

"I love you," he whispered.

She sighed, remembering how she had longed to hear those words while at the same time refusing to say them herself. What a fool she'd been. "I love you too."

They walked together into the bedroom where Hawk laid the baby in her cradle.

"She looks more like you every day." He straightened. "Beautiful, like you."

"You're wrong. She takes after you in every way. Beautiful, yes, but like you. That will never change."

He grinned as he brought his head close to hers. "Care to make a wager on that, Mrs. Chandler?"

She laughed again. "You'll lose."

"Ah, that's something I've learned since the day we first met." He lifted her into his arms. "When you win, my love, so do I. I'll wager my heart on that truth until kingdom comes."

A NOTE FROM THE AUTHOR

Dear Reader:

I began my storytelling career with historical fiction written for the general market. My favorite books to read back then were the sweeping historical sagas that were so popular in the late 1970s and early 1980s. I took great pleasure in immersing my imagination in other times and places. Thus, those types of stories were what I first attempted to write. And, being a romantic at heart, my books couldn't avoid including a love story.

But eventually a greater love story demanded to become a part of my books — the love story between God and mankind — and so the Lord led me into a new career, writing faith-based fiction, both historical and contemporary, for the Christian market, stories that I hope will please Him as well as my readers.

Hawk and Bethany first found their way into my imagination and onto my computer screen about twenty years ago. After all this time, I'm delighted that I was able to revisit these two characters and bring their love story to life on the page in a new and better way. I hope you enjoyed your visit to Sweetwater, Montana, as much as I did.

In the grip of his grace,

Robin Lee Hatcher

www.robinleehatcher.com